BURIED
IN ORANGE

By

John H. Cunningham

OTHER BOOKS BY JOHN H. CUNNINGHAM

BUCK REILLY ADVENTURE SERIES

Red Right Return

Green to Go

Crystal Blue

Second Chance Gold

Maroon Rising

Free Fall to Black

Silver Goodbye

White Knight

Indigo Abyss

Purple Deceiver

CO-WRITTEN WORKS

Graceless

Timeless

ALTERNATIVE ENDING HISTORIC FICTION

The Last Raft

Published by Greene Street, LLC

Print ISBN: 979-8-9869200-2-3

Electronic ISBN: 979-8-9869200-3-0

www.jhcunningham.com

This book is for Bailey and Will Prendergast

Thanks for introducing us to Formula 1,
and for all the fun we've had watching races together.

"To do something well is so worthwhile
that to die trying to do it better cannot be foolhardy.
It would be a waste of life to do nothing with one's ability,
for I feel that life is measured in achievement,
not in years alone."

Bruce McLaren

1937 - 1970

Contents

1. Ch1: COME FLY WITH ME 11

2. Ch 7: MISSING IN ACTION 45

3. Ch 14: UNWANTED HOSTS 99

4. Ch 20: MISTY MOUNTAIN HOP 151

5. Ch27: THE RACE IS ON 203

EPILOGUE 245

ABOUT THE AUTHOR 252

COME FLY WITH ME

1

AS I STARED UP AT THE CEILING OF MY SUITE IN THE LA CONCHA, the question passed through my mind how many nights I'd slept in this bed since moving here nearly a decade ago.

"Buck, are you there?"

I slid my cell phone that had slipped down onto the bed back up onto my chest. "I'm still here, Heather."

"Did you look at your calendar?"

I exhaled sharply as I used my thumb to scroll through my calendar app to the coming weekend and through the next week. Heather had left Key West a few weeks ago and my suite had never felt so empty. She'd lived here with me for a couple of months after helping me solve a local mystery. If we hadn't, I'd be sitting in a Bahamian jail.

"I'm totally clear," I said.

There was a pause on the line. I sat up, realizing that Heather was waiting for more than an update on the lack of bookings for Last Resort Charter and Salvage, the company my partner Ray Floyd and I operated using our three antique Grumman flying boats.

"And yes, I would love to come spend the week with you in New York City." I grimaced after saying the last three words aloud. Heather, I missed, but if I never set foot in New York City again, it wouldn't break my heart.

The sound of her breath intake caused my heart to double-pump. It was the familiar sound she made before her mouth curved into an award-winning smile.

"We'll have so much fun!" she said. "I'll make dinner reservations—and there's a new play I want to see on Broadway." Her giggle tickled my eardrums.

Heather's voice was alive, and I imagined her pacing her Upper East Side apartment, which was ten times larger than my suite here at the La Concha—a fact she reminded me of numerous times during the couple of months she'd endured living with me in the cramped space.

"I think I'll fly commercial rather than putting the hours on one of our planes," I said.

There was silence for a moment before she cleared her throat. "Means a lot that you're coming up, Buck. I appreciate it."

I started to say I owed it to her after all the time she'd spent here, but I bit my tongue. That would not be what she wanted to hear either. "Truth is, I miss you," I said. "I'm looking forward to being with you."

Again, the subtle gasp sounded on my speaker and I imagined her beam.

We chatted a few minutes longer as Heather rattled through a list of her favorite restaurants then the details of the play she wanted to see. I was indifferent to both so suggested she pick her favorites.

When we hung up, I glanced around my two-room suite. It had been perfect for me in the years I was still mentally and emotionally distraught from the failures of my past. But the events of this past year, soaring highs and gut-wrenching lows, had finally forced me to think about my future. I still loved what Ray and I had created with Last Resort, and we'd gotten well accustomed to Big Mama, our new 1951 Grumman Albatross, these past few months, but the long emptiness of my personal life had become painfully obvious thanks to the time I'd spent with Heather. I'd met some amazing women in the past decade, several I cared for deeply and could've imagined making a life with, but I hadn't been ready. The loss of my company e-Antiquity, bankruptcy, the deaths of my parents, learning I'd been adopted at birth, and my divorce from Heather had decimated me to the core, and no matter how many adventures I'd embarked on since then, nothing had filled that void until she and I had reunited.

That thought caused a measured intake of breath and slow exhale of my own. We hadn't said the words yet, and in my case, I was sure it was the last vestiges of fear from losing her previously that pinched my lips tight. But it had become especially evident in the weeks since she'd gone back to New York to fulfill some modeling assignments she'd previously committed to: in my heart, I knew I was back in love with her. I would've never thought it possible. But so many radical factors had led to our divorce, after we'd only been married—or had even known each other—for a couple of years, and we'd both been young and at the pinnacles of our careers. At least my career, anyway. Heather was still a top international model now. Bottom line was that we'd both grown up, gotten to know ourselves better, had numerous other relationships. As if from an invisible yet undeniable force of gravity, life kept pulling us back together through good and bad circumstances, but the good had become a juggernaut eclipsing the rest.

A week in New York City. I suddenly realized my wardrobe of the past decade had evolved to meet my surrounding climate and consisted largely of shorts, flip-flops, fishing shirts, branded Last Resort gear, and linen outfits. September in the City could easily include a wide swing in temperatures, which, along with the quality of restaurants that Heather was planning our meals around, not to mention Broadway, meant I seriously needed to go shopping. There wasn't time for catalogues or internet shopping, either; I had to get my butt into stores here, few of which carried the style of clothing I'd need.

"Crap."

As I reached for my phone to check New York weather, it rang, startling me so much I nearly dropped it. The name on the caller ID made me smile.

"Sir Harry, how are you, my fair knight?"

His snicker deflected my Yankee sarcasm. When the chips had been down for me a few months before, Harry had refused to help for fear of tarnishing his opportunity to be knighted, a decision I originally resented but ultimately understood. Having too often been there to bail me out, he expected me to solve my own problems, which fortunately I had. When the news of how I had managed to do that hit the global news, Harry had been proud and complimentary.

"Good evening, my dear boy."

"Evening for you, maybe. It's just past lunch here at the Last Resort."

"I stand corrected."

Harry hesitated and I suddenly had a premonition that he had something to tell me, which sat me forward. Harry was now in his mid-seventies and overweight from a lifetime of the best foods and wines, with very little exercise aside from his Olympic intelligence that had launched him from a mildly aristocratic upper-middle-class background to what *Forbes* estimated as a couple-billion-dollar net worth today.

"Everything okay, Harry?"

"Yes, yes, sorry for being tongue-tied, but I'm not accustomed to asking for favors."

I smiled. If I could help Harry for once, it would hardly make a difference on the ledger of support he'd provided to me most of my adult life. "Name it, Harry. Happy to help."

He cleared his throat. "That new, er, old, amphibian you acquired recently—is it airworthy, or a restoration project?"

"Fully restored and quite a beauty, I must say. Ray Floyd, my partner, did a great job finding and acquiring her. We call her Big Mama."

"Oh dear. That lovely name aside, what is her range?"

My smile broadened. I knew the name would tweak Harry's reserved nature. "She can fly sixteen hundred and fifty miles with a full payload. Why do you ask?"

"As I said, I'm not accustomed to asking favors—"

"That's because you don't need to, Harry. Everything you've ever needed you've purchased. In fact, what's your current portfolio of companies now?"

"Sixty-four, but as usual, there's a combination of divestitures and new opportunities afoot … but that's neither here nor there." He cleared his throat again. "All right then, allow me to explain. One such potential investment is in a Formula 1 racing team. I'm not at liberty to say which one, but it would give me the largest minority position in a well-established firm."

"Formula 1, as in car racing?" I asked. My brow furrowed. I'd never been aware of Harry investing in any kind of sporting entity, much less racing.

"I don't expect you are much of a sports fan, Buck, but Formula 1 has exploded in popularity. It's been famously popular all over the globe for decades, but in the past few years it's become the rage in the largest consumer market in the world, including the United States. So, yes, as plebian as it sounds, it's a wonderful opportunity that has been extended to me through none other than a member of the royal family. I'm seriously considering it for obvious reasons."

"Aha. The new title has brought some new obligations, perhaps?"

"Hardly." Harry's tone now registered affront. "As I said, it's a rare and unique opportunity, but that's all beside the point of why I'm calling you."

The opportunity to tease Harry was so rare, I had to tweak him a little further. "Oh, I forgot. The favor, that's right."

His long exhale made me wince. "About your plane—"

"You mean Big Mama?" I laughed silently.

"If you must, yes, her. There's a race coming up that will be televised worldwide, and as they do at most of these events, they commence the festivities with a flyover of the hundred-plus thousand people in attendance with different kinds of aircraft, often trailing the colors of the host country's flag."

"Quite the pomp and circumstance for a car race," I said.

"Presidents, prime ministers, and royal families preside over these … car races … as you insist on referring to them, and this particular race is the Italian Grand Prix, which will no doubt include all of the above."

Italy? Now the rationale behind Harry's question about Big Mama's range made sense. I immediately started imagining the course it would take to get from Key West to Italy. Depending on where in Italy the race was held, it could be north up to Halifax, over Greenland and Iceland, and down from Northern Europe, or down across South America and the southern Atlantic, then up Africa to Italy. Lost in a pilot's epic fantasy, my eyes blinked rapidly when I heard Harry repeating my name.

"Buck, have I lost you?"

"No, no, sorry, I was just imagining, ah—where in Italy exactly is the Grand Prix?"

"Monza, just outside of Milan. The organizers have decided upon antique aircraft from the 1940s and '50s to commence the race, which will include some military planes of the day. So, given my opportunity to partner with this historic enterprise, when I heard of these plans, I, um, well, mentioned that I had access to a classic amphibian of the appropriate vintage."

In all the years I'd known Harry, I also had never heard him sound so awkward. While I already cared for him like a relative, it endeared him to me even more. No more teasing. And since he'd always been there for me, not including my last self-inflicted debacle, there was no way I could say no. Plus it sounded like a blast.

"Since it's so big, the Albatross requires a minimum of two pilots, so I have to check with Ray Floyd. But yes, Harry, I'd be honored to help you."

"Splendid, my dear boy! I knew I could count on you. This will truly be a memorable experience and contribute greatly to my affiliation with the team owner."

I wanted to say, *and the royal family*, but I bit my lip and adhered to my no-more-teasing self-admonishment of a moment ago. Italy in Big Mama, that would be quite a trip. I paced the room imagining it all.

"Can you have one of your people send me the details of the event? Which airport the planes will stage from, the timing—"

"That is one of the most exciting details, Buck. The race is this weekend. You'll need come to Europe *molto velocemente*."

I didn't know much Italian, but I guessed that meant very quickly.

A stab of anguish caused my breath to catch in my throat.

Heather.

New York City.

Damn.

2

GIVEN THE MAGNITUDE OF THE TRIP, I decided to go see Ray Floyd, my business partner and friend, to tell-slash-ask him about going to Italy in a couple days. Even though I'd already confirmed with Harry, the Albatross required two pilots, so if Ray wasn't game, I wouldn't be able to go on my own. Plus, given that my quick calculation that it was a five-thousand-nautical-mile trip one way, it would take thirty hours to fly continuously, plus time for fuel and rest stops. It was way too much for one pilot anyway.

I'd confirmed Ray was at our hangar before leaving the La Concha, then drove my 1966 Land Rover Series IIA to the airport. Hordes of people stood outside the main terminal building, which was now under construction to add jet bridges. A long line of eclectic taxis slowly collected many of the new arrivals, while others stood just past the terminal awaiting rideshare pickups. I drove past them and parked in the lot of the General Aviation Terminal, then passed through the building and nodded hello to Doug, the latest flight concierge, who was busy shuffling multiple people out to private planes on the tarmac. I followed one group of four men I guessed to be in their forties outside, and they walked toward a chartered Beech Baron.

I cut to the left and walked down a few hangars until I reached ours. I smiled when I saw our new *Last Resort Charter and Salvage* sign on the door. Inside, I found Ray organizing his multiple tool chests, which had been spread haphazardly around the vacuous space. He looked up when the door closed, then dropped the tools he was holding into the open drawer on the tall chest and walked purposefully toward me. He'd recently shaved off all but a Fu Manchu mustache from his perpetually bearded face, which still caught me off guard since he'd worn the beard as long as I'd known him.

"Everything okay?" he said, as he stopped and placed his hands on his hips.

He was also no longer wearing Hawaiian shirts, another trademark of his for years. They'd been replaced with reproduction t-shirts from classic rock bands, and today's was based on a black-and-white Led Zeppelin poster of an exploding blimp trailing smoke and flames. It occurred to me that it wasn't the best subliminal messaging for future charter customers, but I wasn't going to chastise him when I was here to ask a favor.

"Everything's good—great in fact."

"Great?" His eyes narrowed.

"Yeah, Harry Greenbaum called about chartering Big Mama this weekend."

"Really? Is he going to be in town? I've never met him in person."

I shook my head. "No, we have to fly to him, but you'll finally get to meet him, provided you're available to travel for what may be up to ten days."

Ray's mustache turned up as he curled his upper lip. "Gee, let me check my social calendar." He held his hand up and stared at his blank palm. "Nope, no plans. No charters booked and no hot dates."

I pressed my lips together. I'd never known Ray to go out on a date in the decade we'd been friends. But between his new look and his elevated standing in the community—thanks to the recent opening of our museum dedicated to the Spanish galleon we'd found in the Bahamas, the *Nuestra Senora Farnese*, not to mention the celebrity treatment we'd been afforded after our last find of a unique treasure here on Key West—maybe that would change. The combination of events, circumstances, and adulation had injected an all-time high of confidence in Ray that was a pleasure to see flourish.

I smiled broadly at him, which caused him to squint at me with suspicion.

"Harry wants us to fly Big Mama to Italy to join a formation of classic antique aircraft to kick off the Italian Grand Prix Formula 1 event."

Ray's jaw dropped and his eyes opened wide.

"Italy?" His voice was a decibel higher than usual. "Kick off the Formula 1 race there? Are you kidding?" Another decibel up.

I couldn't tell if he was thrilled or incredulous. "That's right. It's this weekend, so we'd need to get moving damn fast."

He pumped a fist like he was swinging a hammer. "Heck yeah!"

Now my eyes opened wide. I'd hoped he'd say yes, but I didn't expect this level of enthusiasm, given the distance.

"Why do you look so surprised?" he asked. "Formula 1's the hottest thing going these days—they have hundreds of thousands of people at those race weekends. Plus they're televised globally—imagine the promo we'll get for Last Resort!"

Something he said caught me off guard. "What do you mean, 'race weekends?'"

"Those races are three-day events, starting on Fridays. There's a couple of days of practice then qualifying on Saturdays to determine the starting order. Then the races themselves are on Sundays."

I took a step back. "Three-day events? For a car race?"

"Obviously you've never watched one. Most the cars are driven by twenty-somethings from all over the world, and they go over two hundred miles an hour!" He paused, then shrugged. "I recently bought a new gaming system that simulates all the racetracks. I get to pick my favorite driver, and it's like I'm driving their car. It's awesome."

"You even have a favorite driver? How did I not know any of this?"

Ray crossed his arms. "You're normally too self-absorbed, Buck. But for the past couple of months you've been inseparable from Heather, and I'm guessing you had better things to do than watch sporting events on television."

I didn't even have a television. His mention of Heather made me cringe. I hadn't yet told her my plans had changed.

"Do we get to go to the race?" he asked.

That caught me off guard. Harry hadn't said but I assumed so if we were part of the entertainment. I nodded my head. "Yeah, he'll get us in."

Ray pumped his fist again. I hadn't seen him this excited since he reached the highest level of whatever shoot-'em-up game he'd been playing lately. The smile then fell from his face, replaced by a more serious expression.

"It's Monday now," he said. "If we have to be there by Thursday night, we'll need to leave tomorrow morning at the latest."

A smile bent my lips. "So that's a yes, then?"

Ray grimaced. "No, it's a hell yes." He paused and studied my face. "You don't look too excited."

"I promised Heather earlier today that I'd come spend a week with her in New York City starting this weekend."

He frowned. "I'm sure she won't be happy you're blowing her off to go to Italy." He held up both palms to face me. "I'm staying out of that. By the way, what's Harry's affiliation with Formula 1?"

"He said something about a rare opportunity to invest in a team. He thought our participating in the flyover of antique aircraft would help solidify that."

Ray rubbed his hands together so hard and fast, I expected to see sparks fly out from between them. "Hot damn, this'll be amazing!"

"Okay, well, then if you don't mind, start the flight plan so we can get it filed today and leave in the morning."

Ray pointed toward me with gusto. "On it!"

I walked out of the hangar in a daze, feeling like the last one in on a secret. Ray loved Formula 1 racing, go figure. When I got to the Rover, popped the door open, and sat inside, I left the door open so the breeze would air out the hot vehicle.

The next call would be a lot more difficult. I pulled up Heather's number and just stared at it for a moment. She wasn't going to be happy, and I saw no way to make margaritas out of a sour situation.

I hit send and the sound of ringing began on the speaker. She answered quickly.

"Hi! I've already made two dinner reservations and we have tickets for the Michael Jackson musical." She sounded short of breath. "I'm so excited!"

I bit the side of my lip.

"I have a slight change of plans, but with an exciting twist," I said.

Silence followed on the line. I could almost feel Heather's disappointment in the pregnant pause, so I continued quickly.

"Harry called in a marker and asked that Ray and I bring Big Mama to Italy for the Formula 1 race this weekend—"

"In Monza?" Her voice lifted quickly.

"Ah, yeah," I said. "You know about it?"

She giggled. "I dated one of the drivers for a while—nothing serious, Fernando traveled more than me—but I did fall in love with the whole scene and the international aspect of the sport."

Now my jaw hung open.

"Fernando?" It was all I could muster.

"Spanish guy. Very charming, and, well, handsome, not to mention he was a world champion, but that was several years ago—what does Harry have to do with Formula 1?"

I shook my head quickly. Again I felt like the last person on earth to be clued into something.

"Some kind of flyover of antique aircraft over the track at the start of the race," I said. "We're taking Big Mama and we have to leave tomorrow."

I thought I heard a grunt, followed by, "That's lovely, Buck. If you invited me to come, I'd say yes—not to fly in your old plane, mind you, but—"

"I can't invite you, Heather. It's not my shindig." I grimaced in anticipation of her response.

"They are public events, after all," she said.

"Very true, but I don't really know what Harry has planned, and Ray is my plus-one."

"Oh. Charming."

"Takes two pilots to fly Big Mama, Heather. You know that."

It was on the tip of my tongue to share that Harry had some potential investment opportunity brewing, which would likely get us some VIP treatment at the race, but I knew that would just make it worse.

"Okay then," she said. "We'll reschedule New York for when you return from romantic Italy. With Ray," she added.

"If I were going," she continued, "I'd stay at Hotel de la Ville, a nice little boutique inn near the *autodromo* where the race is held, which is where many of the drivers stay. The owner, Gigi, is a friend."

"I don't know what Harry has in mind—"

"If he's staying in Monza, it's the place to be."

"Come to think of it, Harry will probably fly in from Milan on his helicopter," I said.

Quiet followed on the line and I knew I'd disappointed her, not only over New York, but for not inviting her to join us. But I couldn't. We'd be busy flying anyway.

"I'm sorry, Heather. I'll make it up to you, I promise."

"*Buon viaggio*," she said.

I didn't know any Italian, but her statement was close enough to one in French that I did know. Have a good trip.

"Thanks, and I'll keep you posted on our travels."

Click was her response. The line had gone dead.

I started the Rover, and if anyone was watching me, they'd have seen the frown on my face. It had been years since I'd gone to Europe, and flying over in Big Mama with Ray to meet Harry and participate in the Formula 1 festivities would be a lot of fun. Heather coming would have been icing on the cake, but it would be better if we went on our own trip in the future.

If we had a future.

3

THE AFTERNOON WAS A BLUR AS I READIED FOR THE IMPROMPTU trip to Italy. Ray had come up with a painfully long yet efficient flight plan that would take us north to Portland, Maine, in 1,366 nautical miles of flying on day one. From there, day two would be a brutal three-leg trip of 2,044 nautical miles: to Goose Bay in Newfoundland, then to Narsarsuaq in Greenland, finishing in Keflavik, Iceland. From there, if we survived that, we'd fly 1,676 nautical miles on the third day to Edinburgh, Scotland, then down to Linate, Italy—I'd guessed right about the flight time and that it would take three days. If we started at dawn on the last day, it would put us on the ground at Linate Airport, just north of Monza, at approximately four p.m. Thursday.

After he emailed the plan to me, I let out a long exhale, then called him to discuss the details.

"It's all set, Buck." His voice was harried.

I figured that like me, he was busy getting his ducks in a row to facilitate a week away.

"That's a hell of a lot of flying," I said.

"Just doing what we love most, and in our new luxury liner, Big Mama."

Luxury liner? Maybe compared to our other bare-boned antiques, but Big Mama wasn't exactly a Gulfstream jet. "You need help with anything?" I asked.

"I don't have any decent clothes to wear in Italy, much less at the race or any fancy restaurants or hotels," he said.

His statement caused me a pang of anxiety. As I'd lamented earlier, my fishing shirts and linen outfits were also woefully inadequate.

"Where are you going to shop?"

"I want some Ferragamo shoes and some nice Italian pants and shirts," he said.

I nearly blew a snot bubble. "Ferragamo shoes? Really, Ray?"

His loud exhale caused distortion on my phone. "In case you haven't noticed, I'm upgrading my look."

"You mean the classic rock band t-shirts?"

"That's for Key West. Italy requires an entirely different wardrobe."

"You sound like Heather," I said under my breath.

"I heard that," he said. "And comparing me to Heather's a compliment." Ray paused and I could tell he was formulating a greater response. "I'm happy to be your partner at Last Resort, Buck. It's given me experiences I never even imagined I'd have. But it's also given me a level of visibility and exposure I never sought or wanted. That being said, I'm not going to hide from our success, and I'm not going to Italy with some old Jimmy Buffett-wannabe Hawaiian shirts. You know the old cliché, 'when in Rome'? That's not a cliché for this trip."

I was nodding and smiling. Ray continued to amaze me with his increasingly rapid evolution as he fought to shed the tropically-clad chrysalis he'd been swaddled in for most of our friendship.

"And you certainly haven't noticed—or at least mentioned—that I've lost ten pounds. I won't quit until I've lost fifteen more."

I hadn't noticed, maybe because Ray's entire look had changed so much. "That's great, Ray. I'm happy for you."

He paused a moment, then said, "Thanks."

"Okay, butterfly, be free." I laughed. "And let me know if you find any decent clothes on this rock, because I need to do the same."

We hung up, with me shaking my head, but as I'd said, I too needed some new clothes. It took me an hour to review the flight plan, analyze weather along the route, double-check the math on fuel consumption, and study the airports Ray had selected for our stops. As usual, his logic and planning were perfect and I'd made no changes, but he'd expect me to understand everything. In fact, each of us had to have the entire plan dialed in so the other could try and sleep while we took turns as pilots flying.

With that done, I packed what little attire I had that might be suitable for Italy, then texted Ray to see if he'd had any luck shopping. He said yes and steered me to a boutique I'd walked or ridden past many times around the corner on Fleming, just past The Roost.

"No Ferragamo or fancy Italian brands, but other good stuff," was his message.

I'd pick up a few items there then try to shop in Milan or Monza between responsibilities participating in the flight formation of antique planes.

An icon appeared on my phone indicating a new email. I didn't get many of those, so I opened the mail app and found a message from someone named Rafael DeGregorio. I was about to delete it as spam when I saw the word *Monza* in the subject and clicked it open.

> *Mr. Reilly, I'm writing per Mr. Greenbaum's instruction. I'm the flight coordinator for this weekend's opening ceremonies at Monza. I need information about your Grumman Albatross so we can determine the formation with the four other vintage aircraft. Please also provide your pilot license details, experience, and that of your copilot or crew. Photographs of your plane would be appreciated, along with its performance specifications. The formation will meet at Linate Airport (LIN) on Friday, 1 September, and stage from there. We will have three practice flights after our engineers inspect each of the aircraft.*

The email went on to provide contact names and information at Linate and closed with a request to keep Rafael informed on arrival time and progress.

The email made me realize I hadn't followed up with Harry since his original call, so I dialed him now. After a few rings, he answered.

"Buck, please tell me you're not calling to withdraw from this weekend's festivities," he said.

"On the contrary. I'm calling to let you know we've filed our flight plan and will depart at dawn tomorrow. We should arrive at Linate Thursday afternoon."

"Splendid, my dear boy!"

The excitement in his voice was palpable. I didn't think I'd ever heard him more enthused about anything. Ever since getting knighted, he'd stepped up his already world-class game and was now hobnobbing with royalty, the connection he'd said had presented this opportunity to invest in a Formula 1 team in the first place.

I told Harry I'd received the instructions from Rafael DeGregorio and shared that I was now in trouble with Heather for canceling our time together.

"I do apologize for that, but it will be a weekend to remember, I assure you. First class all the way, pit and paddock passes with full access to the team owner's box. Once you are finished flying in formation, I'll have the helicopter swoop you over to Monza."

When had Harry ever been this talkative or effusive?

He fell silent for a moment, no doubt catching his breath. "I do thank you, Buck. And when the festivities are over, I'd like you to return to London with me to spend some time together, one on one."

"I look forward to it, Harry. This will be an ex ... ah ... *citing* transatlantic trip in Big Mama, er, the Albatross ... then flying in formation over a hundred-plus-thousand people. A first, even for me." I'd wanted to say *excruciating*.

I promised to keep him apprised and we disconnected. I sat on the corner of my bed and tried to remember the last time I'd seen Harry. It must have been at least five years since he'd beckoned me to New York City to ask that I help a former presidential candidate locate the remains of his missing nephew. He'd already been quite overweight then and already pushing seventy years old. I feared what his condition would be now, especially after he'd been holed up at his country estate outside of London for a couple of years, in the company of his private chef and ten-thousand-bottle wine collection. Exercise was below him. He had no family; I didn't know for sure if he'd ever been married but recalled he'd once mentioned he had no children.

Regardless, Harry was in top spirits these days, and after all he'd done for me over the past fifteen-plus years, I was both honored and excited to play a part in helping his quest to acquire a share of this racing team, as odd as that seemed to me.

THE NEXT MORNING CAME FAST, and at dawn I took an Uber to the general aviation terminal, where I found Ray already loaded up and waiting inside Big Mama. I stowed my flight bag and the backpack with my limited attire. I'd never had time to shop, so I'd be looking like a fisherman out of water.

Ray powered Big Mama up the runway, and we lit out toward the Florida Straits with the grace of … a fat old Albatross, I guess. Eyes had peered up from the windshields of oncoming cars as I glanced out the right cockpit window down over A1A, which caused me to smile. Big Mama looked like a cross between a squat military transport plane and a pregnant amphibian, and amphibious was exactly what she'd been designed to be.

The sun hovered over the water like an orange wedge on the side of a brilliant green cocktail, and I moved my sun visor to block the right window as the sun both blinded me and caused me to perspire. Big Mama's cooling system had been restored, but it was still woefully inferior to the systems modern planes were equipped with.

After more than twelve hours of flying—with both of us monitoring radio traffic, checking and double-checking our location and the plane's flight data—Ray set her down with a perfect landing at PWM airport in Portland, Maine. We'd stretch our legs, refresh ourselves, grab some lobster rolls, refuel, and catch a few hours of shut-eye before I flew the next leg.

"All's going according to plan," Ray said. Then he grimaced. "So far."

"What's that supposed to mean?" I said.

He glanced over at me with his eyebrow curled. "We're going to fly a seventy-year-old plane over the Atlantic, Buck, and well, anywhere you are, sometimes things don't go smoothly."

I sat back hard in the left seat, craned my head to peer at him, and said, "Seriously? Are you really putting that out there as a suggestion to the universe?"

He pursed his lips. "Don't get all metaphysical on me. I'm just saying…"

I wanted to press him harder but clenched my jaw instead. There had indeed been plenty of instances where plans had changed due to unforeseen circumstances, but that was usually due to events outside my control. Usually.

"We're going to Italy, Ray, not the Caribbean or the Bahamas. A Formula 1 race, for Pete's sake. What could go wrong?"

He shook his head vigorously. "Now you're tempting fate by asking *that* question?" he asked.

"You brought it up, not me."

4

I CHECKED MY PHONE TO SEE IF HEATHER HAD TEXTED or emailed any inquires on our travels. There was a message, but not from her. It was an email from Harry. I read it once and felt my brow furrow.

"What's wrong?" Ray asked.

"Listen to this note from Harry. 'Buck, hope you are on your way. Outside conflict over my potential involvement in the racing team has emerged, and I am anxious to have you here with me. I trust the matter will not escalate into hostilities but do please apprise me of your estimated arrival time. If you cannot reach me, please contact Percy. Harry.'"

I looked up from my phone to meet Ray's eyes.

"That sounds creepy," he said. "Who's Percy?"

"His driver *cum* man Friday." I paused. "'Escalate into hostilities?' Should we be worried?"

Ray mulled over my question. "Harry's always been a corporate raider. Maybe his investing in this team isn't welcome by the team itself," he said. "Let's not worry about it. We have plenty else to be concerned over flying these next three legs."

I thought about what Ray said and agreed that he was probably right. I sent back a brief response advising Harry of our estimated time of arrival, followed by a line I hoped would resonate with him: "Sounds like business as usual in your world of leveraged buyouts and hostile takeovers. Don't get too many people angry with you, Sir Harry. See you tomorrow."

With that I fired up the right nine-cylinder Wright R-1820-76 Cyclone 1,425-horsepower radial engine. The sound and vibration was steady and consistent, just like it should be. Ray and I shared a glance, and I gave him a knowing look as if he shouldn't be so paranoid. I then hit the switch on the left engine, and it coughed for a couple of seconds before sputtering to life and—BOOM—Ray and I both jumped when the engine suddenly backfired.

It caught a second later and jarred the plane with a lurch until the RPMs settled into a smooth cadence. Our eyes again met, and I shook my head at Ray, who tilted his head back on the freshly restored leather headrest. His chief role in our partnership was to ensure our fleet was running smoothly. We couldn't afford engine problems with our aggressive flight plan, and the Italian flight coordinator would scratch us if he thought Big Mama wasn't flightworthy. That would crush Harry, so I tried to push the thought out of my mind.

Ray, on the other hand, wouldn't stop dwelling on the potential issue so easily. We were given clearance to take off and I pressed the throttles forward slightly to get Big Mama rolling.

I had already become accustomed to the height and size differences of the Albatross compared to our other older Grumman Widgeon and Goose. The additional weight made the run-up down the runway smoother, but the weight and girth caused us to use a lot more of the five-thousand-foot runways we typically utilized. Our takeoff from Portland was no different, with Big Mama hitting takeoff speed more than two-thirds down runway number 36 before lifting off the tarmac and into the air. At one hundred feet altitude I raised the retractable landing gear, added power, and toggled the rudder trim to control yaw until we had a comfortable climb attitude, ascending toward our target altitude of 13,500 feet.

Oil pressure was steady on both engines, the battery was charged, the amp draw was good and the exhaust temp within range. So we continued north, with our next destination at Goose Bay, 716 nautical miles away.

"There's something I want to do when we're done with Monza," Ray's voice sounded in my headset.

I clicked my mic. "Yeah, what's that?"

"The oldest seaplane base in all of Europe is on a lake just north of Milan. It's always been on my bucket list to land and takeoff there."

I gave him a sidelong glance. "Which lake?"

"Como."

"Fancy schmancy," I said. "We could buzz Bellagio."

"And George Clooney's house," Ray said.

I glanced over at him and saw the loopy grin on his face. Ray may have shaved off his beard, elevated his wardrobe, and lost some weight, but he was still a celebrity fanboy. He saw me staring at him and lifted his hands palms up. Formula 1 fan or not, Ray had dropped everything to help me accommodate Harry's request, so I couldn't say no to his. Plus, based on Heather's enthusiasm for the sport, along with Harry's connections and pending purchase of an interest in one of the teams, it should be fun.

I nodded to Ray, and he smiled.

Hours later, the approach over Labrador and into Happy Valley-Goose Bay was epic, one that I'd heard other pilots talk about with awe in the past. I added flaps, reduced power, and followed the Churchill River toward the airport famous for being the largest military base in northeastern North America. It was built on a large sandy plateau in 1941, but in another month— two at the most—the borderline subarctic region would be covered in snow. We were fortunate that it was early September. Air traffic control vectored us straight in toward runway 34, an 11,051-foot-long, 200-foot-wide asphalt strip.

I set Big Mama down and barely used a third of the runway, it was so long. The fixed-base operations center, or FBO, was to the right of the runway, and once we'd slowed sufficiently, we turned off on a taxiway and headed toward the general aviation terminal.

"That was an easy leg," Ray said.

"Do they rent gear here?" I asked.

He nodded and I started a list on my phone. Once done, I read it aloud as we waited for the fuel jockey.

"Gumby suits, spare emergency beacon, satellite phone, extra raft, and extra oxygen bottles," I said.

"Gumby suits?" Ray asked. "You really think we're going to wind up in the water?"

The curl of my lip was not lost on him. "Given our course, better safe than frozen."

He didn't argue or look concerned. If anything, I read his expression as questioning why he hadn't already thought of that.

After four hours of flying, I was ready to stretch my legs and hit the head. It was only the first of three stops today, so we didn't have much time for more than fuel, food, renting the gear, and bio breaks. We left Big Mama in the capable hands of the fuel jockey, who directed us toward the rental depot for the gear, and the terminal's sole dining establishment, Robin's Donuts.

All in, we were on the ground for thirty-two minutes. Ray was back in the left seat and used most of the asphalt strip as we were whipped by a steady twenty-five-knot wind that lifted us up less than halfway down the north-facing runway 34. Air traffic control gradually vectored us east where we flew another four and a half hours to the southern snowcapped tip of Greenland and landed at BGBW on the 6,004-foot-long concrete strip of runway 07. Also built in 1941, the Narsarsuaq airport had seen plenty of action in the last few years of World War II.

"Did you know a squadron of PBY Catalina flying boats and B-25 Mitchells were stationed here to escort convoys and hunt submarines back in the day?" I said.

Ray glanced over and yawned. "More than ten thousand aircraft were ferried through this base during the war," he said.

Ray's response didn't surprise me. He was always better prepared and equipped with aviation anecdotes than I was. My job was typically the forward-facing activities of dealing with press, government agencies, and competitors while out in the field, or handling charter customers, whereas his attention was more focused on the finer details. I was sure Ray also knew that Narsarsuaq was considered one of the most dangerous airports in the world due to strong winds and the huge number of fjords in the area. If I knew Ray, and I did, he'd probably planned which legs we would each fly based on his concern about landing here.

Fine with me.

We repeated the same process as at Goose Bay, then once again—less than thirty-five minutes after we'd landed—we were back on the flight deck with both engines running and me in the left seat. "Wish I could've stretched my legs a bit more," Ray said.

"Today's our long one, Ray. You planned it this way for a reason. There's nothing to do at Narsarsuaq anyway. I'd rather get to Keflavik, get a good night's sleep, and leave bright and early for our last two …"—

a yawn interrupted the end of my sentence—"… legs."

"You good to fly?" he asked.

I shook my arms and nodded my head quickly up and down. "I'll be fine." I glanced over my right shoulder to catch his eye. "You nap now and if I get too tired, we can switch in the air."

Ray's expression radiated discomfort. His freshly trimmed Fu Manchu mustache bunched up when he frowned. He hated to sleep while I—or anyone else—flew one of our planes. Hell, I'd rather he was awake, too, because truth be told, two solid days of flying had me dog-tired, but we had no choice. Harry was counting on us to arrive tomorrow afternoon, and that wouldn't be possible if we didn't make it to Iceland before dark. They didn't allow Visual Flight Rules, VFR, night flights there.

I pressed the throttles forward and again experienced the magic of a seventy-plus-year-old, twin-engine propeller plane that appeared vastly underpowered, but wasn't. We rumbled down the concrete runway and gradually lifted into the sky when a crosswind immediately buffeted us. Ray jumped in his seat. I flinched too, but whether from him or the massive plane getting rocked in the wind, I wasn't sure. No words were spoken, but I sat taller and studied Big Mama's gauges and dials to keep from making eye contact with Ray.

Two hours and forty minutes later, we switched positions. Ray hadn't slept, and I was groggy. My eyelids had been getting heavy, which had him on the edge of his seat. The glow of dusk reflected through the cabin from behind us, and we were in a race against the setting sun. Ray added power and I peed in a jug, then dug out a few of the remaining Robin's Donuts. We settled in for the last hour, our heading due east, out in the middle of the North Atlantic, the plane's new but more tropical-weight heater struggling to keep us warm.

I dozed off and the next thing I knew we were on the ground, rumbling along. It was damned close to dark in the cockpit, and I pulled myself up from the slump I'd been twisted in to look out the windscreen. We were moving quickly up the taxiway and I pulled my headset back on and glanced at Ray.

"That went fast."

"For you," he said.

I zoomed out the radar screen and could see the entire island of Iceland. It occurred to me the island was shaped like an inflated puffer fish, with BIKF, or Keflavik Airport, located on the southwestern coast. I rubbed the nap from my eyes and a slow smile bent my lips.

"That was two thousand and forty-four nautical miles of flying today," I said.

"Thirteen hours and thirteen minutes in the air," Ray said. "But who's counting."

"That should be our hardest day," I said. "Seven hundred and fifty nautical miles to Edinburgh in the morning, followed by nine hundred and twenty-six miles to Linate for another ten hours of flying."

"And two minutes."

"What?"

"Ten hours and two minutes flying tomorrow."

I rolled my eyes.

"And that's only if the vibration I've been feeling in the left engine is just my imagination," he said.

My head swiveled toward Ray. "When did you start detecting that?"

"I thought I felt something on the takeoff out of Goose Bay, but I noticed it again an hour ago after you fell asleep. I radioed ahead and they have an open hangar space where we can park Big Mama and check it out."

My head fell back against the headrest. Crap. We didn't need engine problems out here in the middle of nowhere. Harry would be crushed, but even worse, we could be screwed big time.

"Let's get some extra oil while we're here, too," he said.

"You going to add oil while we're flying?"

"No, but if we have to land in the water, then we can try to do it then."

"Oh sure, in the middle of the freaking ocean in twenty-foot seas."

I kept my response to a whisper and hadn't activated the mic. I'd gotten Ray into this, so far be it from me to be the one whining about it.

5

BIG MAMA'S LEFT ENGINE HAD BURNED A DISPRO-
PORTIONATE AMOUNT OF OIL, but Ray had not seen any signs of
leakage, so we were comfortable with topping it off and checking it again
when we landed in Edinburgh. Once we gassed up and bought five
gallons of oil, we walked out of the airport with our backpacks. Reykjavik
is the largest city in Iceland, known for great restaurants and bars. We
could have had made a memorable evening of it, but as pilots flying a
transatlantic crossing in an antique jalopy that might be more appropriate
in a museum, we erred on the side of caution and crashed hard in a small
hotel near the airport.

Up with the orange light of dawn that clung to the horizon like fiery
magma seeping out of the earth's center core, we both took quick
showers, filled our Yeti mugs with hotel coffee—Ray added cream and
sugar and I kept mine black—and we stepped outside into the cold, crisp
Icelandic air. Given that Ray had taken over my shift last night, I took
piloting responsibilities for the first of two legs. Three hours into the
nearly five-hour flight, while we were approaching the Scottish coast, the
vibration Ray had detected the day before reappeared. We monitored oil
pressure for the left engine, which was ticking downward slowly, and
Ray even studied the charts for alternative airports or large lakes where
we could make an emergency landing if need be.

We made it to EGPH, the airport in Edinburgh, where the Civil
Aviation Authority (CAA) vectored us around the city in a square
pattern, between commercial jetliners, as we waited for our turn to land.
The oil pressure was steady, so we saw no reason to seek priority. Having
never been to Europe, Ray kept his face pressed against the right-side
window, calling out observations as we rounded the city and countryside.

"There's a huge castle down there!" he said.

There were castles all over Scotland, but given we were over the old city, I had a good idea what he was referring to. "Is it at the top of the highest point near the downtown?"

"Yeah, that's right."

"That's Edinburgh Castle. It dates back to 1103. The road leading from it down the hill to the bridge that crosses the railroad tracks is called the Royal Mile," I said.

A few moments later as our course took us back over the countryside, Ray shared more observations. "The land's palette is very green. Rolling hills, tiled roofs, and winding roads."

"There are two seasons in Scotland. The rainy season, and July."

The CAA gave us instructions to land on runway 24, so I vectored into our base leg and set Big Mama down on the 8,386-foot asphalt runway. Large commercial jets were lined up on taxiways waiting their turn to depart, and no sooner had we taxied off 24 than a large British Airways A320 set down next to us. We continued to the FBO where we pulled Big Mama up to an open ramp. Ray immediately climbed up to check inside the cowling of the left engine, while I radioed the fuel operator and asked them to prioritize us as we needed to be aloft within thirty minutes. Then I ventured inside to use the head and scrounge us food and fresh coffee.

When I returned with haggis, jugs of water, and our Yetis replenished, I found Ray pouring the oil into the left engine's reservoir.

"Look okay?" I asked.

He gave me a thumbs-up. "Nothing to worry about," he said. "Pretty typical for the Curtis Wright radial engines. Just need to stay on top of the situation."

That was a relief. Ray was one of the top aviation mechanics specializing in old Grummans, and hell, Last Resort now owned three, so he was constantly tinkering, replacing parts, and researching their history. If he was comfortable, I was too. Once the fuel jockey topped us off, Ray took the left seat and we set off on our last leg, destined for Linate Airport just outside of Milan, Italy, 926 nautical miles away.

Five hours and ten minutes later, Ray set Big Mama down at 4:25 p.m. local time. We were both exhausted from ten hours and two minutes of flying all day. We taxied down runway 18, which, at 8,012 feet long, took what felt like forever to get us to Universal Aviation, the fixed-base operator, where we'd been instructed by Raphael DeGregorio to tie down.

As we approached, I spotted other vintage aircraft, which I assumed must be the additional participants in the formation to fly over the autodromo at Monza before the race Sunday. Numerous private jets and several single- and twin-engine planes were also tied down in front of the small general aviation terminal.

"My first time in Italy," Ray said. His eyes were wide.

Linate looked like most other airports, but mountains appeared as smudges in the distance, unlike most of the Caribbean islands we normally flew to.

I pointed to the other classic aircraft and saw an open spot. "There's our tie-down spot."

"Sweet," Ray said. "I don't recognize the types of planes those are."

"Raphael sent me a list of the other planes. Single- and twin-engine Italian warbirds from World War II. There's a Macchi MC.200 Saetta that was used in North Africa—"

"The one painted in tan-and-dark-green camo?"

I nodded. "A Fiat G.50 Arrow—that black plane with the thicker nose that looks like an old Thunderbolt," I said.

"That one looks a little rough."

I pointed to another plane, also black with a white stripe painted around the fuselage behind the cockpit and a white cross adorning its tail. "That's a Reggiane Re.2005 Archer, which is super rare—only fifty-four were built out of the original order for seven hundred and fifty due to production challenges at the end of the war."

"Kind of looks like a British Spitfire," Ray said.

"That's what it was designed to do battle with."

"What's that big twin-engined one?"

I checked the list on the email from Raphael DeGregorio. "That must be the Savoia-Marchetti SM.82 *Marsupiale*. Another World War II vintage Italian aircraft."

Ray smiled. "What's the old joke about the vintage Italian army rifle for sale, 'only thrown down once'? Wonder how much action these planes saw."

"I'm just hoping they're airworthy and don't cause any issues for the Formula 1 flyover Harry has his heart set on."

Ray rushed through the post-flight checklist so he could set his feet on Italian soil.

Thirty minutes later, we'd checked in with Raphael, who was thrilled at our arrival, and he briefed us on the plan for meeting the next day to go over the schedule then practice formation flying with the other planes. With the logistics now established, we took a taxi into Milan to the Bulgari Hotel where Harry had rooms waiting for us, and where we'd meet him for dinner.

I'd texted Heather earlier to let her know we'd arrived safely, and all I got back was *Good.*

While Ray marveled at the ancient architecture of the crowded, massive, and least interesting big city in Italy—at least to me—I rested my head back against the seat and closed my eyes. The three days of flying had been exhausting, but now here, I planned to enjoy spending the time with Harry, which—since we were participating in the pre-race festivities on his behalf—made it even more special.

I felt an elbow in my rib, which caused me to jump. "Buck, we're here at the hotel," Ray said.

I sat up, my eyelids fluttering. I'd fallen asleep. A porter had opened our doors and was removing our scant luggage from the car's trunk. My watch read 6:08, which meant we had to hurry as we were supposed to meet Harry down at the restaurant at 6:30 for a very early meal, by Italian standards. But Harry had other obligations to attend to later, and as exhausted as Ray and I were, that was fine with me.

Ray's and my rooms were adjacent to each other, and we agreed to meet at the bar in fifteen minutes. When I stepped inside my room, a familiar scent tickled my nostrils.

Or was it my imagination?

On the bed was a black pair of men's slacks and a shirt with a brand new pair of Ferragamo loafers.

"What the hell?"

On the other side of the bed I saw luggage. Fancy luggage—a pair of Louis Vuitton suitcases.

"Shit!"

I'd somehow entered someone else's room.

As I stood frozen, I heard a sound from … the bathroom? Or another room in the suite. Was it a giggle?

The smell … the giggle.

I walked forward slowly, with a sensation I imagined a cat burglar must experience breaking into an occupied home. Beautiful alternating gold and black ceramic tiles led to a bathtub—full, with bubbles spilling over the edge.

Another giggle—I turned quickly to my right—and my jaw fell open.

"Benvenuto in Italia."

Heather stood to my right, dressed only in a sheer camisole, her blonde hair on her shoulders, her blue eyes sparkling under the halogen lights.

My mouth dropped open as she closed the distance, the camisole falling open in the few strides it took to reach me.

She wrapped her arms around me, and I was filled with instant joy, followed by a growing sense of dread.

"What are you doing here?" I said.

She leaned away from the embrace, her smile now gone.

"I mean, oh my gosh, I can't believe you're here!"

Her smile returned slowly, and she pulled me closer, her hands already at work on the buttons on my shirt, followed by my belt.

"You need a bath after all that flying." Her voice was a hoarse whisper.

I buried my face in her hair—the smell I'd noticed when I entered the room. I breathed it in deeply.

My pants fell to the tile floor and landed on top of my Patagonia fishing shirt.

"Don't worry, Buck. Harry called and invited me after you told him you had to break our date in New York."

Somehow when she'd been undressing me during our embrace, she'd shed her camisole and stood naked before me. The same nervous quiver passed through me, just like the first time I'd seen her with no clothes on, and she looked every bit as spectacular these dozen years later.

She took me by the hand toward the steaming bath.

"I'll wash your back," she said. She pumped her eyebrows. "And your front."

The smile on my face narrowed my eyes. I stepped into the hot water just after she did and pulled her close.

"Guess we're going to be late for dinner," I said.

"No one will be surprised at that, my dear."

After the lengthy bath, where we made sure every inch of each other's bodies was massaged and cleaned, we dried off then hurried to get dressed.

"I can't believe you went shopping for me," I said.

"I've been here two days and done nothing but shop. It's been perfect."

My next thought was that Ray would be jealous over my wardrobe since he'd been so determined to dress in style. My dirty clothes were balled up in the corner. Cargo pants, orange fishing shirt, and Pilar Rum t-shirt.

"Thanks, dear." My voice was quiet in the small, lavishly decorated room.

Heather was now dressed in a tight-fitting red pencil skirt and matching low-cut top, her hair miraculously still perfect, and since she wore hardly any makeup, she was ready just as fast as me.

We found Ray and Harry under a broad umbrella outside on the patio, set with several tables for al fresco dining. I heard Ray talking about Formula 1 as we approached, but when Harry spotted us, he stood and bowed to Heather. My heart fluttered when I studied him. Always a heavy man, he had visibly gained weight since I'd seen him last, a couple years before the pandemic. He wore a tweed suit with a muted tie and dabbed continuously at beads of perspiration on his forehead. My heart skipped a beat out of concern for my former investor and family friend who had known my parents since before I was born.

Heather gave Harry a hug and a kiss on the cheek.

Harry grinned widely, his trim Van Dyke beard arched up and revealing his brown, crooked teeth. I took a step toward him and extended my hand. He took it in both of his and squeezed tight. If I didn't know Harry better, I might have thought I'd seen tears well up in his eyes.

"Buck. I'm so pleased to see you. And very grateful you made the journey in your classic plane." He nodded toward Ray. "Mr. Floyd here told me about the arduous crossing."

"Good to see you, Harry." My smile lingered, and the joy I felt at seeing him was tempered by my concern for his condition, dangerous for a man in his early seventies. "And thank you for inviting Heather to join us."

"It is always a pleasure to see your former better half," he said.

I pointed to Ray. "Turns out Ray's a big F1 fan, and well, Heather, ah ..."

"Used to date one of the drivers," Heather said. "I already told Harry, Buck. It's no big deal."

Harry sat back down but his smile still radiated. "Do sit, dear boy. I'm afraid I don't have a lot of time before I must leave to meet principals of the firm I'm in discussions with."

I sat across from Harry, between Ray and Heather. There was already a bottle of red Barolo wine on the table, and a bottle of prosecco in an ice bucket. I told Harry we'd already connected with Raphael and were in the loop for tomorrow's meetings and practice flights, which I expected would delight him. But his face had grown serious, and he didn't even acknowledge my statements.

"Everything okay, Harry?"

He took in a shallow breath, and I could hear a rattle in his chest common among people carrying so much weight. It caused me to wince.

"Forgive me, Buck ... all of you, for that matter." He bowed his head a moment, then looked me straight in the eye. "The conflict I mentioned to you before has escalated to, well, let's just say an unpleasant level of dissension."

Ray shuffled in his seat next to me.

"*Dissension* isn't a helpful word, Harry. Can you be more precise?" I said.

He pursed his lips, then reached for his glass of red and took his time, sniffing and savoring it as we all stared at him. Ray's mouth was open, and Heather sat back in her chair, more amused than concerned. Ray and I had speculated previously that it was likely some kind of competitive situation related to Harry's deal, but he did seem rather put off by whatever the truth was.

"You said earlier that you hoped the situation—whatever it is— would not escalate into hostilities. Is that what's happened, Harry?"

He gave me an impetuous smirk. "You know how business deals go." He cleared his throat and used considerable effort to sit his girth up straighter. "And yes, *hostile* is an appropriate term I would use to describe the external negotiations."

"Related to your buying into this Formula 1 team?" I said.

"Quite," he said. "Williams Racing is a historic team, and their celebrated past has attracted all types of suitors."

"Williams is one of the classics," Ray said.

I placed my elbows on the table. "Can you please be more specific, Harry? Is the seller hostile, or is a competitor hostile?"

He yanked the napkin from his lap with a flourish then dabbed at his lips. "More the latter, I'm afraid, but it's not exactly a competitor." He held a pudgy palm up to prevent more questions. "I have a meeting with them tomorrow, so no more speculation until after that, if you don't mind."

"But what is the—"

Just then his phone rang—very loudly.

"Excuse me," he said.

He lifted the phone to his ear. "Yes?" He nodded once then turned the phone over and pressed the button to terminate the call.

"That was Percy. I'm afraid I'll have to depart early."

Percy was Harry's longtime driver and man Friday.

"But Harry—"

He interrupted me as if I hadn't spoken. "Chef Lorenzo has prepared a feast for you, so please do enjoy it. Everything here is on my account, and you are my guests, so really, enjoy yourselves."

He turned his attention back to me, his eyes serious. "I will plan to see you at the Williams facility in paddock tomorrow where we can speak in greater detail." He reached down to the side of his chair and retrieved three identical red leather zip-up satchels, each bulging wide. "Here are your all-access credentials for the hospitality suite, paddock, pit and all festivities."

"Ray and I are supposed to meet Raphael back at Linate tomorrow morning at ten for briefings followed by our initial formation flights. What time is the meeting you mentioned and when will you be at the track?"

Harry stood, and once he was on his feet, I realized I'd forgot how tall he was. Six-one, as I recalled. He had the presence and size of a very well-dressed brown bear. He stepped to the side, reached down, and took a cane from the back of his chair. That was new. He'd never used a cane as far as I knew.

Harry bent down and gave Heather a peck on the cheek. "So lovely to see you again, my dear."

"And you, Harry." Heather said. "Thank you again for the invitation and hospitality."

I stood and Ray followed suit. Harry walked around the table toward Ray first and extended his arm. He towered over Ray and was at least twice his weight. "Thank you for coming to assist Buck flying the plane, and I do hope we get to talk more."

Then to me, he hesitated, didn't meet my eyes, but reached around my shoulder for a quick, awkward hug. "Thank you, dear boy. I do so very appreciate you being here. I'll see you after your practice."

Words stuck in my throat as I sensed something far more important was at play than Harry asking us to participate in the historic flyover at the start of the race. But he was already moving away from me, and I'd hesitated, unable to ask him the pointed questions that were rattling inside my head with a building pressure.

"Harry, let me walk you out—"

He held his palm up, again, now with his arm extended fully like a running back giving a defender the stiff arm. "No, please, stay here and enjoy Lorenzo's fabulous cooking. We can speak in more detail tomorrow. Plus, I have rooms for everyone at the Hotel de la Ville in Monza, which as Heather knows, is *the* place to stay for the race there."

With that, he nodded quickly, turned to the left, and rather than entering the interior restaurant, followed the path that led around front to the hotel where Percy would no doubt be waiting in Harry's Rolls Royce.

"That was weird," Ray said.

I turned to face them. Heather was sipping bubbly; Ray's eyes were narrow and he had his arms crossed. Weird indeed.

"Why do you guy boys look so surprised?" Heather asked. "Harry's a billionaire business titan. Do you think he got there by luck? Or by not being involved in hostile takeovers? No way." She shook her head and took another swig of prosecco. "Plus, Formula 1 is as cutthroat as businesses come. There's only ten teams and the sponsorship money, TV rights, and global branding is worth billions. Other syndicates have been trying to buy their way in for years. The ante just to show up at the table is two hundred million dollars, and even with that, most of the teams are rejecting major players from getting a seat at the table, so Harry having the opportunity to buy into an existing team, and one with the pedigree of Williams, is almost unheard of."

"Williams are every bit as historic a team as even Ferrari," Ray said.

I ignored Ray, still focused on Heather. "What's your point?"

Heather glanced from me to Ray then back as if I were daft. "The point is that there's no doubt a ton of other groups who would like to be in Harry's position."

A swarm of waiters arrived carrying trays and plates of food that had been custom-made for us, each complete with an array of fresh pastas, delicate fish, meat, and vegetables that together looked as if they should be headed for a photo shoot or TV show. As the serving staff swirled around our table, placing the plates, removing others, and filling wine and water glasses, our discussion about Harry's visible concern settled. Heather seemed to have a logical perspective, so we let the moment pass and lost ourselves in one of the best meals I'd ever consumed.

Exhausted from the three days of flying, but restless, Ray and I succumbed to Heather's plea to walk over to the Duomo a few blocks away to see the ornate, triangular cathedral bathed in brilliant light amid the large public square where the fourteenth century church was set. As we walked through the streets toward the Duomo, the location of which Heather somehow knew by heart, I had a strange sense of being watched.

We arrived at the square to find hordes of people all with the same idea, and it was far too crowded to navigate, so we stood on the edge, peering in and admiring the illuminated edifice that towered high above the crowd. The same sensation of being watched again caused the hair on the back of my neck to stand up, and when I turned around, a pair of men turned quickly away but held their ground. I glanced past them to where their attention was now turned and saw nothing for them to be staring at other than closed shops and office spaces.

What the heck?

A pull on my sleeve turned me quickly back around. Heather was pointing up to a balcony across the street, facing the Duomo and the square. A huge orange sign proclaiming *Aperol spritz* glowed like an open flame, and based on Heather grabbing both my and Ray's hands and pulling us toward the sign, it was clear that like a moth, she could not ignore its magic.

As we crossed the road and entered the building where the Aperol bar was situated on the second floor, I glanced back at the last moment and saw that the pair of men had followed us. Dressed in black, with close-cropped hair and tight, dark beards, they appeared almost military in stature.

What the hell? Why would they be following us? I'd grown accustomed to fans stalking Heather, but these two didn't look like fashionistas or paparazzi.

Heather tugged hard on my hand, as we passed quickly through the building lobby and up the open staircase toward the orange luminosity of Aperol. I kept my eyes on the front door as we ascended the steps, but the pair of men hadn't reappeared.

Had it been my imagination? Must've been.

Why would anybody be following us in Milan, Italy?

6

HEATHER AND I HAD A MEMORABLE NIGHT in our suite at the hotel. As tired as I'd been, her quest for romance was unquenchable, and sleep didn't come for hours after we'd returned from enjoying multiple sweet, orange-colored Aperol spritzes by the Duomo. Ray and I had to be back at Linate Airport early in the morning to meet Raphael DeGregorio and the pilots of the other antique planes to practice our formation flying for Sunday's race. Heather had no interest in that, so she'd arranged for a driver to deliver her and our collective luggage to our next stop, the Hotel de la Ville in Monza. We agreed to meet later at the track where the race teams would be practicing in preparation for the weekend. She promised to guide us through what she described as the VIP labyrinth into the Paddock Club where Harry would be waiting.

I arrived at the restaurant to meet Ray for a quick breakfast, but he'd finished long ago and had a cold double espresso and a croissant waiting for me.

"Better eat that on the run," he said. "We can't be late for the briefing."

I downed the espresso, palmed the croissant, and followed Ray through the hotel lobby, past reception and out to meet the driver that Harry had arranged. Traffic toward Linate was congested, and brilliant red Ferrari flags were everywhere. Red was clearly the color of the day among pedestrians and occupants of other vehicles, and our driver informed us that since we were initially headed toward Monza, traffic would be thick until we turned south toward Linate.

"The Tifosi are thrilled for team Ferrari to be so close in the points with Red Bull, and hopes are high for either Charles Leclerc or Carlos Sainz to win the Grand Prix," he said, glancing back over his shoulder and ignoring the brake lights ahead of us.

I turned to Ray and my squint prompted a smile.

"Charles is Monegasque, and Carlos is Spanish," Ray said. "But they're the two Ferrari drivers, both in their twenties, sickeningly handsome, wealthy beyond belief, and rock stars here in Italy—worldwide, for that matter."

He glowed when he spoke. The spark in his eyes was different than when he talked about old planes, or even video games. How had I never known him to be a Formula 1 fan?

Damn. This sport really was a phenomenon.

"*Tifosi?*" I whispered.

"Fans," Ray said. "For Ferrari and their drivers." He squirmed in his seat, and I immediately knew that Ray was Tifosi.

Jeez.

The driver was correct: when we turned south toward the airport traffic thinned, and we arrived just in time for Raphael's briefing. He was older than I expected, chain-smoked cigarettes, had his own espresso machine in the small conference room and spoke English at high speed, fueled by the constant flow of nicotine and caffeine. The other pilots were Italian and spoke sufficient English to allow conversation, but more importantly, so they could communicate in the universal language of air traffic control. Once introductions were complete and we'd all enjoyed the close-up inspections of each other's planes, Raphael ushered us back to the briefing room.

"Given the size of the planes, the Albatross will be on point, with the Savoia-Marchetti and Regianne off the left wing, and the Fiat G.50 and Macchi off the right wing. Each plane will be fitted with canisters to release red, white, or green smoke—it's very important that you remain in formation, and at the exact altitude, otherwise the streaks of colors intended to produce the Italian flag will be a mess, this entire effort a failure, and me a laughingstock."

Ray glanced at me and raised a single brow. I'd already decided to let him be pilot in command so he could do what he does best and plan every detail of the flight. Between Harry's visible concerns and my sense that we were being followed last night, I was already having difficulty concentrating on the briefing. After another thirty minutes of instruction, Raphael led us out to the flight deck and our planes for our first run-through.

"You've got the left seat," I told Ray as we walked.

He said nothing, but the corners of his mustached mouth lifted in what I knew to be a smile. At Ray's urging, we were both wearing red polo shirts emblazoned with Last Resort Charter and Salvage logos on the chest. I hadn't thought of it before, but when Raphael smiled at us as we walked and said the newest word in my limited Italian vocabulary—*Tifosi*—I realized Ray had pre-planned our attire for a dual purpose.

The flight formation performed admirably on our first maneuver together. As it turned out, Raphael was acting as copilot on the Macchi in the rear-left position. Even though we all had pre-printed flight plans, he called out each vector like a coxswain. I studied the area chart as Ray flew, and called out landmarks as we flew at low altitude over the town of Monza, then around the eight-thousand-acre Monza Park, the largest in Europe, and continued around the *Autodromo Nazionale Monza*, the racetrack where the Grand Prix was being held. We both craned our heads to take in the odd-shaped track, wide and circular on one end, narrowing to a tighter radius curve that turned back toward the long straightaway on the opposite end. Even though it was only a practice day, there were tens of thousands of people around the track, and a tight concentration of trailers and multistory condos behind the main straightaway and multistory enclosed grandstands.

"That's the paddock where all those trailers are located," Ray said. "The teams are organized from end to end based on the standings, with the leading teams on one end and those with the fewest points on the far end."

"Points?" I asked.

"Each race has a winner, but the top ten of the twenty drivers all get points in both the constructor's, which is the car manufacturer, and the individual driver's categories. The winner of a race usually gets around twenty-five points, and the person in tenth place gets one point. Late in the season, a champion is crowned once it's mathematically impossible for anyone to catch them. Same with constructors."

I surveyed the scene from above. There were a huge number of vehicles associated with the race teams below us. "How often do they race?" I asked.

"The season goes for nine months and takes place all over the world, literally, from Bahrain to Budapest, Montreal to Monaco, Japan,

Saudi Arabia, Brazil, England, Austria … the list goes on. There's usually a race every week, or at least every two weeks."

"They move all this equipment around the world every week?"

"That's right, and as you can imagine, the logistics are a nightmare. But that's one of the reasons they have such a huge global following."

Our ragtag formation of vintage warbirds completed our first practice without mishap, and back at the airport, we agreed to meet in a few hours to practice again. The same driver who had brought us here from Milan was again out in front of the airport to bring us to the Autodromo in Monza. The trip north would normally take thirty minutes from Linate, but it took an hour due to traffic. And it was only a practice day at the track.

When we finally arrived at the first gate, our driver used my credentials to get us to the entrance closest to the paddock, where we used the badge designated "Friday" to pass through an electronic gate. Inside were dozens of people drinking champagne, wine, and cocktails, others seated in F1 driving simulators, trays of food circulating, and a retail booth with collectibles from each team— none so predominantly displayed as those from Ferrari.

"These simulators are exactly what the drivers use to practice driving the different tracks when they're home," Ray said. His excitement was palpable.

"You want to try one?"

His eyes went wide. Already a video wizard, Ray jumped at the chance to try the driving game, and when one became available, he slid into the low-slung seat. An attractive woman wearing an *F1 Experiences* shirt stepped up to him and asked if he'd like instructions.

I pulled out my phone and called Heather. After a few rings, she picked up.

"Are you here?" she asked.

"We're in the big tent where you first enter the paddock. Ray's playing a driving game. Where are you?"

"I'm at Aston Martin, but Harry said for us to meet him at the Williams building," she said. "When you leave the tent, go inside the paddock building and take a right, then look for the exit into the area where all the big trailers and teams have their three-level buildings."

"This place is huge," I said. "How am I supposed to find the Williams building?"

Heather snickered in my ear. "You may be the only one here that doesn't know the name of every driver, instantly recognize the logo of every team, and understand the pecking order of the placement of buildings."

I bit my lip until a lightbulb went off in my head. "The location is determined by where the team is in the standings." I held my breath.

"Very good, Buck. You're learning." She giggled again. "Sadly, Williams is on the far end of the paddock."

I absorbed that and realized it must mean they were in first or last place. Heather had said 'sadly' so I guessed the latter. "Because they're in last place in the points."

"That's right, but maybe if Harry invests in them, they'll have more capital for engineering improvements to compete with Red Bull, Mercedes, Ferrari, and the rest."

I glanced over at Ray just as his simulated car entered a corner with too much speed, spun out, and crashed.

"Okay, we'll head that way," I said as I disconnected the call.

I tapped Ray on the shoulder just as he was about to start another virtual race on the Monza track. His shoulders slumped and he rolled his eyes, then struggled to stand up and exit the low-slung simulator.

"Come on," I said. "We're going out among the real race car drivers."

His eyes lit up bright again, and we followed Heather's directions, through electronic gates that read our credentials until we were out in the paddock. Television crews were everywhere interviewing young and old men, some in fire suits, which had Ray gaga naming names I didn't know and would quickly forget. I scanned the three-level buildings lined up adjacent to each other down the length of the paddock.

Ray caught me staring at one. "Inside those buildings are areas for offices, hospitality, bars, dining, and a wide array of other functions. They're for the teams themselves and their guests. The public and press are not welcome."

People swarmed the open space in front of the team buildings, all wearing the coveted paddock passes, amid a sea of interview crews and even men in team uniforms pushing trolleys of massive racing tires. On the opposite side of the buildings were one- and two-story trailers I could see into on the lower level. They contained a massive number of tires, each with red, white, or yellow stripes on the outside, plus some with treads and green stripes. Pausing to stare through one such trailer, I saw another, narrower corridor outside on the far end. Beyond that were security-protected entrances to what I deduced were the actual pits.

Next to me, Ray was absorbing the same details, but he had a sappy grin on his face like a kid at the North Pole spying on Santa's Workshop. I spotted a blue-and-white building at the end with a big W on the front. I took Ray by the elbow and urged him through the paddock. Up ahead another interview took place, but it wasn't a young driver or an older team executive. It was a beautiful blonde woman—

"Is that Heather?" Ray asked.

"Of course it is."

We walked up and stood behind the man holding the microphone and asking her questions. The interviewer's British accent reminded me that Harry was probably waiting for an update on our flight-formation practice.

"Are you here to support Fernando?" the interviewer asked.

She hadn't spotted me or Ray yet, so the air caught in my lungs as I awaited her answer.

"No, no, that was long ago," she said. "I wish him the best with his new team, though."

Good answer.

I stepped to the side of the interviewer and she spotted me, then waved off further questions. Curious to see how she'd act here, I waited. Without delay, she closed the distance between us and gave me a quick kiss and a hug.

"Finally, you're here!" she said.

I noticed the interviewer say something to the cameraman, who turned toward us, lifting his television camera. I stepped forward, put my arm around Heather's waist, and pulled her forward toward the Williams tent.

"Have you seen Harry?" I asked.

"No, I was visiting with old friends until you arrived."

I wanted to ask about Fernando but took comfort in the way she'd answered the reporter's question. Still, it wasn't lost on me that she was recognized here in the paddock. How long had she and this Fernando guy been an item anyway? And how long ago?

We arrived at the first-floor entrance to the Williams building. When I pulled the door open, I was greeted by an unfriendly looking beast of a man with tattoos on his arms and neck but wearing a very tight-fitting Williams polo shirt.

"Help you, mate?"

I held up the cluster of badges on the lanyard around my neck.

"We're guests of Harry Greenbaum."

"Harry who?" the doorman said.

Another man stepped forward, equally large and intense-looking but wearing a sport coat and an earbud connected to a coiled, clear tube that disappeared inside the collar of his shirt. "How do you know Sir Harry?" he asked. His expression was heavily tilted toward scowl as opposed to hospitality.

"We're old friends."

"Your name?" His accent was also British.

"Buck Reilly, and these are my—"

"Oh, sorry sir, I've been waiting for you."

"And you are?"

"Jones. Can you come speak with me in private, please?" He nodded to an open area where there were a couple of white leather couches and armchairs. The man's intensity caused the hair to stand up on my arms, and I had the sudden feeling that something was wrong. We followed him, and when he turned back toward me, he must've spotted Heather and Ray, as if for the first time.

"Who are they?" Still the grimace.

"They're with me—also guests of Mr., er, Sir Harry."

He pulled his phone from his pocket and slid his thumb across the screen. "Names?"

Ray started to speak and I held my hand up. "Ray Floyd and Heather Drake. Is there something wrong?"

His eyes shifted from the screen on his phone, which he then slid back into his breast pocket while his eyes locked onto mine. He squinted as if trying to read my mind, or at least my expression, then exhaled harshly.

"Sir Harry's missing."

MISSING IN ACTION

7

"MISSING? WHAT THE HELL'S THAT SUPPOSED TO MEAN?"
I ASKED.

"He was supposed to be here two hours ago and hasn't shown up,"
Jones said.

"Well, maybe he had a meeting, or went to get some food—"

"No, mate, I don't think so. I was at our designated meeting point
thirty minutes early to check it out, and he never showed. No call, no
text, nothing."

I shared glances with Heather then Ray, both of whom had
confused expressions on their faces.

"You said you were there early to check it out. What were you
looking for?" I asked.

"My job's security, mate. I check everything and everybody
associated with the client I'm assigned to—"

"Assigned to?" I asked. "So you aren't a regular employee of
Harry's?"

"No. Apparently, he's never had a security detail before. We were
just hired last week. I've been with him every day since." A satisfied grin
bent the corners of his mouth, but his eyes remained hard. "Saw you all
with him briefly at the hotel restaurant last night."

Harry's concern that the situation here was getting aggressive
washed over me like a hot breeze. My stomach turned and I had to
breathe slowly from my mouth to overcome the sudden nausea.

"Do you have any idea who has been hassling Harry and why?" I
asked.

Jones's expression didn't change, the sneer a fixture on his lips. "I'm
not at liberty to discuss any details with anyone unless authorized by Sir

Harry."

I stepped toward Jones, who was an inch shorter than me but thicker and ten years younger. "How's he supposed to authorize anything if you lost him?"

"I didn't lose him—"

"You're *assigned* to him, aren't you? His private security detail? What the hell else would you call the fact that you can't find him?"

Jones bit his lip and his eyes narrowed to slits. "Watch your tongue, Buck Reilly."

From behind me, I heard Ray clear his throat, but my eyes were locked on Jones's as the nausea had morphed into anger that swirled like water reaching the boiling point.

"Ah, Buck?"

I turned just enough to see Ray but kept Jones in my peripheral vision, uncertain what he might do.

"We have the second formation practice in an hour. We need to get back to Linate."

"I can't go now, Ray." I exhaled slowly and his body sagged an inch. "What should I do?"

"You go and get Raphael to fly with you as copilot. Heather and I will search the paddock and hospitality suites for Harry."

Ray's mustache curled in on itself as he bit both lips between his teeth. "This flyover is important to Harry," he said.

"I know, you're right. Go ahead, it's fine. Call me when you're done and hopefully we've found him enjoying some Italian wine and the company of a beautiful woman."

Ray nodded slowly, then stepped forward and squeezed my shoulder. "Good luck and keep me posted. I'll come right back here when we're done."

Ray rushed off and left me and Heather with Jones.

"Have you alerted the Carabinieri?" I asked.

"The police won't do anything for twenty-four hours," Jones said.

"How many other people are a part of your security detail?" I asked.

"You're looking at it." He stretched his ropey neck, and more tattoos peered out from the collar of his shirt.

"Have you advised your employer yet?"

"Yes. Protocol requires us to check in if a meeting is not kept, then hourly until contact is reestablished."

"What if it's not reestablished?" Heather asked.

"Additional forces will be sent."

"I suggest you ask for those additional forces now, Mr. Jones," I said. "We'll go search the area for him."

"Right," he said. "I'll remain here and establish this as our base of operations."

As I was about to walk away, more questions came to mind. "What exactly was Harry so worried about that he hired a bodyguard?"

"As I told you, that's privileged information."

My jaw clenched again. Jones was trying my already frazzled nerves. "Clearly, I'm here as a special guest of *Sir* Harry Greenbaum, whom I've known my entire life. I think you can rest easy that I'm inside the circle of trust."

Jones stared hard at me with no change in his expression, but I could almost see the slow wheels moving behind his glassy eyes. "Right, well, it had to do with threats made in connection to his potential involvement with this race team."

That correlated with the vague mention of increased hostilities Harry had mentioned. "What kind of threats, and from whom?"

"I don't know all the bloody details." Jones glanced from side to side, clearly losing his cool now. "Something to do with another syndicate seeking to parlay Sir Harry's opportunity to squeeze their way into the Formula 1 market. That's all I know, but he did share that this other group may get violent if he didn't concede to their demands, which is why he hired Tactical International, the firm where I work."

Lovely.

Harry was already a self-made billionaire, had recently been knighted, and had more money, toys, palatial homes, and companies than anybody could ever dream of. Why the hell would he risk his life over the opportunity to invest in a damn racing team?

Jones and I exchanged cell numbers and agreed to touch base every thirty minutes, or sooner if either of us learned more. With that, Heather and I exited the Williams building and were again engulfed in the crowded goings-on of the paddock. We stood by the door as I tried to gather my bearings, having no idea what to do next. I turned to Heather.

"You've been to some of these races, I assume. What should we do?"

"That Jones creature hasn't called the police, so we could do that, but we could also speak with the VIP concierge upstairs to ask if they have seen him today."

Heather and I walked through the whole paddock searching, but there was no sign of Harry. She was interrupted a few times by press and even a couple of drivers as they rushed toward the pits. I wondered if one of them was Fernando, but they all looked too young.

I felt the phone vibrate in my shirt pocket and saw "Jones" on the screen.

"Any news?" I asked.

"Spoke with track security."

"And?"

"His card has not been swiped to enter the track yet today."

"Well, I guess that means he's not here," I said. "By the way, why weren't you with him this morning rather than meeting him here?"

"Those were his instructions. I left ahead of time to come check out the track, and he was to follow."

"How did you get here?"

"I've got a car."

"What about Harry?"

"His bloody Rolls Royce and driver are here with him."

Of course, Percy. Harry always shipped his Rolls and, more importantly, Percy, his driver, everywhere he went. I hung up on Jones, scrolled through my phone directory and pushed the name when it popped up.

"This is Percy speaking. How may I help you?"

"Percy, it's Buck Reilly. I'm inside the track at Monza. Where are you and Harry?"

He cleared his throat on the other end of the line. "Hello, Buck, so good to hear your voice." He hesitated, and I waited for the answer to my question. "Sir Harry is also there at the racetrack, and I'm outside in the parking lot."

I shook my head. "No, he's not here, and according to security, he hasn't entered the track using his credentials. Would he have had another way in?"

"That's most odd," Percy said. "I dropped him at the entrance to the paddock nearly three hours ago. Perhaps security has the wrong information."

"I don't think so, Percy. This gorilla of a private security guard hasn't heard a word either and believes that Harry's missing."

"Oh no," was all that Percy could mutter.

Heather and I exchanged a glance. The phone was on speaker. She shook her head, then suddenly an incredible roar of sound exploded from behind us that caused me to jump. The roar continued and Heather leaned closer to me.

"Practice has started."

Shit, I couldn't hear anything on the phone now, so I held it up to my ear and spoke loudly. "Percy, can you meet us at the entrance to the Paddock Club where you dropped Harry so we can talk further?"

I could barely make out his response but thought I heard the word *yes*, so I took Heather by the hand and started back through the crowd toward where Ray and I had entered earlier. The circuitous route was anything but direct, no doubt by design, to force everyone up past the hospitality suites in the paddock building back down the steps and into the tent where the bar, simulators, and souvenir stands were located. I glanced to see if Ray was there, back on one of the driving simulators rather than on his way to Linate, but saw nothing more than happy, shining faces.

We walked back through the same turnstiles where we'd entered— which I was now grateful for since there was electronic documentation of anyone who swiped their card as they came and went. We stepped back into the daylight to find the burgundy Rolls Royce that Harry had owned as long as I remembered, with Percy seated behind the wheel on the far-right side watching for us.

As I walked toward the Rolls, Percy lowered the passenger window. "I'm so glad to see you, Buck," he said. "And Ms. Heather. Sir Harry was thrilled that you both came to join him here."

Heather and I climbed in the back of the mammoth antique vehicle. It suddenly dawned on me that my fondness for antique vehicles— planes in my case—was also enjoyed by Harry, albeit with classic antique British automobiles. The spacious car had nearly as much room as the

Big Mama cockpit and dwarfed the cabin area of both my smaller planes, Betty and the Beast.

"Percy, something crazy is going on here and I have no idea what," I said.

"Oh dear. I am very concerned, sir," he said.

It dawned on me that Percy was nearly as old as Harry, in his mid-seventies, and while now was not the time, I couldn't help but wonder whether he was too old to drive—at least safely.

"In the interest of time, I'm just going to be straight-up and to the point, Percy," I said. "I apologize in advance."

As proper as Percy was, his eyes remained clear, and he showed no sign of upset or surprise. He was the consummate professional.

"What the hell's going on with Harry and this damned racing team?" I said.

I went on to reiterate that Harry had noted concerns over escalated tensions and repeat other esoteric statements he'd made in the hope Percy could shine a light on the situation. "You're with Harry more than anybody, Percy. We must assume he's missing—so please, what can you tell me?"

Percy's shoulders lifted with a deep breath, and as they lowered, he said, "You know I've sworn an oath of secrecy to Sir Harry, which I have upheld for nearly fifty years now."

"Yes, but—"

Heather placed a hand on my chest, and I turned my head to face her. She held her index finger up to her lip, as if to say, "Be quiet and give him a minute."

I sat back against the plush burgundy leather.

"However," Percy continued, "I do share your concerns over his safety. And, since it's you, Buck, I will share what Sir Harry has told me, and moreover, what I have overheard while he was in the car and on the telephone."

"Thank you, Percy, please." I sat forward again.

"Another consortium has been seeking to bully Sir Harry into being silent partners in his investment in the racing team. They have escalated their requests from cordial to demanding—and now, I fear, to violence."

"I don't get it, Percy. Why is he so intent to risk his life over this opportunity, if you want to call it that?"

I had previously overheard him discuss numbers with the sponsor, and it does sound quite lucrative, but, ah …" Percy hesitated.

"But what?"

"This particular racing team is practically a British national treasure. The former owner for whom the team is named, Sir Frank Williams, dominated the sport before the big companies spent unlimited funds on their engineering, cars, and teams. He was knighted for his successes, but not long after he passed away, his daughter reluctantly sold the team—which was heavily in debt—to an investment fund based in America."

"It was controversial and shrouded in mystery—nobody is certain who the actual owners are today, at least the public isn't," Heather added.

I glanced at her, grateful that she was well versed in the sport.

"However," Percy said. "There are rumors unsubstantiated in the public that the investment firm is involved on behalf of certain British royals who are the actual owners of the team."

"Is that true?" I asked.

Percy hesitated, our eyes met in the rearview mirror, and he nodded deeply in the affirmative. "Sir Harry was invited on an exclusive basis by the owners to have a first right to invest in the team, as more funds are required to match the expertise of the leading constructors. And given his new stature as a knight, I daresay he felt both honored and obliged to accept the offer to co-invest with the new owners to further entrench himself with those close to the monarchy."

"Sounds like some kind of *noblesse oblige*, but to the rich, not the poor."

"Quite."

"And this other syndicate wants in on Harry's opportunity to back-door their way into the sport?"

"I believe that is correct." Percy cleared his throat. "But it is slightly more complicated given that his offer to invest expires at the end of the race here in Monza. If Sir Harry does not close by then, the owners already have a backup contract signed with a suitor of their selection, and even if the owners wanted to give us more time, the contract will automatically become prime and close if Sir Harry's does not. So timing is of the essence."

"Does he want to invest and participate?" Heather asked.

"I must say I have not seen him more excited about an opportunity in quite some time. Whether it is because of the meteoric popularity of the sport, the invitation from the royals to participate, or the potential for great remuneration, I cannot say," Percy said. "But I expect it is a combination of all these considerations."

"Then why hasn't he closed the deal already?"

Percy grunted and seemed to stoop over the steering wheel. "The solicitors have been very rigid on the contractual documents, I'm afraid, and while Sir Harry is most excited for the opportunity, he did not achieve great success in business by being emotional over transactions." He paused for a moment, then sat up straighter. "From what I could tell though, the contract is very close, and he did not think it would be an impediment to finalizing the transaction by the deadline."

"You said the deadline is by the end of the race?" Heather asked.

"Correct, ma'am."

Heather turned toward me. "That will be around five o'clock local time on Sunday."

I glanced at my watch. It was now nearly one-thirty on Friday. "So we have two days to figure this out before that deadline, which— investment aside—is also the deadline for whomever is trying to force themselves into Harry's deal."

I slapped the headrest on the seat in front of me, causing both Percy and Heather to jump.

"We have to assume these people have grabbed Harry and will do him harm if he doesn't cooperate." I leaned closer to the front seat. "Do you have any idea who this other syndicate is?"

"Sir Harry has not shared that with me."

Just then, I felt the vibration of my cell phone from in my pants pocket. The screen read "Unknown."

Accustomed to the occasional spam call, I nearly ignored it, but then thought of Harry missing and slid the icon across the screen.

"Hello?"

"Buck Reilly?"

The voice had some kind of accent, one that rolled the first letter of my last name. A chill suddenly made me grip the phone harder.

"That's me."

"Remain calm and listen to everything I tell you."

I held my breath. Concern must have registered on my face because Heather leaned in closer to try and listen and Percy craned sideways in the driver's seat to watch.

"We have Herr Greenbaum. You are to keep that information to yourself. Do not tell the authorities—"

"Whoa, what the hell are you talking about?" I asked.

"Do not tell anyone at the Williams organization," the man continued, "and do not contact anyone in Herr Greenbaum's organization."

Heather mouthed the word, *Herr?*

My stomach twisted. "What do you want?" I asked.

"You will carry through with the acquisition, and provided Herr Greenbaum is cooperative and submits to our wishes, he will be released. If not, then he will not be so fortunate."

"Who the hell are you and why're you doing this?"

"No police, no Williams executives, and no lawyers, Herr Reilly. And you do as instructed with the contract."

Click.

I lowered the phone.

"Harry's been kidnapped." Heather's voice was a whisper. "Jones was calling the police and coordinating with Williams's security team for help."

"That's exactly what that guy said not to do, Heather."

My mind swirled in a vortex of surprise and concern for Harry, then it suddenly registered that I needed to try and control the situation or Harry would be in extreme danger, possibly even killed.

"Was that the man who took Sir Harry?" Percy asked.

Percy had been part of Harry's organization longer than anyone, but there was no way I could not tell him.

"Yes, it was."

The urgency in my voice must have led Heather to place her hand on my leg and squeeze it, again seeking to calm me down.

"Sounded German," I said.

Percy's eyes opened wider. "Sir Harry referred to the person he has spoken to several times as 'Herr Himmelman.'"

"Bingo," I said.

"There are no German teams in the sport now," Heather said.

"I thought Mercedes was a big deal here?" I said.

"Yes, but that group is actually British, and run by an Austrian," she said.

Everything here had turned into a shit show. Seemed like the super-rich fighting a game of high-stakes investment, further fueled by the opportunity to partner with royalty. For someone as fixated on the pomp and circumstance of being a Brit, Harry would clearly love to have this happen, but as Percy said, only if he felt good about the business terms. "What do they want?" Percy whispered.

"I need to call Jones," I said.

He answered after one ring.

"The kidnapper just called me," I said. "They have Harry and said we need to keep the situation quiet or they'll kill him."

"Track security alerted the police and they're requesting that you return to the Williams building."

"Shit. The guy said not to alert the police, Williams or ... anyone."

"Too late for that," Jones said.

I exhaled hard. "What's track security have?"

"They haven't said. They want you here before they tell me anything further."

"On the way now, but listen Jones, don't mention that they called me ... in fact, totally downplay his disappearance."

"But—"

"No buts, just do as I say."

I ended the call and turned back to Percy. "The police want to meet with me. I'll call you back as soon as we see what information they have. We need to keep our cool and give this a little time to learn what the hell's going on here."

"Godspeed, Buck," Percy said. "I daresay Sir Harry's fate is in your hands."

Great.

8

THE PADDOCK WAS FAR LESS CROWDED, but the thunder of noise from the racetrack remained deafening, so I assumed everyone was watching the practice. Heather and I hurried back to the end of the team buildings, and from the outside, the gray Williams' one seemed as quiet as the rest. But when we stepped inside, we found the room full: three uniformed Carabinieri, consisting of two men and one woman, along with another man wearing a dark sports coat, another wearing a Formula 1 shirt, and an attractive woman with bobbed blonde hair, who appeared to be in her early forties and wore a white Polo shirt with *Williams Racing* emblazoned on her chest.

Jones stood in the middle of them with an expression somewhere between anger and embarrassment. All talk ended when Heather and I walked inside.

"Excuse us, sir, there's an investigation going on," the woman in the Williams shirt said.

"That's Buck Reilly," Jones said.

All the faces lit up and turned our way. The Williams woman, who I further noted was trim and athletic, stepped forward and placed her hand tenderly on my bicep. "Mr. Reilly, I'm Claire Robbins with Williams Racing. I'm terribly sorry. You must be very concerned."

My first thought went to what Jones had told them about the kidnapper calling me.

"Harry's been known to disappear from time to time, so I wouldn't say I'm concerned, yet, but has there been any news?" I asked.

Claire turned toward the man in the dark sports coat, who cleared his throat. "Signor Reilly, I'm Luigi Mazza, head of security here at Monza. We do not have any news, but we are reviewing security footage from the main paddock entry area from early this morning." He paused. "It is too soon to file a missing person's report, but given Sir Harry's stature, the Carabinieri are concerned, even if you are not."

My mouth was suddenly bone dry, and I reached for a bottle of water atop a counter spread with bottles of wine, Ferrari champagne, and bowls of snacks. As I drank deeply from it, Claire again turned to face me.

"If there is anything we can do to help you," Claire said, "we will avail all our resources to do so."

I was again surprised by her concern for me. "I'm sorry," I said. "Do we know each other somehow?"

Her eyes grew wide momentarily. "We have not had the pleasure, but of course we know who you are from Sir Harry."

I turned to glance at Heather. Her expression also showed confusion.

"Because we're doing the flyover at the start of the race?"

Claire's face bunched up as if she had a mouthful of sour candies. "Why no." She let loose a nervous giggle. "Because you're named in the investment documents."

Her words hung in the air, and I was so surprised, a five-count passed before I finally said, "What?"

She canted her head at a slight angle. "I hope I'm not spoiling a surprise, but yes, you are listed as Sir Harry's successor if something should happen to him."

"I'm—?" I suddenly felt a sharp sting on my thigh and jumped. Standing slightly behind me, Heather had pinched me.

The man on the phone had instructed me to continue with the contract. I hadn't understood what he meant, but now …

The police studied me with greater scrutiny, as did Jones.

What the hell? I swallowed, hard, and took in a deep breath.

"Yes, of course. Harry and I are very close."

It took a beat for Claire to recover, but then she smiled broadly.

"I should say so."

There was side talk in Italian between the uniformed officers and the other men, then they all turned toward us. The police started to walk out, and Luigi Mazza, the head of security, looked me directly in the face. "We are returning to our command center. We will either return or call Mr. Jones with any updates once we have finished reviewing the security footage."

Mazza requested my cell phone number, which I provided him, and I thanked them all for their efforts.

"I'm sure it's nothing," I said. "Harry will undoubtedly return with crates of exquisite foods for everyone to enjoy." I watched as the head of track security and the Carabinieri exited the luxury building.

Heather looked up into my eyes. "What should we do now?"

"Can I speak with you for a moment, Mr. Reilly?" Claire said. "In private."

"Of course, but Heather can join us."

Claire led us into a small conference room outfitted with blue leather furniture and a white circular table. We all sat, and I decided to heed Heather's multiple pinching admonitions to shut up and hear what Claire had to say.

"We are truly at a loss, Mr. Reilly. I have no idea what to say."

"Please call me Buck. And this is Heather Drake—"

"Of course, I recognize Ms. Drake," Claire said. "Allow me to provide a bit more background on myself. I'm the niece of the team founder, Sir Frank Williams, and I've been part of the discussions with Sir Harry."

"I understand there is a deadline to finalize the contract by the end of the race," I said, "and if Harry does not reappear, you have a backup contract from the next suitor already executed and ready to go."

She winced at my directness. "Yes, that is true. There's already a ceremony planned. Our team is under great pressure to improve and to be restored to our former glory, and the funds from the investment are critical to making that happen." She paused. "But not only the capital. Having a partner of Sir Harry's stature will also be very beneficial."

I leaned forward, away from Heather's grasp, unable to prevent myself from fishing for information. "My understanding is that there's another syndicate, a German one, that's been pressing Harry to allow them to co-invest with him—"

Her eyes narrowed. "That's news to us, but I'm sure you know that per the contract, that is not allowed without our board's unanimous consent."

She again presumed I knew more than I did. And why the hell was

I named in the contract anyway? Did Harry think I had the money for this? Even if he did, from what Claire said, the board would have to approve it … but wait, my name was already in the contract, so they must have done so.

Had they done due diligence on me?

Or Googled my name?

Good grief. It wasn't long ago during the process of Harry knighting that he didn't want any public connection to me for fear of being passed over. Now he was listing me as his successor? What the hell?

Claire's eyes suddenly lit up and she glanced up into my eyes. "Of course, since you are named in the document, you could sign and finalize it at the ceremony on Sunday afternoon should Sir Harry ask you to do so."

A lump formed in my throat. Would Harry have given me signing capacity? Even if he did, how could I commit to an investment on his behalf and arrange for funds to be transferred—however much that might be?

I conjured a smile. "I'm not sure I ever heard the final agreed-upon figure for the investment."

"It hasn't changed since we were first introduced to Sir Harry. Same figure that's in the private offering memorandum that was drafted for him and him only—except including you, of course."

I cleared my throat. "Of course."

Heather shuffled next to me, and I suspected she recognized I was trying to learn the dollar amount in question.

"Would it be possible for Buck to get a copy of the contract so he could contact their solicitor?" Heather asked.

Claire dropped her shoulders in a matter-of-fact manner. "I don't see why not." She pursed her lips. "I don't have a copy here, but I can have one emailed and print it for you."

"That would be most appreciated," I said. "I'll contact our lawyers to confirm signing capacity as well."

"Excellent," Claire said. "Nothing is more important than locating Sir Harry, but he was so excited for this opportunity, we would hate for him to be disappointed by missing out due to the time stipulation."

"Remind me again when the deal officially turns into a pumpkin?"

I asked.

"Excuse me?" A light chuckle followed. "Oh, as in Cinderella, the fairytale. Interesting colloquialism. The contract must be signed at the ceremony just after the race on Sunday, or the backup contract will be electronically finalized and the opportunity lost."

Another thought hit me. "Can you say who the backup contract is with?"

She winced. "I'm afraid I cannot, due to the confidentiality agreement." She paused and glanced around, but there was nobody but the three of us in the small conference room. "I will say that the other suitor is one of financial necessity who lacks the panache and excitement that will accompany involvement by Sir Harry, even though they have agreed to pay twenty-percent more than his sum."

I absorbed her statements, which left a lot of room for speculation. My paranoid mind had naturally questioned whether the backup investor might be the one who had taken Harry, but I decided not to press Claire further at this point given that she assumed I knew much of this anyway since I was named in the bloody document as Harry's successor.

A knock on the door caused me to flinch, which brought a sudden smile to Claire's lips. She opened the door to find Jones standing there, his cell phone in hand.

"Track security has news," he said.

Claire waved him inside then closed the door again. The small room suddenly felt significantly more cramped. Jones handed me his cell phone, which I took, switched to speaker mode, and laid on the table. News might actually be a bad thing, given the kidnapper's demands, so I had mixed emotions for what would come next.

"Buck Reilly here."

"Mr. Reilly, it's Director Mazza, track security—"

"What news do you have?" Tired of formalities, I interrupted his preamble.

"We have found, how do you say, footage of Sir Harry from this morning."

"Where was he?" I asked.

"It was when he arrived at the VIP entrance."

Silence filled the line.

"I'm listening?" Impatience altered my voice.

"The footage shows Sir Harry exit his Rolls Royce, then walk purposefully across the street toward the VIP entrance where he was greeted by two men. They spoke to him for a moment, and we cannot be sure, but Sir Harry may have turned back toward his car. But a silver van pulled up between them with the side door open. He hesitated, but each of the two men took one of Sir Harry's arms and helped—or lifted—him into the vehicle then entered after him. The vehicle then drove slowly off."

My mouth had dropped open and I was mouth breathing. It was not lost on me that Claire's and Heather's expressions were as surprised as mine. Jones bit his lip, no doubt embarrassed by his failure to ensure the safety of his ward and confused by my instructions to remain silent.

"Sir Harry's Rolls Royce was still there after the van departed, but then shortly after, it turned into the carpark where it has been all morning since."

I took in a deep breath, the kidnappers' instructions ringing in my ears. I was at an inflection point: either ignore their demands and help the police or play along a little longer to see what happened next. I exhaled hard, my gut telling me to do the latter.

"Could mean anything," I said.

"What does that mean, sir?" Mazza asked.

"Harry has friends and business interests all over Italy. Did everyone really expect him to sit at this racetrack for days on end and eat popcorn and hotdogs?"

Mazza hesitated on the phone, then said, "So you are not concerned?"

"Have there been any phone calls or demands from his supposed captors?" I asked. "No, there haven't. So let's everyone just relax here and not read too much into the situation."

"Nobody has contacted you, Signor Reilly?" Mazza asked.

I turned to see Jones and he shook his head as if to imply he hadn't said anything to them. "Me? No, why would they?"

"According to management at Williams, you are listed as his successor in the agreement." He paused. "Are you a relative?"

Relative? What the heck? "Harry was the largest investor in my former company," I said.

"e-Antiquity?" Mazza asked.

A sudden jolt of adrenalin hit me. Would the authorities think I might be involved in Harry's disappearance?

I cleared my throat. "That's correct. Many years ago," I added.

"The company went bankrupt, from what I read online, yet you are his successor in what has to be a multimillion-Euro investment?"

Heather's eyes opened wide at the comment, and I felt my eyes strain too.

The room spun for a moment, and Mazza asked another question that was lost on me while I tried to get my breathing under control. All eyes were focused on me, but rather than asking him to repeat it, I wanted information from him.

"This van seen in the video footage, were you able to get a license plate number?"

"No, the angle only showed the side of the vehicle."

"Were there any distinguishing marks?" I asked.

Mazza hesitated and I realized there must be something. No doubt he was trying to determine how much to tell me—there was whispering in Italian on his end of the line—must be with the Carabinieri.

I winked at Jones. "You're his security detail, right? Can you get some answers here?"

Jones pushed forward between Claire and Heather to be closer to the table. "This is Reggie Jones from Tactical International, Sir Harry's personal bodyguard. I need you to send me screenshots of the two men and the van, please, immediately."

More discussion in Italian on the other end of the line.

"If you really are concerned there is foul play," I said. "Get Jones the information so we can—"

"This is now a police matter, Signor Reilly—"

"Let's not overreact, okay?"

Jones raised his hand as if to tell me to stop. "I am registered with local law enforcement and our company has executive privilege in matters such as these, so you are obligated to provide me with the information I requested immediately, Director Mazza."

The Italian conversation on the other end of the phone had become more intense but then stopped suddenly. "I will text you the photos momentarily, Signor Jones," Mazza said. "But back to you, Signor Reilly. Please remain there as the authorities wish to question you further."

"Sure, I'll be here," I said, then pressed end on the phone to await the photos.

"Can't anyone raise Sir Harry on the cell phone?" Claire asked. Then to me. "I'm so sorry for all the confusion, Buck. I do hope it does not detract from the ceremony."

"Indeed," Heather said. Her face had turned ashen—whether concerned for Harry's fate or for the multi-million Euros—I wasn't sure, but she was otherwise steady.

The constant drone of racing engines had subsided, and I saw through the window that the number of people flooding into the paddock had increased. A *ping* sounded and Jones held his phone up to his face.

"They sent video and photos," he said.

"Let me see them?" I said.

Harry was clearly recognizable exiting his car and walking, waddling really, across the narrow road to the VIP entrance. The two men, burly bastards with dark hair and dressed in what appeared to be black business suits, stepped up to him. The quality was too grainy to read Harry's expression, but he clearly tried to walk away from them before the van—a Mercedes Sprinter—pulled up and stopped. We watched as they helped—or shoved—Harry inside and followed him. The van door slid shut just as the vehicle pulled away.

It looked like there was a logo or words on the rear corner of the van, but again, the image quality was too poor to discern any details.

"Damn it!" My shout startled everyone, and I realized I was blowing my effort to mask my concerns in front of the woman from Williams. "Can your company have this footage enhanced, Jones?" Then to cover my tracks: "I think I recognize that van as one I'd seen pick Harry up before."

"We should be able to, sir."

Before handing him his phone back I forwarded the photos and video to my phone. When I felt it vibrate in my pocket, I knew the data had arrived and I returned Jones's phone to him.

My phone suddenly rung, and I pulled it from my pocket. The name on the screen was again "Unknown."

I walked quickly toward the door. "Be right back."

Once outside, I glanced around and, seeing no sign of Mazza, answered the phone. "Hello?"

"You have been observed speaking with the police, Herr Reilly."

"Harry's a missing billionaire. People are concerned. I'm downplaying it."

"Very wise. Now please return to your airplane at Linate, immediately. Instructions will follow. Come alone."

A click followed, and the heavily accented voice, which I again recognized as decidedly German, was gone.

I stood there with the phone pressed against the side of my head, realizing I had already chosen the path of going it alone and trying to decide quickly how to handle the situation. I lowered the phone.

"Another fine mess," I said.

"Who was that?" Heather asked. She had followed me outside, along with Jones and Claire.

"It was, ah, Ray. There's a problem with Big Mama, er, our plane."

Jones's eyes lowered to a brief squint.

"I'm terribly sorry about all of this," Claire said. "I need to get upstairs to brief our chief executive. Would you like to join me while we wait for the authorities?"

I took in a short breath and exhaled it quickly. "Heather, you and Jones go. I'll be up in a minute. I need to make another call and use the restroom."

Claire opened the door and led the way. Jones glared at me for a moment then followed reluctantly. Heather turned to me after they were gone.

"Did they call again?" she asked.

"You stay here and see what you can learn. Try to keep the police calm—"

"Buck? What are you doing?"

"I need to go—"

"The Carabinieri told you to wait here."

"No, track security did. Once I leave the track, they have no further jurisdiction."

She grabbed both my arms in her hands. Her grip was strong.

"Where are you going?"

"I need to play along in order to save Harry." Our eyes connected. "I'll keep you posted."

"Buck—Buck?"

I'd already turned and hurried into the crowd. If the authorities arrived here before I could get out, I'd be held for questioning. The throng was now thick with people swarming through the paddock, no doubt seeking their favorite driver or team principal. I rushed forward and sought to blend in with a group of people moving toward the VIP tent at the far side of the paddock. A moment later, Director of Security Luigi Mazza and the same group of Carabinieri from earlier jogged past us, their eyes fixed on the Williams building.

Once to the VIP tent, I texted Percy to meet me at the corner of the road just up from the VIP entrance where I'd noticed the Sprinter van turn right. Then I stepped up to the souvenir stand and bought a red Ferrari hat with the number 16 on it, along with a Ferrari t-shirt of the same color, and pulled them on in an effort to avoid the same cameras that had captured the fateful moment when the men grabbed Harry.

I'd done nothing wrong, yet, but since when did that matter when the shit hit the fan in my world? Plus, I didn't know who to trust and had never had any success waiting for the authorities to solve problems.

Harry was gone, and his captors had contacted me twice with instructions.

I'm on my way, old friend.

9

AFTER NAVIGATING THE TIFOSI-CLOGGED ROADS OF MONZA, Percy made fast progress south down the A52 highway to the airport exit near Parco Forlanini. The old Rolls Royce was spacious and comfortable inside, but my mind was focused far from creature comforts. Percy's and my conversation was sparse. Given his recollection that the person who'd badgered Harry about the Formula 1 opportunity was named Himmelman and had a German accent, I used the time to search for information on the name in relation to criminals in Germany, Switzerland, and Austria. I found nothing.

There were thousands of Himmelmans—a traditionally Jewish name that meant "heaven man"—not that that was particularly helpful. I let Ray know I was on my way, but he had been just about to take off with Raphael DeGregorio and the other planes for the next formation practice. As we closed in on the airport, I again realized that Linate was large and commercially oriented with little architectural distinction. Unfortunately, it was best known for the worst airline crash in Italian history: in 2001, a private jet taxiing onto an active runway in the fog had collided with a Scandinavian jetliner, killing all 114 people aboard both planes. That was one of Ray's fast facts meant to illuminate me on our initial approach yesterday, but it had resulted in giving me agita instead.

The general aviation terminal was small, equally indistinct, constructed of silver metal panels and clear glass with operable windows, giving it the air of an antiquated design. Percy glided to a stop in front of the terminal, and the old Rolls felt like a luxury train car floating on cushy suspension. I removed the Ferrari t-shirt and put it on the seat next to the hat.

"Shall I wait for you?" he asked.

"I have no idea what to expect here, so don't bother. I'll call or text you to report whatever I learn. If you don't hear from me in an hour, please call me. If I don't answer, call the police."

"Good luck, then." His voice was deep, somber, and—while always professional—now tinged by fear. Or maybe resignation as if he'd always expected something to go wrong, sooner or later.

I placed my hand on his shoulder. "Hang in there, Percy."

With that I stepped out of the battleship-sized vehicle and pushed the door closed. I glanced around but saw no sign or hint of why I'd been directed here, nor anyone who might be here to meet or capture me. Had the message meant to instruct me to climb back on my plane and leave Italy? That wasn't happening.

I wasn't concerned about my own safety but probably should've been. Italy was far, far away from Key West and the Caribbean, and the stakes at play were much different than my typical pursuits finding lost treasure or souls, competing against adversaries that, while dangerous, often had limited resources or intelligence. On the contrary, based on the goosebumps on my arms, this situation felt far more ominous and above my pay grade.

After standing outside for a moment, I pulled open the glass door and entered the long, narrow lobby of the terminal. A man, seated ramrod straight in a leather chair next to the only column in the center of the room, jumped up the moment I stepped inside. He walked purposefully toward me, but I saw he had a slight limp. He was neither tall nor short, muscular nor skinny. Dressed in a black suit, white shirt, and black tie, he immediately struck me as a mortician. I only hoped he wasn't here to preside over Harry's funeral.

Or mine, for that matter.

The man walked toward me with calm confidence. As he got closer, I saw that his expression was neither cocky nor shifty, just determined. No facial hair, and the hair on his head was dark brown, nearly black itself. He wore round eyeglasses in thin, black frames. He stopped five feet from me, and his expression was inscrutable.

"Herr Reilly?"

"And you are?"

"You came in your partner's car, I see."

His statement caused me to lean away from him. "Partner?"

"Yes, in the contract." His expression didn't change an iota. "Herr Greenbaum is alive and safe but is being detained so that we may conclude our negotiations without distraction."

"Who are you and what do you want from me?"

"My name is not material, as I am only here to deliver a message." He paused. "An invitation, actually."

"My dance card is pretty full, *Herr* Mortician, but what do you have in mind?"

The man squinted slightly for a brief second but ignored my provocation.

"You are designated as Herr Greenbaum's proxy, and we know that you are authorized to act on his behalf in the investment contract, should he, shall we say, become incapacitated."

"Let's *not* say that, *shall* we?" I took a step closer to the prick, who held his ground.

"Your reputation precedes you, Reilly, but under these circumstances, I encourage you to control your emotional impulses, animalistic urges, impatience, and sarcasm in order to save the life of Herr Greenbaum."

I bit my lip and stepped a couple steps short of wiping the floor with the expressionless twit who had immediately burrowed under my skin like a chigger.

My deep inhale caused the first hint of a smile on the Mortician's pale face. Yeah, first point for you, asshole. I matched his smug grin. "What's the plan, Fritz?"

"You are to join us at a meeting at Lake Garda."

"Where's that?"

A slight, condescending glance caused me to grit my teeth.

"To the northeast, approximately one hundred kilometers away."

"When's the meeting?" I asked.

"As soon as we arrive. You are going to fly us there in your antique aircraft. Your associate, Herr Floyd, has returned, and is on the flight deck with the other collectors of ancient machinery."

Shit.

Ray's not going to like this.

In an effort to shift the momentum, I walked past him and said, "Fine, let's go."

His hard-soled, black leather shoes made a click-*whoosh* sound from the way he dragged one of his feet. At the reception desk at the end of the long lobby, I showed the pass that DeGregorio had provided all the formation pilots to a pudgy, bored-looking woman wearing a Signature Flight polo shirt. She gave us a quarter nod and I continued past, through the small locker and break room and out a propped-open metal door. Most general aviation terminals of any consequence had similar offerings the world over, the main difference being the age of the buildings that contained them. That and geography, of course.

Click-*woosh*, click-*woosh*.

"Reilly," the Mortician said from behind me.

I stopped and turned to face him.

"I will wait here while you alert your partner of the plan. Do not mention the details to any of the others, or you will put them all in peril. Is that clear?"

I gave him a two-finger salute off my forehead, spun and continued onward to the impromptu debriefing that Raphael DeGregorio was giving on the tarmac behind the planes, all lined up like a hand-colored photo from a World War II history book. Big Mama wasn't as old, but her classic flying boat lines were similar, yet significantly larger, than her distant Widgeon and Goose relatives from the same era as the rest of these warbirds.

Ray saw me coming, and I realized he was looking past me to where the Mortician stood near the entry to flight services. Honed by years of averting trouble of my making, Ray didn't miss much.

"Reilly, nice of you to join us," DeGregorio said. "Can we count on you for Sunday, or should I arrange for backup from the Como Seaplane Base?"

My mind was far beyond the reason for our being here, but I didn't want to alert or alarm any of them for fear that the Mortician meant what he said about putting them in danger. "I won't let you down, but we do have some other business to attend to."

I turned to face Ray, who had the pinched look of someone expecting bad news.

"Ray and I have to take a quick trip on behalf of Sir Harry, so we'll be taking Big Mama on a short flight."

I kept my eyes on Ray as I spoke. He pursed his lips.

"The fourth practice session will be tomorrow at nine a.m." DeGregorio said. "Don't be late."

I gave him a sidelong glance and nodded. "Probably would be a good idea to have some backup to help Ray if my work for Sir Harry causes me delay."

DeGregorio grunted and shook his head.

Ray and I walked toward Big Mama at the end of the flightline closest to the general aviation terminal, and the Mortician started walking toward our plane.

"What's going on, Buck?"

I cleared my throat. "Real quick, as I don't want to put you in danger, this guy's a representative of some cartel that's holding Harry until he agrees to include them in his deal."

"Holding him—as in against his will?"

"Yep, that sums it up." I said.

"Where are we flying to?" he asked.

"Lake Garda. Water landings are legal there too, right?"

"Would it matter?"

"Not really." The Mortician was just on the other side of the plane now, walking our way, the click-*woosh* even more evident with his faster pace. "Don't ask him any questions."

The black-clad messenger rounded the tail and stepped up to us where we stood next to the ladder that led to the aft hatch on the port side. He looked from me to Ray then back again.

"I'm armed, so please, no foolish heroics," he said.

Ray's brow furrowed. "Nice to meet you too."

I nearly smiled. Sarcasm had always been my way of facing adversity, buying time, or showing disdain to jerks like this one. But few had been as menacing as the Mortician, who seemed as cold-blooded as could be, and I had little doubt he meant what he said.

"Climb inside," he said.

Ray went first and I followed him. It would be easy to overpower the twit, but there was no point in that. I needed to help Harry, which at the moment meant flying this a-hole to Lake Garda. Ray had already gone to the cockpit and sat in the left seat. He was studying his area map of Northern Italy, no doubt assessing where Lake Garda was situated.

"I have already filed a flight plan," the Mortician said. He reached inside his jacket pocket and produced a folded-up printout of the flight plan.

I gave it a quick glance. It wasn't very far away and would take us back over Monza to the northeast. When I looked up again, the man held an automatic pistol aimed at my chest.

"Take your seat, and let's go."

His lack of emotion and efficiency of movement, save for the click-*woosh*, made me think this was a normal part of the man's job. I followed orders.

"You can put that away," I said. "I'd have already broken your neck if I didn't need you to take us to Harry."

Another smirk. The Mortician appeared to like it when I talked dirty.

I remembered my instructions to Percy, which included for him to call the police if he hadn't heard from me in an hour. After all, there was no point in cowboying this further if Harry, Ray, and I were all captives. I bit the side of my mouth.

"Listen, Fritz, I need to text our driver that he can leave, or he'll be calling the police."

The Mortician stared at me with dead-fish eyes. "Don't say where we're going."

If he knew more about flying, he'd realize the flight plan he'd filed already established that, plus air traffic control would track my plane, but I wasn't going to point that out to him.

I read the text out loud as I typed it. "Percy, Ray and I are taking the plane for a ride to practice for Sunday. Everything's okay. Will check in later." Then to the Mortician. "That okay?"

He nodded and I hit send.

Ray reviewed the flight plan, compared it to his area chart, then entered the sequence of waypoints into the GPS before starting the left-side Wright R-1820 Cyclone nine-cylinder engine, which caused Big Mama to slightly lurch to the left. I donned my headset and the Mortician followed suit, seated in the front left seat of the main cabin.

He clicked his mic on. "Land where conditions allow, but in as close proximity as possible to the GPS location noted at the end of the flight plan."

"Ten-four," Ray said.

"Can you tell me anymore about the meeting I've been summoned to?" I asked.

"No."

Ray and I exchanged a glance. His deadpan stare spoke volumes.

Perfect.

10

THE COUNTRYSIDE BELOW US WAS COMPRISED OF VARYING SHADES OF GREEN, and I realized we were flying over Monza Park. The autodromo where the Formula 1 practice was being held was off to the left, and large groups of people were spread out around the pinched oval track. Mountains filled the horizon to the north; our heading was northeast, so we were headed toward them. As we flew, several lakes appeared intermittently, and I wondered if any were large enough to land on. After another fifteen minutes, the ground turned brown below us, but the reflection of the sun upon it made me realize it was a vast lake, which I assumed to be Garda given our flight time and Ray's reduction of Big Mama's altitude.

From 5,500 feet up, the lake appeared very wide at the southern end but tapered to a much narrower northern configuration. Our altitude continued to drop after Ray added more flaps and reduced airspeed. A glance back at the Mortician found him staring intently at me, the gun still in his hand. Not much of a sightseer, this one.

Ray vectored Big Mama to the eastern side of the lake where large villas dotted the shoreline. Different-sized villages were situated around the lake, and I saw a vast castle on a southern isthmus. Based on the huge parking lot near it, I assumed the castle must be a popular tourist attraction. Hotels, large and small, were perched near the water and, in some cases, up in the hills above the lake. We circled the designated landing spot close to the western shore, and based on the Mortician's specified endpoint, I wondered whether our destination was the large sprawling hotel there on the coastline.

"Grand Hotel Fasano." I read the large sign prominently displayed on the wall facing the lake.

Ray vectored back east, and with Big Mama banked onto her left wing, he carved a tight turn to the left. I knew he did it to check for boat traffic or impediments that could damage the plane, or worse, anything we could strike upon making our water landing. There were a few islands on the lake, one with a massive fortress-like castle on it that appeared to be very old but in excellent shape. I couldn't help myself, so I clicked my mic and turned back to the Mortician.

"What's that place?"

"The home of the Borghese family. It dates back nine hundred years and remains the center of their empire."

His voice was bored as if empires were commonplace. In Europe, however, they had been, but few remained. The Borghese name rang a bell, and if my memory served me properly, one had been a Pope back in the early 1600s.

Ray continued the tight arc of the turn until we were facing west again, and the Grand Hotel Fasano was visible in the distance. I leaned forward and scanned the water, now coming at us quickly, for boats or obstructions, and glanced at the course plotted on the GPS. Ray was right on target but needed to set Big Mama down quickly to make sure we had enough water to stop the massive plane.

We touched down into the light chop and there was no porpoising or heavy bouncing, the weight of Big Mama settling heavily into the water. The Mortician showed no change in expression and appeared focused on nothing but completing his mission without issue. Friction from the pull of the water, along with Ray reducing the speed and pitch of the props, reduced our momentum and soon we were no different than any other boat cruising the lake toward its destination. Well, conceptually, anyway. Amphibious flying boats were far rarer these days, and while seaplanes were common and allowed to land on the Italian lakes, Big Mama drew attention from boaters who approached us but thankfully remained at a reasonable distance. Boaters often liked to come close to Betty and the Beast, but they were a fraction of the size of the far more imposing Big Mama.

Now close to the Grand Hotel Fasano, Ray reduced the speed even further.

"Get ready to deploy the anchors, Buck."

I turned back to our passenger. "Are we staying, or picking Harry up and leaving?"

"Listen to Herr Floyd and deploy your anchor."

"Guess that means we're staying," I said under my breath.

I climbed under the instrument panel and into the broad space there. I confirmed that the anchor was tied down, its rope coiled cleanly to ensure throwing it would be orderly, then popped open the hatch above my head. Wind hit and blew me back a step until the middle of my back rested against the edge of the hatch. The beauty of the Italian countryside froze me for a moment as I glanced up and down the shore and up above to hilltop villages.

Too bad it wasn't me and Heather flying here for a romantic getaway.

"Throw it, Buck!" Ray's voice sounded from inside the hatch.

I grabbed the Danforth anchor and twisted at the waist, then sprung it forward to hurl the pronged metal claw forward, where it disappeared below Big Mama's nose. A couple of seconds later, the sound of it hitting the water resounded. Once the line quit feeding out through my right hand, I pulled it back until the anchor held, then turned back to see Ray though the windscreen in the cockpit. I gave him a thumbs-up, and he reversed thrust by changing the pitch of the propellers. Big Mama's slow progress forward ended, and as she began to go slowly backward, I closed the hatch and crawled back out from under the instrument panel onto the flight deck. I stood back up and found the Mortician staring at me intently over the business end of the pistol.

"I need to place a stern anchor too," I said.

He waved the gun to the side, instructing me to pass.

The desire to give him an elbow to the temple as I passed him was hard to suppress, but I bit my lip and continued through the cabin. After retrieving another anchor from the storage locker, I glanced out the right window then the left to assess how much if any current there was. Seeing none, I popped the hatch on the same side and again threw the anchor, waited for the line to go slack, then pulled it taut. Once I was satisfied it was secure, I tied off the line on the cleat on the interior fuselage and glanced out through the open hatch toward shore.

A classic wood launch was heading for us from the direction of the hotel. The boat's bow was lifted, and white wake spread out on both sides behind it. Our welcoming committee, no doubt.

Back inside the cabin, Ray was finishing up the post-flight checklist and turning off the battery. With that, he stood slowly and turned to look down the fuselage. The Mortician had moved next to me, his gun still brandished.

Ray glanced at him, then me.

"Shall I wait in the plane?" he asked.

"One of our men will keep you company, Herr Floyd. Do not use the radio or your cell phone for any reason," the Mortician said.

I covertly curled my lip for only Ray to see, who pursed his in reply. I could almost read his mind. *No heroics, Buck,* was what I imagined.

The wood launch, which had a cabin and canopy that covered much of the rear deck, pulled up to Big Mama, its bow facing directly toward our open hatch. A man with the longest beak-like nose I'd ever seen shimmied along the port side of the boat. He was also dressed in a black suit, and I wondered whether this was some type of uniform he and the Mortician were wearing. Like the Gestapo. That thought caused me to swallow.

The man on the bow of the boat, younger and more fit than our passenger, tossed me a line that I caught and pulled to draw the boat closer.

"Give the rope to Herr Floyd," the Mortician said.

I did as I was told, and Ray wrapped the line once around the cleat next to the hatch. The boat was rising and falling in the chop, and I wanted to get it away from Big Mama as soon as possible to prevent it from impaling the fuselage, so I held my hands up as if to question what they wanted me to do. The man on the bow waved me forward, so I sat on the bottom of the hatch, waited until the boat lifted on a wave, and slipped forward onto the pitching deck. The Mortician followed a moment later, and Beak-nose climbed aboard Big Mama to keep an eye on Ray.

Once I had shimmied down the side of the boat and stepped down onto the deck, I glanced back at Big Mama and saw Ray staring out past his keeper. We held a long gaze, and I nodded. A second later, he nodded back.

After collecting the bow line, the Mortician lowered himself onto the deck next to me and I turned my attention to the others on board. There were three of them, all dressed the same, again igniting my suspicion that they might be in uniform. Rather than engaging with these men, though, given that they were clearly muscle—or in the case of the Mortician, trusted errand boys—I sat on the rear bench seat for the short ride back to shore. The captain backed away from Big Mama, then placed one of the boat's two inboard engines into reverse, while nudging the throttle slightly forward on the other so it spun quickly around and faced toward shore.

None of the men spoke to or acknowledged each other as the boat's bow lifted slightly and we accelerated toward shore. My mind wandered to think ahead to what I might find. Above all, I wanted to see Harry to ensure he was safe, then help however I could. The only problem was that I had absolutely no idea why I'd been beckoned or what I could do to solve the situation.

But I'd find out soon enough.

11

TWO OF THE MEN FROM THE BOAT—THE MORTICIAN, and another, burly man with close-cropped blond hair, thick neck, and dark glasses—escorted me off the boat, down the private dock, across the manicured lawn, and into the Grand Hotel Fasano. It was a high-end, sprawling facility that had a small beach in front of its patio dining area, where women wore chic dresses and men snappy sports coats with colorful pocket squares as they sipped prosecco and smoked cigarettes.

The click-*swoosh* sound caused me to redirect my attention forward to try and anticipate where we were headed and what the agenda would be. Inside, the hotel was elaborate and spacious. Gilded moldings, frescoed walls, and marble floors gave off the feel of a castle. The Mortician led us down an open staircase with ornate gold-and-black railings to the lower level where signs for the spa and conference center pointed in opposite directions. We turned left toward the conference area.

"Here I thought I was going to get a massage," I said.

I felt a push on my back from the thick-necked man behind. "*Silencio,*" he said.

The men steered me into a waiting area equipped with pale-blue leather couches, more frescoed walls, and a painting on the ceiling I assumed to be Gabriel blowing his horn. I wished he were blowing alarm bells.

Thick-neck placed his hand on my shoulder and urged me onto the love seat perpendicular to the sofa, then stood to my side. The Mortician approached the closed door, leaned his head closer as if to listen for a moment, then stood erect and subtly knocked three times.

What seemed like five minutes passed before the door opened and another black-suited man nodded us forward. Thick-neck tapped my shoulder and I stood and followed the Mortician inside where four men were waiting. Three wore black suits, and one was dressed in a grey, almost silver suit. Rather than a tie, he had a brilliant blue silk scarf around his neck. He was seated at the table in front of an open laptop computer.

"Mr. Reilly," Blue-scarf said. His accent was also German. "Thank you for coming."

"I don't recall having a choice," I said.

We remained standing, and Blue-scarf gave me an impetuous smile.

"Choice is exactly why you are here."

"Where's Harry?"

"And whichever choice you make now will set loose a domino effect of ramifications, no matter which way you go."

I stared at Blue-scarf for a long moment. "Once I see Harry, we can talk about these choices you're referring to."

"Forgive me for not introducing myself," he said.

"Himmelman, isn't it?" I asked.

His eyes narrowed, then he closed the lid on the computer and the impetuous smile returned. "Depending on what you know about me, you may have learned that I never give up when there is something I want." He paused. "And I do mean *never*."

The truth was I hadn't learned shit. Percy had told me Himmelman's name, but it was so common, I'd learned nothing else. But I didn't want Blue-scarf—er, Himmelman—to know that, so I decided upon an educated guess. "Not much really, other than that you've been hassling Harry about his opportunity to invest in the racing team. Which the authorities are aware of in case anything happens to him," I said. "Or me."

"Our negotiations have been in secret, Mr. Reilly."

"Hostile negotiations?" I asked.

His smile vanished and his eyes glistened as he leaned closer to me. "Deadly."

Himmelman sat in an elaborate wood chair that had the grandeur to have served as a throne for some tinhorn dictator. He nodded to Thick-neck next to me, who again placed his hand on my shoulder—gripping it so tight I winced—steered me over a step, and pressed me down into a smaller chair in front of Himmelman.

"Where's Harry?" I said.

"In a safe place," Himmelman said.

One of the men in black suits—I'd lost count, but there had to be ten or more of them—entered the room with a cup of tea on a saucer and placed it on the table next to Himmelman, who didn't acknowledge the delivery, thank the man, or break eye contact with me.

"What is it you want from him?" I asked.

"We require his cooperation."

"On what?"

"To partner with you in the racing team investment."

"Doesn't seem like Harry wants you as a partner," I said. "Can't imagine why."

"Yes, back to the choices we spoke of upon your arrival."

I was holding my hands together, wet with sweat, and I again felt way outgunned, underprepared, and damn close to helpless given the circumstances.

A burst of anxiety-fueled adrenalin made me throw my hands up. "What am I supposed to do about it?"

The smirk was back. Yeah, kudos, asshole. You have me totally outnumbered here or I'd beat the truth out of you and use that lovely blue scarf to wring your neck.

"Sir Harry has named you as his successor in the contract, so I wish to … *encourage* you to speak with him."

"About what? Capitulating to your demands?"

"To make myself clear, if you are unable to convince him, he will die."

The same rush of adrenalin pressed me back in the uncomfortable wood chair.

"And then," Himmelman continued, "you, as his successor, will sign the papers or meet the same fate." His eyes bore into mine and I could tell he was seeking to read my body language. I did everything possible not to pee my pants.

I cleared my throat and slowly crossed my legs as if we were old friends sitting in front of a fire, swapping fond memories over a digestif. "Sounds like you'd then have two dead bodies and no signed contract," I said then faked a yawn.

Himmelman's eyes narrowed and his nose twitched as if he were a rat sniffing out food. Or fear.

"That may be so, but since you and Sir Harry would both be deceased, it would be a rather hollow victory for you. More like falling on your collective swords. And for what? Our money is good, and we are determined."

"Let me speak to him, in private, to ensure he's safe and to discuss his thoughts," I said.

Himmelman pulled a thin cell phone from his jacket pocket and pressed a single button. A man answered instantly in German, and Himmelman responded in German, a language I didn't speak nor understand. A moment of silence later, another voice sounded.

"Hello, who is calling, please?"

I dropped my crossed leg and sat forward. "Harry, is that you?"

"Buck, dear boy, I'm very sorry to have drawn you into this rather nasty business."

"I'm sitting here at Lake Garda with Himmelman and his battalion of black-suited storm troopers." I watched Himmelman's eyes as I spoke, watching for any reactions that could lead to someone getting harmed—like me. "He explained to me what he wants."

"I am sure he has, but his demands are impossible," Harry said.

My stomach dropped and I had to take a deep breath so I wouldn't lose it.

My chief goal was to save Harry's life, which would indirectly save mine too. And probably Ray's also. "It's just a racing team—"

"No, Buck, it's much more than that! The main principals are dear friends and related to the monarchy. I cannot do anything to jeopardize their reputations, cast aspersions on their operation, or bring shame to the Crown. I would sooner perish."

Himmelman sat forward. "As will your successor here, Charles B. Reilly the Third, if you both refuse to sign the document providing my syndicate with the controlling interest."

"And then you will still have nothing, my dear Himmelman," Harry said.

Himmelman stared off into an empty corner of the room, apparently bored by Harry's and my similar responses.

"I will have no loose ends either, and will then approach the next team desperate for money to keep up with Red Bull, Mercedes, and Ferrari. One of them will no doubt recognize the multiplier effect of my plans, and they will make more money than they ever have before."

"Money is not my interest, dear chap," Harry said. "And I have well documented our discussions for the authorities to discover in the case of my sudden, inexplicable demise."

Himmelman now smiled boldly. "I wouldn't call a massive heart attack inexplicable, especially for a man of your gross body weight, Sir Harry." His head twisted quickly to face me. "And Mr. Reilly here, well, flying antique aircraft is certainly a risky business, and one as old as his Grumman Albatross crashing into the mountains would not be a surprise, would it?"

The phone crackled for a moment, then Harry's voice sounded, albeit weaker and harder to hear. "The race, and the ceremony for executing the contract, is two days away, Hans. If we do nothing, the team will automatically accept the next offer. It will all be done electronically on DocuSign; there's nothing you can do about it."

My hands were now tingling and discomfort gurgled in my abdomen. "Sounds like we have a stalemate here, gentlemen," I said.

Himmelman's attention turned back toward me. "No, it means more convincing methods of persuasion are required for Sir Harry—" He then broke into German, issuing what sounded like a command in a harsh voice.

The sound of a loud *whack* came through the speaker of the cell phone, followed by what sounded like a whimper.

"Harry, are you okay?"

Another *whack* followed.

"Harry? Harry?" I said.

A rough laugh sounded next. "Don't worry about me, Buck. They may land on the oldest base of water-driven torture to seek capitulation, but I was trained back in flight school to pilot through no matter what."

Harry's voice had been emphatic and determined, but his statement made no sense at all.

"What do you want me to do, Harry?" I said.

"Keep this all confidential, Buck, or you will put others in danger as well." He paused. "It makes me ill, same as that placid time in Saint

Barths—"

Himmelman slapped his hand against the table. "Keep it quiet indeed. In fact, if either of you leak information to anybody, cry out, or make a foolish attempt to impede my efforts, then the other will be tortured until they beg to be killed." His ice-blue eyes stared into mine with pure determination. "Is that clear?"

I nodded quickly.

Another *whack* sounded on the phone.

"Yes, quite clear." Harry's voice sounded far away.

Himmelman ended the call. His stare was controlled, and his hands were steady as he placed the phone back in his breast pocket.

"You had better listen to your *dear friend*, Mr. Reilly. Sir Harry must think very highly of you as he has made you the successor on a hundred-million-Euro investment should something happen to him, like the sudden heart attack I mentioned."

Hundred million? Adrenalin finally exploded through me at an uncontrollable rate, and I lunged for Himmelman—

Black vultures swooped in on me so fast, Himmelman didn't even blink as he reached for his cup of tea—

WHACK, WHACK, WHACK!

Pain shot through my back and outstretched limbs as I reached for Himmelman, but his guards were so well trained and responsive to threats, I didn't get within three feet of him.

WHACK, WHACK, WHACK!

I crumpled to the floor, with pain shooting through my limbs and torso, until everything mercifully went dark.

12

THE SOUND OF BIG MAMA'S TWIN ENGINES eventually roused me back from the beating. I was crumpled over in a rear right aisle seat until the sudden smell of ammonia sat me up straight as I swatted at my nose.

I whacked someone's hand, and when my eyes focused, I saw the Mortician and Thick-neck, who must've loaded me onto the plane, which Ray had already started, no doubt anxious to fly out of here as soon as possible. My eyelids fluttered. The Mortician again waved the smelling salts below my nostrils, and I turned my head.

"I'm awake, I'm awake. Enough with that already."

Past the Mortician I saw Thick-neck pulling the anchor from the rear hatch. When he had it inside, he dropped it onto the teak deck, which caused a loud *clunk*. I craned to see if he'd damaged the flooring but came face to face with the Mortician's gun instead.

"Pull the front anchor, Herr Reilly. We need to get you back to Monza promptly before the Williams team managers become concerned." He narrowed his eyes. "You are now the prime investor and must conclude the transaction."

His words sunk in.

My eyes suddenly opened wide. "Have you hurt Harry?! Is he all right?"

"Too many questions, Herr Reilly." He waved the pistol toward the flight deck. "Go, now!"

I stood, still groggy, my limbs aching from getting beaten and the back of my head tender from whatever they used to knock me out.

Would they have killed Harry? They said they would, but had they?

I made my way into the cabin where Ray was focused on monitoring boat traffic and appeared ready to go once I pulled the anchor. His eyes grew wide when he got a look at my face, which ached and felt puffy so probably didn't look too good, either. Once in the forward hatch, I made quick work of pulling and storing the anchor and closing the hatch, then crawled quickly back into the right seat and buckled up while Ray added power and began our runup.

A moment later we were hurtling down the imagined runway into the easterly wind and light chop, but Big Mama hardly bounced at all. Her twenty-two-thousand-pound mass plowed through the waters like a cruise ship. Once we reached the critical speed, Ray slowly pulled back on the wheel and Big Mama broke free of the earth's grasp. She immediately yawed to the left, which was a normal characteristic on the takeoff roll for an Albatross. Ray countered it by applying the right rudder to offset the P-factor caused by the right engine being at full throttle, which straightened Big Mama out. Ray pulled the wheel back further, and I watched the instrument panel as we climbed steadily at 115 knots.

As soon as I donned my headset, the Mortician's voice sounded in my ear. "Well done, Herr Floyd. Depending on what happens to Herr Reilly, we may employ you and your plane for the convenience it offers."

Ray and I turned our heads to face each other. His left eyebrow was arched at a sharp angle. I held my index finger to my lip. Nothing Ray could say or ask could help the situation, and if the sick feeling in my gut was correct, Harry may have been murdered already.

"When you return to Monza, you will tell the head of Williams that you saw Herr Greenbaum at a social function and he authorized you to sign the document."

I stared straight ahead through the windscreen at the large cumulous clouds that floated like gaseous icebergs in our path.

"Do you understand me, Herr Reilly?"

I pressed the mic button with nearly enough force to crush it. "Not until I know he's safe."

There was no response.

"You hear me, asshole?" I asked.

I looked over my left shoulder to see the Mortician still holding the gun.

"We will blow up your plane, and—"

"You leave Big Mama out of it. Plus, if she doesn't fly in the formation to kick off the race, the Williams team will know something isn't right."

"And Fräulein Drake will also be in jeopardy until you comply."

I sat back in the right seat and closed my eyes.

What kind of shit show did you get us involved with, Harry?

Then I realized that after all the crap I'd put him through over the past decade, losing millions of his dollars and always asking for loans and favors, this was fitting payback.

If he was still alive, I couldn't let him die, but if he was alive, he wouldn't ever talk to me again if I capitulated to Himmelman's demands. It wasn't Himmelman facing the stalemate; it was me.

PERCY RETURNED ME TO THE SAME VIP ENTRANCE where I'd entered this morning, and where Harry had been kidnapped by Himmelman's men. I told Percy to stay out of sight—which wasn't easy given the burgundy Rolls Royce—and to keep his phone on in case we needed help.

"And Sir Harry is safe?" he asked.

I winced, which he must have noticed in his rearview mirror, because his mouth dropped open.

"I spoke to him on the phone but didn't see him." I paused. "Suffice it to say that Harry probably took a similar beating as I did. These people are very serious. Deadly serious. I need to figure out how to turn the tables on them, and fast. But we need to keep this *entre nous*, Percy, got it?"

With that, I gave Percy a squeeze on the shoulder. Then Ray and I got out of the Rolls Royce and didn't look back as we entered the VIP tent, flashed our credentials, and hurried through the tent of games, bars, and souvenirs, back through the labyrinth of doors and corridors until we were back in the paddock and walking quickly toward the Williams facility at the end.

"I met the pilot for the Williams team at the airport," Ray said. "He told me that Harry is close friends with the managing partner for the Williams Racing team."

We hurried past a TV crew interviewing two men in red fire suits, which caused Ray to pause a moment, but I kept going. He hurried up to my side a moment later.

"That was Ferrari drivers Charles Leclerc and Carlos Sainz," he said.

My eyes were fixated on the gray three-story condo at the end of the paddock with the large W mounted on top. "Did the pilot tell you the managing director's name?" I said.

"Yes, he … did." Ray was huffing and puffing. "Matt … Sterling. He runs Pinnacle Ventures, which manages the team for an anonymous owner."

"That must be Harry's friend from the royal family."

Given the number of people in the paddock, including other drivers getting interviewed, I assumed practices must be over for the day. I asked Ray if that was accurate.

He consulted his watch. "Yeah, the second practice probably ended an hour ago."

"What's next?"

"Tomorrow's Saturday, and they'll have some Formula 2 races in the morning. Then the third practice will happen around lunch with qualifying a couple hours after that."

"What time's the race on Sunday?"

"Three o'clock."

As we walked up to the front entrance of the Williams building, I could see Jones, Harry's rent-a-bodyguard, looking through the window.

"And the race takes two hours?" I asked.

"Yeah, that's usually the case, subject to yellow and red flags, of course."

"We have to assume we have until five o'clock at the latest to save Harry and this deal he cares so much about it may kill him."

"What are we going to tell security?" Ray asked.

I stopped short of the door and turned to face him. "Nothing. We can't say a thing, or we put Harry's and, ah, well … other lives in jeopardy too."

To his credit, Ray didn't wince, whine, or shudder. In fact, his reaction caused me to take a step back.

Ray's smile appeared almost evil under his Fu-Manchu mustache. "Then we need to find him, and fast."

I smiled back and slapped him on the shoulder. "Attaboy."

Jones from Tactical International pushed the door open, and rather than having the conversation out in the paddock, we pushed past him inside the condo. Heather was walking down the internal staircase ahead of Claire, the niece of the Williams team founder, and locked her eyes onto mine. She closed the distance quickly.

"Where have you been? You were gone for hours," she asked.

"We had a meeting with the, ah, advisor handling Harry's investment in the team."

Heather's brow furrowed and she held her fist up to cover her mouth as she quickly studied my bruises. She knew there was trouble but not exactly what, so my matter-of-fact response must have signaled her not to mention them in front of Claire.

"Is Matt Sterling here?"

"We were just with him upstairs," Heather said.

"I'll take you to meet him," Claire said.

We climbed up to the next level, where a nice dining area, kitchen, and a space with white leather sofas created a plush spot to relax and watch out over the paddock. She continued up another flight of steps to the top floor, which was largely open air and equipped with a long bar and multiple TVs showing interviews down in the paddock we'd just left. There was a long white couch and white stools at the bar.

"Matt is in the conference room meeting with the Team Principal," Claire said. "When they're done, I'll introduce you."

"Where did you go?" Jones asked. "Track security was in a titter that you'd left without waiting for them to speak with you further."

The door to the conference room opened, and Claire hurried over before anybody had walked out. I leaned closer to the bodyguard. "I'll fill you in after we speak with Sterling. There's work to be done."

Jones stood taller, his eyes a bit wider and the corners of his mouth pulled back in surprise. "Right," was all he mustered.

Claire spoke with the tall, handsome man with premature gray hair whom I presumed to be Sterling as they stood outside the conference room door. The man said something final to the other man who'd left the room—must be the Team Principal—another tall man with short brown hair and, if I had to guess, in his early forties. They exchanged curt nods and the latter man disappeared down the steps before Sterling turned his gaze toward us and mustered a broad smile.

We walked toward each other, and he extended his arm five feet before reaching me.

"Mr. Reilly, a pleasure to finally meet you." His smile was genuine and his blue eyes sharp like a hawk's. "I'm Matthew Sterling, chairman of Williams Racing."

"Nice to meet you, sir."

"Sir Harry has spoken fondly of you, but frankly, we were very surprised to have you codified as his successor in the agreement."

I nodded and thought, *not as surprised as me.*

"Any news of his whereabouts? There's talk that he may have been abducted?" Sterling looked at Jones when he said that.

Track security and the Carabinieri must have spread the word hoping to stumble onto something.

"I spoke to Harry," I said. "He's fine."

Both Sterling's and Jones's eyes opened wide. Jones stepped closer.

"Wonderful news, such a relief," Sterling said. "Had he gone to town for a proper meal?"

I concentrated on keeping my face neutral. "He had other business to attend to, but he asked me to reassure you he has every intention of finalizing your agreement."

"Splendid, splendid, the entire ownership group will be very pleased. The infusion of capital is critical to our next technological endeavor to make the team more competitive in the midfield," he said.

That statement made me pause for a moment. "Midfield only? No aspirations to win it all?" I asked.

Sterling's eyes narrowed and his face became serious.

I felt Ray edge forward behind me. "Buck's new to Formula 1," he said. "Midfield is highly competitive with other teams like McLaren, Aston Martin, Alpine, and Haas. The higher the constructor finishes in the standings, the more money they receive, so every step up is increasingly lucrative."

"Quite," Sterling said. Then he shrugged with a sudden giggle. "Given your relationship with Sir Harry, and since you're named in the contract, you will be considered one of the team owners as well. So all the vagaries of the sport will become part of your DNA, like they have mine."

"Your group just purchased the team a few years ago, isn't that right?" I said.

"Correct. Our partnership seeks to restore the team back to the founder's level of success while ensuring to preserve its British heritage."

He flashed a quick smile. "No offense, of course. In fact, my investment firm, Pinnacle Ventures, is based in New York City and my wife is American. This year we also have the first American driver on the grid since 2013, so we greatly value our cousins across the Atlantic and recognize the value of the sport's growth and acceptance in the States."

As Sterling spoke, I could feel a presence behind me. With a quick glance back I found Jones hovering close, his hot breath beating against the back of my neck.

"I am new to the sport," I said. "But my partner Ray here is quite the fan."

Ray stepped forward with his hand tentatively extended. "Really a pleasure to meet you, sir. As Buck said, I'm a big fan."

Sterling gave him a curt nod. "Well then, glad to hear Sir Harry is on board." A wry smile twisted his lips. "Of course, since you are also a principal, you can sign the agreement at the ceremony should Sir Harry still be tending to other affairs," he said.

I forced the corners of my lips to turn up, but if Sterling looked closely, he'd undoubtedly notice the concern in my eyes. "That would be fun for me, but Harry's looking forward to doing that himself. He has until the end of the race on Sunday, correct?"

"Yes, that's correct. We have a special celebration planned." He paused. "It would be tragic if for some reason you were both late, and the electronic process went forward with the backup contract."

I winced. "You can't change that?"

"I'm afraid not. It's how the bidding process was structured by the investment bank. After interviewing the many qualified bidders—and as I said, there were several—the short-listed parties were given the opportunity to put forth anonymous bids. Once those were filed, the names of the bidders were revealed to prevent any fixing. But I'd be lying if I didn't say Sir Harry was the preferred partner all along, thanks to his connection with the other owners and, as I said earlier, in our interest to preserve the team's British heritage."

"Understood," I said. "Harry, er, *we* won't let you down."

The shrill sound of a phone ringing caught all our attention. I turned and saw Jones pull his phone from the breast pocket of his sports coat. He looked at the name that appeared on the screen, but I couldn't see it.

"Yes?"

Whoever was on the other end of the line spoke for a minute, then Jones gazed up at me. "Yes, he's back here at the Williams building."

More talk from the caller.

"Right. We'll be here waiting." He then pushed end on his phone and replaced it in his pocket. "Mazza, head of track security. He and the proper authorities would still like a word with you, Mr. Reilly."

Sterling stepped forward. "Please feel free to use the conference room on the ground level. I'm sure they'll be pleased to know Sir Harry is safe and no doubt adding local wines to his collection." His big smile and sky-blue eyes were disarming.

"I'm sure," I said.

If only it were true.

13

WHILE JONES, HEATHER, RAY, AND I WAITED IN THE DOWN-STAIRS CONFERENCE ROOM, the security professional eyed me coldly. "Where was Sir Harry when you spoke to him?" he asked.

I swallowed. I'd debated back and forth whom to trust, how to keep Harry's deal alive, and to honor his wishes of not sharing specific details with the authorities, the latter of which had been accomplished by exaggerating his status with Sterling. But if we were going to try and find Harry, I'd need Jones's help. And even though Himmelman's threat was clear that if I uttered a word, Harry would be tortured and killed, I needed Jones's help.

"Harry's being held by some German cartel who are threatening to kill him, and me, if we don't agree to include them in the ownership entity to invest in the team."

At first hard, Jones's expression morphed to anger. "Damn it."

"We need to keep this under wraps or it will screw up Harry's plans and, worse, get him killed."

"What are we going to do?" Jones asked.

"I looked up Tactical International when I was riding back here from the airport. Big firm, lots of assets and levels of protection," I said. "Can you get reinforcements?"

Jones's eyes narrowed. "Already on the way."

"Armed?"

"To the teeth."

A flourish of activity sounded below, and we hurried into the reception area to find Mazza and the same two Carabinieri who had been here with him earlier.

Mazza eyed me, Jones, Ray, and Heather up and down as we each reached the bottom of the stairs. "Signor Reilly. We have been waiting for you," he said.

"How can I help you?" I asked.

"Are those bruises on your face?" he asked.

"Got tripped in the crowd."

He leaned back a few degrees and held his gaze steady, hiding what I could tell was surprise. "You left with Signor Greenbaum's driver," he said. "Where did you go?"

My brain processed numerous responses, angles, truths, and lies all at once as I tried to discern how honest to be with the head of track security and his police bookends. I needed help, but bringing him into the loop would be a sure way to have the situation balloon into one I could no longer control; therefore Harry's life, if not mine, would be at greater risk. But at the same time, I didn't want to make myself complicit in the situation by withholding facts.

"I had to get to Linate Airport to practice our flyover with the squadron."

Mazza's eyes narrowed. I heard Jones clear his throat behind me. Now that he was in the loop, he too would be concerned for self-preservation.

"We saw the planes circle Monza Park." He paused. "They appeared shortly after you left, and, well, the drive to the airport—"

"That was me in the plane," Ray said. "Buck was running late."

Mazza glanced past me toward Ray, seeing him as if for the first time. "And you are?"

"Ray Floyd. Buck's partner at Last Resort Charter and Salvage."

The corners of Mazza's mouth turned down. "Last Resort, is it?" He grunted.

"I waited at the airport for Ray to return," I said.

Mazza turned to face the male Carabinieri and spoke quickly in Italian. The Carabinieri, who wore a name tag I hadn't noticed before that read "Donatello," nodded and said something under his breath.

"We will speak with Signor DeGregorio, the flight leader," Mazza said.

"What, you don't believe me?" I asked with an edge to my voice.

"Signor Greenbaum is—"

"Fine," I said. "Signor, er Sir, I mean, Harry is fine. I spoke to him on the phone. He's ah, shopping for wine—a winery, actually."

Out of the corner of my eye, I noticed Jones shift his weight from one foot to the other. I swallowed, recognizing that now I was lying to the Italian authorities and the path I had inadvertently chosen would be very hard to retract.

"Wine, you say?"

"The van that picked him up is a distributor from somewhere up near Lake Garda."

Mazza didn't respond, just focused on my eyes, and it took every ounce of concentration not to blink, twitch, or fidget. "Strange," Mazza said. "This morning, Greenbaum's driver, Signor Percy, told Officer Donatello that a German group had been pressuring him about a pending investment and he was afraid they had abducted Greenbaum."

Percy hadn't told me that.

Could Mazza be bluffing?

I crossed my arms. "Who might that be?" I asked.

"We were hoping you could tell us, Signor Reilly."

Images of the Mortician and Himmelman pulsed through my mind, along with their threats and the aching wounds on my back and face.

"No idea, but if that's the case, I hope you're on the lookout for them. Harry is the eternal optimist and doesn't think anyone would ever harm him."

Mazza nodded past me. "Is that why he retained Tactical International?"

I half-looked toward Jones but then stopped. "Hundreds of thousands of people come to these Formula 1 races, Mazza. A billionaire like Harry needs to take precautions in situations like these."

Mazza pursed his lips for a moment, then stood taller. "Wealthy people need also to be careful of the company they keep, isn't that so, *King* Buck? Especially if these so-called friends would benefit as a result of the wealthy person's demise."

A sharp intake of breath caused me to flinch. Son of a bitch had been doing his research. I licked my lips.

"No doubt," I said. "Harry will be back later. Please keep us apprised about anything you learn of these Germans you're referring to. If Harry's in danger, we'll increase our security measures." I turned to gauge Jones's expression, which I was happy to find blank. "Isn't that right, Mr. Jones?"

"Damn straight. Sir."

After giving me a long, dissatisfied glare, Mazza turned and walked back toward the crowded paddock with the two Carabinieri in tow. They walked right past a driver in a green fire suit who was being interviewed by a press crew and didn't even look at them as they walked by. I knew Mazza didn't believe me, which could make me a suspect if matters deteriorated further.

Way to go, Buck. Lying to the Italian authorities about Harry going missing. It was foolish, but Harry had demanded secrecy. I just hoped he would either agree to let these Germans co-invest or find a way out of wherever he was being held.

When I turned to face the others, Ray and Jones would not meet my eyes. Heather looked past me, and when I glanced over my shoulder, I realized she was watching the green-clad driver's interview. I realized the driver was looking in our direction, too. He donned a big smile and waved. I turned to see Heather smile and wave back, and when she noticed me watching, her smile fell away.

I shrugged. "Is that Fernando?"

"Sure is," she said.

"Hmm. Pretty short," I said.

"Most of the drivers are, but he makes up for it with charisma and charm."

"I'm sure."

Jones cleared his throat. "Lying to the police could become a problem, Reilly."

"Harry would be killed if I didn't." I let that sink in, then asked, "Does Tactical International have access to intelligence or law enforcement data banks?"

"Yes, but that will require some information to research, not just—"

"The head guy's name is Hans Himmelman. Brash, cocky son of a bitch. Ask your people if they have anything on him. We need to understand our adversary and see how we can get to him."

"Will do," Jones said. He appeared comfortable taking orders; my guess was he had been British military. "A dozen men are on their way here now, too. But they're search and recovery types, not researchers."

"Good. If we learn anything about Himmelman, maybe it will give us some clues on where to direct your special operators. I met him at Lake Garda, but I had the impression that Harry wasn't there."

"Based on what?" Jones asked.

"Just a gut feeling."

"Right. Let me know if you think of anything else or they contact you again, and I'll tell you when my team arrives."

I gave him a curt nod, then turned to Ray. "Let's go talk to Percy and see if we can jog his memory."

"I'll stick around here and see if anything comes up," Heather said.

I again turned my attention back to where the interview was being conducted with her old beau, Fernando, but he and the TV crew were gone. She saw me and connected the dots.

"I'll stick close to the Williams people," she said.

"Okay." Then to Ray. "Let's go."

Ray and I worked our way back through the crowd. He oohed and aahed at a few people he saw and named names, but not being a race fan, I didn't know anybody. Some of the names were foreign, like Verstappen, Gasly, Leclerc, and Zhou. The international nature of the sport produced drivers from all over the world.

"What did Harry say when you spoke to him?" Ray asked.

"He said some weird stuff. I couldn't tell if he was trying to give me a clue or they'd drugged him and he was delirious."

"Like what did he say?"

Ray and I walked side by side except when we had to squeeze through groups of people, like now, but by the time he hurried back up to me again, I had recalled Harry's statement.

"Something about 'landing on the oldest base of water torture,' and how it reminded him of being in flight school back in the day."

"I didn't know Harry was a pilot," Ray said.

"That's the thing." I paused. "He wasn't."

"So maybe it was a message of some kind. What was that about oldest base of water torture? Did he say anything else?"

"Yeah. I guess he was referring to waterboarding—and yeah, he said another weird thing right before Himmelman hung up the phone. He mentioned the time he got ill at some—what was the word he used—*placid*, that's what it was, some placid time in Saint Barths," I said.

"Saint Barths?"

"Harry was there with me, Jack, my former partner at e-Antiquity, and a number of other investors just before the company cratered, but we were on a yacht that was anything but placid. What about the reference to flight school?" I asked.

Ray suddenly grabbed my arm and we both stopped.

His eyes were the size of saucers. "I told you the oldest seaplane base in the world is in Italy," he said.

"Where is it again?"

"Lake Como."

A bolt of lightning flashed in my brain. "That must be it! Let's go there."

I started pushing through the crowd, and Ray hurried to keep up with me.

"It's a couple of hours' drive from here," Ray said. "And the lake's very long—and we don't know where to look."

"We'll get Big Mama and fly there, then."

I saw Ray smile next to me.

"Good idea."

UNWANTED HOSTS

14

PERCY AGAIN DROVE US TO LINATE AIRPORT, BUT THIS TIME he had the old Rolls Royce cruising at top speed. As he drove, he confirmed telling Mazza about the German group potentially abducting Harry. "I wanted to be as helpful as possible," he said.

"Of course you did, Percy, but when I spoke to Harry while at the hotel in Garda, he told me to keep everything confidential so nobody else would get hurt."

"Dear God, poor Sir Harry," Percy muttered.

"You did nothing wrong, but from here on out, let's abide by Harry's wishes and keep all this on the down-low." I paused. I didn't want to burden Percy with too much information that could put him at risk, but at the same time I wanted to give him hope. "Ray and I have a clue we're going to follow up on."

"With your plane? So they have taken him to another location?" Percy asked.

"We're going for a ride to think things through. Keep an eye on your phone for news or in case we need you."

"Of course."

I sensed a change in Percy's voice and looked at his reflection in the rearview mirror. Was that a tear on his cheek?

"Thank you, Buck," he said, then swiped his cheek.

As Percy and I were talking, Ray had been reviewing landing procedures on Lake Como, texting the owner of the Aero Club Como after he received the name and contact information from Raphael DeGregorio in another text. I heard Ray's phone ping and turned my attention to him.

"It's from the guy at the seaplane base—his name's Carmen Micciche."

"What did he say?"

"He said we can land Big Mama on the lake and provided me with the GPS coordinates for Aero Club Como's dock, ramp, and hangar."

"Perfect."

"Lake Como?" Percy asked.

I grimaced. So much for protecting Percy. "That's right. We have reason to believe they may be holding Harry there."

"Sir Harry does like to stay at the Bellagio a few times a year. He flies there from the seaplane base since it's a two-hour drive north from Como through very narrow roads." He cleared his throat. "I drive up there so he has local transportation, but it is a very challenging motorway full of blind corners and passages so narrow only one vehicle may pass at a time."

Ray and I exchanged a glance. That explained Harry's knowledge of the seaplane base there. Harry's other odd statement occurred to me, and given that now Percy was inadvertently in the loop, I wanted to know if it meant anything to him.

"I think Harry was trying to give me a clue on his whereabouts with an odd statement he made at the end of the call," I said.

Percy glanced at me in the rearview mirror.

"He mentioned a 'placid time' on Saint Barths where he'd been ill. Does that mean anything to you?"

Percy hesitated, but I could see his eyes squint in the mirror. "No, I'm afraid not."

We took the exit toward the airport at high speed, the old Rolls tracking steadily, but as the large body of the vehicle leaned hard to the left, it gave me another idea.

"Ray, since Harry used the seaplane base in Como, ask that guy Carmen Micciche if he knows him, and if so, if he's seen him lately."

"We will be arriving at Linate in moments," Percy said.

"Maybe Raphael can help," Ray said.

"Okay, hold off on calling. Let's wait until we get inside."

Percy entered the airport grounds maintaining higher than legal speed, and I hoped we wouldn't get pulled over. After navigating the serpentine roadway, he screeched to a stop in front of the general aviation terminal.

"Thanks, Percy," I said. "Keep your phone handy and I'll let you know what we learn."

"And I'll call you if we need an escape plan," Ray added.

"Piece of luck, men!"

Now we were familiar with the terminal and, more importantly, the people there knew us. So when Ray asked where DeGregorio was, we got the information without filter. We found him on the flight deck, tinkering with the Macchi we had found out belonged to him. When he saw us, his expression contorted to one of wrinkled surprise.

"There's no more practice today," he said. "What are you two doing here?"

Now that we were going on offense, I was going to need the help of some select people, like Raphael DeGregorio. "Sir Harry, the principal who had asked us to join your flight formation, may be missing," I said.

He stood up straight. "Missing?"

"That's right, and we believe he may be in danger."

DeGregorio's entire body language had changed. His hands were on his hips, he stared straight at us, and he was clearly concerned. "He is a wealthy man, yes? Are the police searching for him?"

"We don't want to sound too many alarms, so no, but we are."

He threw his hand up in the air. "Italian law enforcement are weak and disorganized anyway." His face grew even more serious. "What about the flyover? This is of national importance."

"I'll be here, don't worry," Ray said.

My lack of response was response enough.

"How can I help?"

"You gave Ray the name of the man who owns Aero Club Como—"

"Sì, Carmen Micciche. He's like a brother to me."

"Would you mind calling to ask if he has seen Harry, er, Sir Harry?"

DeGregorio's face again became a topographic map of doubt. "Carmen? How would he know anything?"

"Sir Harry frequents Como and charters a plane from the club to take him to his hotel."

His eyes know grew wide and he nodded slowly. "Ahh, that makes sense, but if he's missing—" He interrupted himself and held a hand aloft. "I'll stop asking questions and do as you ask."

From his pants pocket he removed a very early model iPhone. His index finger hovered over the keyboard for a second before he stabbed at it multiple times. The volume was loud on the phone so I could hear it ringing even as he held it up to his ear.

Someone must have answered because DeGregorio's face was instantly animated, and he glanced quickly toward me and flared his nostrils. He then launched into rapid fire Italian that I had no way of following. I did hear him mention my and Ray's names, the word *Grumman*, then very slowly, "Big Mama," at which the other man, presumably Carmen Micciche, must have laughed as DeGregorio rolled his eyes. After what I guessed was a question on the other end, our intermediary again launched into a lengthy description and I again heard my name, followed by Como and Sir Harry. As soon as he mentioned that name, Micciche must have interrupted him.

"Stop, stop," DeGregorio said in English. "I'll put you on speaker."

Ray and I leaned closer.

"Hello? Hello?" DeGregorio said.

"I'm here," Carmen said. "And yes, I just saw Harry—forgive me, we are old friends who don't bother with formalities."

"*Bene, bene*," DeGregorio said. "Signor Reilly, what would you like to ask Carmen?"

I took the phone from his hand and held it closer to my mouth. "Hello, Carmen, we appreciate your help here. Harry's also a very dear friend to me and my parents before me."

"You're that treasure hunter, no?" Carmen said.

I winced. What had Harry told him about me that made me so memorable?

"Ah, yes, Harry was our main investor." I held my breath.

"*Sì, sì*, he spoke of you often. He was very proud of your accomplishments."

Past tense, of course. e-Antiquity had gone bust a decade ago now.

"Yes, Harry always enjoyed our adventures back in the day," I said.

"No, no, he still spoke of you long after your company went bankrupt. I would tease him because his previous exuberance caused me to invest—hey, you know, I'm always looking for some extra cash."

I watched Ray's expression as Carmen spoke. He closed his eyes for a moment and gave a slight shake of his head. Good grief.

"But I sold the stock at the peak after you found the Serpent King in

Guatemala. I figured how could you top that, right? And I was right, yes?"

I smiled. Whew. "Yes, you certainly were. Well again, we appreciate your help here. Harry has gone missing and may be in danger—"

"I just saw him this morning!" Carmen shouted. "He was aboard another charter, a plane I didn't recognize, a beautiful Caravan on floats. I was upset because I always fly him, and he didn't even stop in for an espresso like he normally does, but yes, it was him no doubt about it."

Ray's eyes lit up and I felt adrenalin surge into my system.

"That's great to hear, but you say you've never seen the plane before, so you don't know where they went?"

"That's right, I've never seen it, but one of my charter plane pilots told me he saw a beautiful Caravan land in Torno."

I turned my attention to DeGregorio and mouthed the word *Torno?*

"It's maybe a third of the way up the lake on the eastern shore, halfway to Bellagio," he said.

Percy said Harry stayed in Bellagio, but it wouldn't make sense for them to go where the staff would know him.

Carmen continued. "Our charter continued up past Torno and vectored around where we always do for tours, and when the pilot came back south, he saw the Caravan taking off again."

"So maybe they dropped Harry off in Torno?"

"I have no idea, Signor Reilly, but hey, you're the treasure hunter. If you could find the tomb of the Serpent King, you can find that out, too."

I ignored his comment. "What is there at Torno where they may have gone?"

"Several hotels and private residences. The road there is narrow, and the hills climb steeply from the water." He paused. "Now that I think about it, my pilot said the Caravan was in the water in front of the il Sereno hotel, which is the nicest one there, so maybe they were dropping Harry off for a meeting."

Something about the name of the hotel made me pause. Il Sereno. What was it that Harry had said, something about "same as that placid time in Saint Barths?"

My eyelids suddenly spread wide. *Placid* was another word for *serene*, and in Italian, *serene* was likely *sereno*. "There's an il Sereno hotel in Saint Barths," I blurted.

DeGregorio frowned and Ray's eyes went wide to match mine.

Then Carmen spoke on the phone, which surprised me, and I almost dropped it. "*Sì, sì,* that is true. I think they have another hotel in another luxury location but can't recall where."

All that mattered was that he confirmed my recollection that there were hotels with the same name in Saint Barths and Lake Como, which broke Harry's code.

I clutched the phone so tight I was afraid it would crumble. "Thank you, Carmen. We're headed to Lake Como now, so keep an eye out for our Grumman Albatross."

"Big Mama?" He laughed.

"That's the one. We'll be looking for the il Sereno hotel, based on what you said—Torno is a little ways up the lake from Como."

"That's right, it's a beautiful, square-shaped building very close to the water. A combination of light-brown wood and concrete, very *moderno* and artistic. From the air you will see the large rectangular swimming pool right on the water's edge on the south side of the hotel. Nothing else like it until you get to Bellagio."

I pumped my fist and Ray had already started walking toward Big Mama.

"*Grazie,* Carmen and Raphael, I very much appreciate your help," I said and handed the phone back.

I jogged after Ray, my heart sprinting ahead of me.

Come on, Lake Como.

15

FROM THE AIR, LAKE COMO WAS LONG AND SINEWY, and the town that bore its name was on the southernmost shore. Mountains sprung up on both sides of the dark, deep water, and palatial villas dotted the eastern and western shores, while the town of Como hung from the southeastern corner of the lake like a babe suckling a teat. I had Googled the location of Aero Club Como while Ray flew Big Mama on what turned out to be a very brief flight. The Aero Club was also on the southernmost shore of the lake and Ray had vectored so we'd fly right over it.

As we approached, I spotted a series of large buoys in a straight line from a ramp into the water. Two old single-engine float planes were tied up to a dock, and another plane was taxiing to the north away from the ramp. Ray flew low as the pattern here was only at one thousand feet above the lake, and there was no doubt anybody at the Aero Club would have heard the roar of Big Mama's twin engines. Given Carmen's long tenure here and love for classic planes—which I'd seen on their website—he'd enjoy seeing an Albatross on approach.

Now out over the lake, Ray vectored around a peak on the eastern shore where the body of water angled due north. We were low enough to see cars driving on the road, and I realized what Percy had said was true. The roadway was very narrow, two lanes at best, but periodically the landscape and buildings encroached on the road narrowing it to a single lane. The homes here, set on terraced plateaus down the steep hill of the eastern slope, were lovely, in some cases astonishing.

"Torno's just up ahead," Ray said. "I'll go around once just to eyeball the hotel."

"No!" I shouted. "Land ASAP before we get to the hotel, so nobody sees us. Himmelman's henchmen know what Big Mama looks like. If we get spotted, the jig's up."

"Shit," Ray muttered under his breath, but our Bose headsets made his voice crystal clear.

He added half flaps and our descent sharpened, with our nose now straight toward the water.

"Watch for boats or hazards," Ray said.

"I'm watching!" I lied. I'd been studying the eastern shore looking for the artsy box of a building and swimming pool by the shore, but now I deviated my attention below—

"Boat below!" I shouted.

Ray quickly reached up and added power, then pulled back on the wheel to increase our angle of attack. We passed dangerously close to the antique wooden boat, so close, in fact, I saw a flash of two people seated in the boat duck from the oncoming behemoth.

Ray added full flaps and edged the wheel forward, and just as Big Mama settled into the calm water, I spotted what had to be il Sereno up ahead. I pointed it out to Ray, and he responded quickly with measures to slow Big Mama down. Now that we had assessed the options, we agreed our plan would be for him to nose up to the dock where I would jump out and he'd back away and wait out on the water.

I knew I had to share my plan with Ray before it was too late. I cleared my throat and he glanced at me with impatience since I'd hurried him so much.

"Listen, my goal here is to talk Himmelman into swapping me for Harry."

Ray's mouth fell open. "What?"

"Harry's old and fragile, and he's the main event. Everyone wants to see him at the race, and it'll reduce the heat on the situation. Mazza will back off and—"

"Are you crazy?"

I bit my lip for a moment. "Probably, but I have a better chance of enduring whatever they throw at the captive than he does." I paused. "So, with any luck, it will be Harry coming back to the plane, not me."

"Then what?"

"Harry will know what to do."

Ray stared at me, then held out his hand. I took it in mine, and he gave me a firm shake. "Good luck then."

With that, I climbed under the instrument panel, got back on my feet, and with the nose hatch open, climbed out and prepared to jump off onto the dock. A dozen patrons and an equal number of staff stood by the pool or up one level where an outdoor dining area overlooked the water. Another epiphany struck that no matter where we landed, by coming up to the hotel's dock slowly and as quietly as we could, Big Mama had the equivalent subtlety of the Loch Ness Monster creeping to shore. As I slid to the end of the nose, I said a quick prayer.

Surprise may very well have been lost, which meant time was of the essence.

Ray moderated the power, feathered the props, and slowly edged up to the end of the dock where, without hesitation, I launched myself forward, jumped out and dropped ten feet onto the wood planking. The dock pitched hard to the right when I landed, causing me to roll forward in a somersault so I wouldn't wind up in the water. Like a crazed gymnast I stood right up and was surprised that the crowd applauded.

Perfect.

Enacting my simple plan, I wasted no time and ran forward up the dock, then turned left into the al fresco dining area where an open door led inside the hotel. The applause continued and I felt my face burn, flushed with blood, embarrassment, and determination. Inside the hotel, a man wearing a suit and carrying an empty service tray stared at me with his mouth agape.

"Where's the reception area?" I said, half out of breath and loudly.

Still in shock, he raised a finger and pointed to a staircase in the middle of the room that was as artistic as the hotel's exterior, with thick wood treads suspended by ropes. I dashed onto the stairs and took them three at a time until I reached the top.

The lobby was sophisticated in warm hues of wood against dark, cold stone. I spun in a circle until I found a reception desk off to the side in a wide corridor that turned to the right where it must have led back outside. I could still hear the engines of Big Mama; Ray must have been backing away from the dock. Out of breath, I hurried to the young man and woman standing behind the desk: him in a black suit and tie and her in a black dress. They appeared unfazed and wore smiles, apparently accustomed to all kinds of distraught guests and ready to help.

"Good after ... noon," I said, still out of breath.

"Good afternoon, Mr. ...?" The man had to be in his late twenties and appeared ever confident.

I ignored his question. "I'm looking for my, ah, friend, Sir Harry Greenbaum."

Neither of their expressions changed. The young woman, a brunette, stared down at what must be a hidden computer screen blocked by the counter. A moment later she looked up with a disappointed expression on her face. She didn't need to say anything, so I tacked on.

"He's a guest of one of his business partners, Hans Himmelman."

The man's eyebrows suddenly arched. "Ah, I'm sorry, sir, but Mr. Himmelman's party just left, maybe thirty minutes ago."

Damn!

"Was there a, ah, tall, portly—quite portly—man with them? Tweed suit, VanDyke beard, bald with bushy gray hair on the sides? That's my friend, Sir Harry."

Now they both smiled, and the man adopted a pedantic smirk. "I'm sorry, sir, we are not allowed to share information about our guests."

I stood tall, now breathing regularly, and glared at the pair. "He wasn't a guest. They came earlier for a business meeting—only five or so hours ago."

The smirk faded, and the man glanced toward the woman, who was considering the information. Finally she gave him a barely perceptible nod.

The young man cleared his throat. "Yes, in fact, a man matching your description was with the Himmelman party. They left by car."

"Did they say where they were going?" It was rhetorical, but I had to try.

"I'm afraid not, sir, but there are only two choices: south to Como, or north to Bellagio and beyond."

I bit my lip and tried to contain the disappointment; I felt like a pierced balloon. An idea struck. "Do you know which car they were in?"

The man lowered his head slightly and shook it slowly from side to side. "I'm afraid not, sir."

Crap.

"But you could ask Rudi, the valet," the young woman said.

Standing tall again, I placed my hand on the counter. "And where can I find the valet?"

In a sweeping gesture, the young man rolled his arm toward the corridor that disappeared to the right.

I nodded in appreciation and pulled a twenty-dollar bill from my pocket. "And your name?"

"Charles, sir."

"Thank you, Charles."

I hurried down the corridor and followed it right through an open door, then outside down a slate path and across a pedestrian bridge. On the right was the pool and lake; on the left was a stone wall with formal landscaping built into the hill. I hurried forward and saw a small building at the end of the path and an arch with a parking area ahead. Two red Ferraris were parked side by side, along with a large Mercedes and a beautiful black Porsche. It gave me a momentary pang for my former life back in Virginia when e-Antiquity was at its peak and my personal transportation was a black Porsche 930 Turbo Carrera.

At the small gatehouse, I saw a man seated at a table looking at his phone. When he saw me, he stood quickly. Another twenty-something male in a dark suit and tie.

"Rudi?"

"Yes sir?" His voice was high-pitched, whether from surprise or late puberty I couldn't tell.

"I'm late for my group—the Himmelman party—Charles said they just left thirty minutes ago."

"Yes, yes, that's correct, sir. They left in the other Mercedes, but ah, this one's still here. Do you, um, have the ticket?"

If the car was still here, that meant some of them must still be too. But according to Charles, Harry had already departed.

"No, not with me." Different fabrications pulsed through my mind until I landed on one. "Did they head back down to Como, or were they on their way up to get an early start for drinks in Bellagio?"

He smiled. "They didn't say, sir, but I did hear the mention of an airplane, if that helps."

A long exhale deflated me again. "And the others?" I pointed toward the other car.

He held up his hand, palm up. "I'm not sure, sir."

"Okay, thanks."

I retreated from the direction I came but found an outside stair that led to the pool patio. Lost in thought, I was almost to the dock when two men in dark suits stepped in front of me.

"Subtle arrival, Herr Reilly. We've been in the boat anticipating you."

It was the Mortician, flanked by the thick-necked beast of a man from the hotel in Garda. These guys really got around. I spotted a highly varnished antique wood boat at the south side of the boat dock and realized it was the same one Ray had nearly landed upon when we arrived. Too bad I had steered him clear. Subtle arrival indeed.

"I was hoping to find Harry and Himmelman here." I said. "I'd like to exchange myself for Harry. Let him go do the deal with Williams, and I'll be your hostage."

The Mortician's eyes narrowed, but they were not smiling.

"How gallant of you, Herr Reilly, but that is not an option," the Mortician said. "In fact, you have disobeyed the Principal's instructions of non-interference that he imposed back at Garda, so now Herr Greenbaum will be punished. As will you."

"That's Sir Harry to you, *Herr* Himmler."

His eyes narrowed further, unamused at my reference to the former head of the Nazi SS back in World War II.

He said something in German, followed by a bone-chilling leer. Thick-neck moved toward me. "You're coming with us," he said.

I glanced toward the pool on my left, spotting a beautiful woman sunning in a skimpy bikini, and I smiled and nodded to her. Thick-neck couldn't help but follow my gaze, and I suddenly dropped my shoulder and crashed into him like a fullback running over a linebacker toward open field. He was knocked off balance just enough for me to get past, down the few steps, and onto the dock. On cue, Big Mama, whose propellers had been spinning slowly as Ray floated offshore a hundred yards, surged faster.

"Herr Reilly!" The Mortician's German voice sounded from behind me.

Ray would never get here fast enough, but the would-be assailants were caught off guard and had yet to follow me. I initially planned to dive in the water and swim for it, but then I saw their boat line was only loosely wrapped around a cleat and the keys were in the ignition. I jumped inside, and rather than wasting a second to untie it, thereby allowing them to catch up with me, I sprang for the key. Thank God the outboard engine fired up right away.

Pointed out toward the lake, I jammed the throttle forward just as I heard Thick-neck storm down the dock. The boat lunged forward but was jerked momentarily back toward the dock when the slack on the single line grew taut. The engine's power won out, ripping the cleat from the varnished wood hull, along with a good foot of the hull itself, which sprang back toward Thick-neck and hit him in the chest, launching him backward and into the water on the other side of the dock.

Adrenalin got the better of me. "Later, assholes!"

I spun the wheel until I was pointed toward Big Mama, who was closing in fast. All of a sudden, the boat started listing heavily to starboard, and I glanced back to see water rushing in through the huge gash in the beautiful antique boat's gunwale. The rope must have ripped more wood off than I could see.

It was taking on water fast, adding weight and shifting the center of gravity of forward, which, before long, caused the prop to lift out of the water. With another fifty yards to go, I realized I wasn't going to make it. I glanced back at the dock; the Mortician and I locked in a momentary stare. He raised a fist, and as the engine cut out from water entering the cowling, I heard him yell.

"Damn you, Reilly!"

If I only had five Euros for every time I'd heard that statement, I'd have my ass in the sand on some swanky beach. Thrown off balance, I dove awkwardly into the lake, surprised at how cold the water was. The boat disappeared under the surface behind me as I treaded water. Without further delay, I began a steady freestyle stroke toward Ray. If I wasn't mistaken, I heard the engines change in pitch and at a glance saw the propellers slow.

I swam hard around the port side of Big Mama's never-ending fuselage and once again realized just how large she was, especially while on the water.

My concern how I'd get on board was immediately solved when a rope ladder splashed in front of me. I saw Ray wave once from the open aft port hatch; then he disappeared, hopefully up into the cockpit to get Big Mama back under control. I swam to the rope ladder, grabbed hold, and—as the engines increased in pitch—fought my way up rung by rung. The drag of the water now pulled at me as Ray maneuvered toward the south, until it felt as if the ladder would be ripped from my grip.

"Let me … climb … on board!" My shout was lost in the sound of the props.

Back on shore, I saw Thick-neck had commandeered another boat, a small wooden one likely used by hotel guests, with the Mortician, off-balance, trying to climb aboard.

Ray must've seen that too, hence his dragging me through the lake.

The water pulled at me with increased force, but galvanized by the reality that if I fell from the ladder the two goons would get to me before Ray could turn around, I gritted my teeth and focused all my remaining strength on the next rung, pulling myself up just enough to get free from the pull of the icy water. I climbed up—off-balance and rocked by the end of the ladder dragging over the waves of our own making—until I reached the hatch, lifted myself in, and fell to the cabin floor.

"Pull the ladder in and shut the hatch!" Ray yelled.

Ray had never been big on empathy. I caught my breath, crawled back to the hatch, hoisted the ladder, threw it on the teak floor, and slammed the hatch shut. As soon as he heard the metal door clank closed, Ray added power and Big Mama skidded over Lake Como with the grace of a runaway hippopotamus. I pulled myself forward, my hands digging into each of the cabin's seatbacks until I reached the flight deck. I fell into the right seat just as Big Mama pulled free from the water's grasp, and as Ray eased the wheel back, we angled toward the blue sky above.

I righted myself in the seat and, with shaky arms, clasped my five-point seatbelt and shoulder harness. With that, I fell back into the seat, closed my eyes, and fought to get my heart rate under control.

Once I donned my headset, Ray wasted no time to start asking questions.

"Learn anything?" he asked.

"Yeah, they'd been there, but we just missed them."

"Where'd they go?"

I turned toward Ray, whose expression soured at the sight of the sarcasm I felt dripping off my face—or was that the cold remnants of Lake Como?

"They didn't leave me a note."

He grimaced. "What do we do now, then?"

My cell phone was positioned on the instrument panel in a Velcro pocket I'd attached there with a suction cup, and I saw a text flash on the screen. With a heavy arm, I grabbed it and swiped it to life.

"Jones sent a text," I said.

"What's it say?"

I bit my lip to prevent more sarcasm, inhaled a deep breath, then read it aloud. "'We found data on Himmelman. He's Austrian, not German, and is a known criminal with a diverse portfolio.'"

"No surprise there," I interjected, then continued reading. "'He lives in Vienna but also has what is reported to be an impenetrable mountaintop compound near Val Gardena in the Italian Dolomites.'"

"No shit?" Ray said. "This is starting to feel very James Bond." He glanced at me and frowned.

"Don't say it, Ray."

Another text came through from Jones. "'Our team has arrived and can be dispatched immediately once we have intel on the target.'"

"He's so military," Ray said.

After a few deep breaths, I almost felt human again, albeit a soggy one. "The valet at the hotel heard them say something about a plane as they left with Harry. They're too far ahead of us by car, and who knows what little airstrip exists around here where they may have parked that Caravan."

"Maybe Carmen or Raphael DeGregorio could help us," Ray said.

I thought about it for a second. "You mean to see if they filed a flight plan?" I asked.

He smiled. "Even criminals have to fly by the rules."

"Good point."

Ray's phone was connected to the audio system so we could communicate on it via our headsets and microphones. He dialed the number, and after a few rings, the familiar voice of Raphael DeGregorio sounded loudly in my ears.

"Hello, Ray? Did you find your friend?"

I pointed to Ray, still too fatigued to explain it all again. He recited the limited news we'd learned and asked Raphael if he could check flight plans for a Cessna Caravan taking off from somewhere around Como and, if so, see where it was headed.

"Roger, my friend, I'll call you right back."

The line went dead, and we both stared at the instrument panel as Ray flew slowly south, back over Como, then vectored to the east, staying clear of the Malpensa airspace, and headed back toward Garda. In what seemed like a very short time, his cell phone rang, and he carefully swiped the screen to accept the call.

"Success!" DeGregorio's voice boomed in my ears, causing me to wince. "The plane is registered in Vienna to some corporation, but it isn't headed there."

I clicked on my mic. "Where's it going?"

"Ahh, Signor Reilly." I could almost hear him licking his lips. "The plane is on its way to Cortina d'Ampezzo in the Dolomitis, up near the Austrian border. The old airfield there is now for private use only."

Ray and I turned to face each other. Neither of us were smiling.

"Great job, Raphael," I said.

"Shall I alert the authorities?" he asked.

Ray's eyes opened wider as he stared at me and awaited my answer.

"No, that won't be necessary," I said.

Ray shook his head, then ended the call.

"What was it Jones said, 'an impenetrable mountaintop compound?'" Ray asked.

"Head east, Ray. I'll find the coordinates for Cortina d'Ampezzo."

The exhale from his sudden deep breath caused static in my ears.

"Of course you will, Buck. Of course you will."

16

THE FLIGHT TO THE DOLOMITES WAS BACK OVER LAKE GARDA then north into the tall, jagged mountains that provided both a natural border and security for Italy through centuries of regional aggression. I'd never spent any time here, but as a student of history, I knew the region had changed hands multiple times between the Germans and Austrians and their imperialistic efforts.

I had plugged the coordinates into the GPS, which charted our course, and we stayed at as low an altitude as possible since we didn't have a flight plan. I was still soggy and the air was colder here, so I cranked up Big Mama's heating system.

"Are you going to rouse the troops Jones flew in?" Ray asked.

"No, I'm afraid they'll get Harry killed."

"Oh, and we won't?"

"They need us alive if they hope to insert themselves into this racing deal."

"They only need one of you alive, sounds like to me."

I glanced sharply at Ray and thought about his statement. "That may be so, but I think they know if one of us gets killed the other won't exactly be cooperative."

"It's a dangerous game we're playing here, Buck. We don't even know who these people are—aside from running a criminal empire, per Jones."

"I haven't figured out their angle yet," I said. "But it must be more than just wanting to own a piece of the team. That's too mundane for a group like this."

"The clock is ticking, and according to Matt Sterling, there's no way to alter the deal or timing. Can't you just sign the document and get it over with?"

"And where am I supposed to get a hundred million Euros to pay them? Signing the document is one thing; perfecting the deal's another."

Ray scooted forward in his seat and laid his head back against the headrest.

"Good point. Hadn't thought of that."

"I don't know anything about the terms and whether the signature triggers closing, releases funds from escrow, or just creates the obligation to pay within a certain time frame. Remember, I knew nothing about this before we got here, and I still have no idea why my name's in the contract."

It donned on me that Claire Robbins, the niece of the Williams race team's founder, had said she'd email me the contract. Had she?

I checked the emails on my phone.

There was an email from Claire Robbins with an attachment. I tried to open it, but I only had one bar of cell service and the file was too big.

Damn.

Ray checked our course and began to reduce altitude as the airport at Cortina d'Ampezzo was only a few more miles ahead. My cell phone rang, again sending a shrill sound through our headsets. I grabbed it quickly just to stop the sound.

"Hello?"

"Where the hell are you?" It was Heather.

"We're flying east at the moment," I said.

"What happened back at the hotel?"

"How did you know about that?" I asked.

"Ray texted me when you went to shore. He said you were going to try and trade yourself for Harry. For God's sake, Buck!"

I turned sharply toward him, but he ignored me and focused on prepping for landing.

"I need to call in our approach," Ray said.

"Buck," Heather interrupted. "Please let the police handle this. You're ill-equipped and have no idea what you're doing."

I bit my lip for a moment. "I can't, Heather. They're threatening to torture Harry now. He may not even last until the ceremony on Sunday."

"Then let Jones help. He said he has an army at his disposal."

Ray tapped his fingers on top of the wheel. Had they conspired on this when I was running through il Sereno?

"Like I said, I can't do that."

"Why not?" she asked. "You'll get yourself and Ray killed if you keep this up! You're no match for an Austrian crime cartel—what the hell are you thinking?"

"Because it's Harry, that's why. I can't sit back and entrust his safety to local authorities who don't know or give a shit about him or to mercenaries whose failure to do their jobs led to his getting kidnapped."

Ray turned away and looked out the left window. I was pretty sure he was shaking his head.

"But what I can do is reconnoiter Himmelman's mountain lair. If it comes down to needing to send in our forces to rescue Harry, they'll need intel on what they're facing."

Heather let out a loud exhale. "So that's where you're going?"

I rubbed the couple of days' worth of growth on my beard and debated how to respond. If something happened to us, it would be wise to at least have somebody know our whereabouts.

"I'm sure Ray would tell you anyway, so we're flying to an airport in the Dolomites."

"Cortina?" she asked. "That's only open for select private use. Next closest one is Venice."

I grimaced. "I don't want you in the middle of this either, Heather."

I realized we shared locations on our iPhones. But, again, that was at least some form of insurance, so I decided not to cancel it.

"I'll be the eyes and ears here in Monza," she said. "Jones is here and can send his team in to help if you learn anything."

I ended the call, and Ray immediately switched to the radio and alerted air traffic control of our location and intent to land.

"Roger, Grumman N41RF," a voice responded. "Proceed to runway eighteen and watch for VFR traffic. All else is clear."

"Roger, Cortina."

As we descended into the valley, the mountains now surrounding us felt even larger. The airport was at an elevation of 4,262 feet and the range had elevations up to nearly 11,000 feet; this was tricky flying with crosswinds, updrafts, and poor visibility. A few of the higher peaks, all of which were bare rock, were covered with snow. That was another scenario I feared: what if we got snowed in up here? What would happen to Harry if neither of us could sign the damned agreement?

Ray vectored and announced he was on base leg; we could see the airport ahead amid what appeared to be a large town nestled in the valley between a series of huge mountains. Wind buffeted us and he fought to keep Big Mama on course. The old gal had a large, stout fuselage that was anything but aerodynamic, so in circumstances like these, she gave a rough ride.

As Ray masterfully executed our landing checklist, my mind centered on finding Harry. But how would we do that? Jones never said where the exact location was, only that it was near Val Gardena. The famous ski town was meant to host events associated with the 1944 Winter Olympics planned for Cortina, but due to the war the games weren't held. Ultimately the Olympics were held in the area in 1956, but since the late sixties, it had been the site of an annual World Cup downhill race.

Based on the map app on my phone, Val Gardena was approximately forty-five minutes by car from Cortina, and there were only a few hours of daylight left. When the sun dropped behind the mountains, it would be like hitting a light switch.

A last-minute gust blew Big Mama off course just fifty feet off the ground, but Ray expertly countered with the aileron and rudder, set us back into position, and set the Albatross down hard on runway 18. We stuck, so he reduced power further. His purposeful actions in the cockpit gradually brought me back to the present. I studied the couple of planes on the tarmac and spotted a Cessna Caravan on floats next to a late model Falcon 6X jet. I exhaled hard at the sight of the jet, flashing back to e-Antiquity's heyday when I traversed the world in similar planes.

"There, that must be the seaplane they came in."

"Heather was right, there's not much going on here," Ray said.

Ray was guided to a tie-down location on the same row as the Caravan but at the opposite end. Given the other planes here, Big Mama would stick out like a lemon among oranges. There was just no way to hide an antique flying boat, especially an Albatross.

When had the Caravan arrived? Could Himmelman and his goons still be here? And Harry too?

I squirmed in my seat, anxious to get out and try to find them. The airport was small and may have been luxurious back in the day, but at this point it was hardly well appointed. The FBO had already radioed asking if we needed fuel or anything else.

"Lodging?" Ray asked.

The answer was affirmative, and unless I had quick success, we'd be stuck here until morning anyway—or at least Ray would. If I couldn't find them here, I'd head to Val Gardena to search for Harry there. They'd already known we'd come looking at il Sereno, so they'd be expecting us, which—if I played it right—could be okay. I'd learned long ago that when up against a far superior and better equipped adversary, it's best to make them think you're predictable but then, when the moment arises, do something so crazy—some would say so *stupid*—they'd never expect it.

But you can't plan crazy; it just happens.

Big Mama came to a stop at our assigned tie-down location, and Ray shut down the twin engines and turned in his seat to face me.

"You do whatever you need to, and I'll stay here near Big Mama to keep her ready for a hasty departure."

We locked eyes. I knew he wasn't being a wimp or trying to avoid trouble. He was doing what Ray always did: thinking how best to stay ahead of the curve. That was one of the reasons he was my best friend and partner at Last Resort Charter and Salvage.

"Okay, buddy. If I'm not back by, say, noon tomorrow, alert Jones to have his team come find me, and hopefully Harry."

Ray extended his fist, and I bumped it with mine. I then unbuckled, climbed out of the right seat, made my way through Big Mama, opened the hatch, lowered the ladder, and set foot on ground at Cortina d'Ampezzo. No sooner was I standing there than Ray retracted the ladder and close the hatch without another word.

At private airports, the FBO was the one-stop shop for most pilots' needs. You planned your flight there, arranged for a car or accommodations, paid your tie-down fees, purchased fuel and sundries, and, if taking a charter, met your flight crew. Based on what I saw here, it might be limited to fuel and a concierge. The FBO entrance was ahead, but that's not where I was going.

There was a demarcated walkway behind the few planes tied down here, so I walked in front of the planes trying to stay out of sight. When I was close to the Cessna Caravan on floats, I slowed and glanced around. It was the second to last plane in the row, with the big Falcon just past it. Since it was on floats, the plane stood much higher than a typical one on wheels.

With nobody in sight, I walked up to the single-engine Caravan like I owned it and walked slowly around it as if I were doing a preflight check. But rather than checking pitot tubes, flaps, and rudder, I reached up and put my hand on the engine cowling.

It was still warm.

My tropical attire did little to combat the chill in the air, so the heat of the engine was comforting, illuminating, and concerning. The people who had flown here aboard this plane could not be far away. A shiver passed through me.

I continued around the plane and, after a fast glance around, stepped up onto the starboard pontoon to peer inside the cabin. It appeared clean as a whistle. I didn't spot a speck of debris, and the seat belts sat folded and organized on the six seats in the back, fewer than its capacity. I inched forward on the pontoon until I could see into where the copilot would sit on the right side. Again, nothing.

Upon closer inspection I saw a notepad mounted to the instrument panel. There was writing, including the words *Como* and *Torno*. It had to be the same plane that had dropped Harry there and presumably retrieved him earlier today.

A hydraulic hum and *whoosh* of air sounded behind me, causing me to turn quickly. The hatch on the Falcon dropped open and stairs extended toward the tarmac. I glanced up toward the lighted cabin, feeling like a kid caught with his hand in the candy jar. What I saw caused me to clench my teeth. Standing there, with the afternoon sun reflecting off his glasses like the orange glare of death, was the Mortician.

"Herr Reilly, how nice of you to come find us."

He walked slowly down the steps, favoring his left leg. As I pondered smart-ass retorts, Thick-neck appeared in the open doorway of the jet.

"How'd you beat me here?" I said.

"They came and picked us up just after you left." He smiled. "The Caravan's cruising speed is 186 knots, which I assume is faster than your antique."

Big Mama's cruising speed was 150 knots.

Crap.

Thick-neck hustled down the steps quickly and was on the Mortician's ass by the time he reached the tarmac. Still standing immobile on the pontoon, I smiled at the men. In Como they said they'd beat Harry due to my meddling, and my appearing here now would only make matters worse. I smiled, but there was no charming these guys.

"I thought this Caravan was a beauty, but that Falcon? Holy Mother of Jesus, you guys really travel in style."

"You're making matters worse, Reilly."

I took that as a prompt to step down off the pontoon, which I did slowly so as not to arouse Thick-neck's undoubtable thirst for revenge after I'd knocked him into the water back at il Sereno. Once on the ground, I turned to face them.

"I told you back in Como that I'd like to trade myself for Harry. The head of the Williams Team is concerned over his disappearance and could prevent them from going forward with the transaction, which could impact all our interests in getting this deal done." I paused. "He has a message for Harry."

The Mortician's face was as inscrutable as ever, but I did notice his eyes narrow slightly.

"Tell me the message," he said.

"Can't do that, Fritz." I shook my head. "Is Harry on Himmelman's jet there? I could take his place, and then Harry could return to Monza to smooth everything over."

The Mortician turned slightly and addressed Thick-neck in German. The bowling ball of muscle retrieved a cell phone from his pocket and hit a speed dial button. A moment later he too was speaking what to me was gibberish—a shame given Harry's and my lives hung in the balance and the conversation likely could have a definitive impact on our collective shelf life. The call was brief, and Thick-neck spoke with confidence to his black-clad associate.

The Mortician gave me a toothless grin. "It must be your lucky day, Herr Reilly."

"How so?"

"The Principal has granted your wish."

I stepped forward toward the plane. "Great. I'll stay here and Harry can leave."

As my mind launched forward and I tried to remember where the button was on a Falcon to close the hatch, and as the instrument panel appeared in my memory, my plans for rescuing Harry were quickly doused by three black Mercedes G-Wagons that pulled up from around the FBO toward the Falcon.

"We are going to the Promontory," the Mortician said.

I stopped in my tracks. "Please. The Principal at the Promontory? That's a hell of a tongue twister, there, Heinrich."

His left eye squinted. "Only in English." His thin-lipped smile was menacing. "We have better ways to twist tongues at the Promontory."

The G-Wagons stopped next to us. The one in front had four men in it, all dressed in black. The one in the middle held only a driver, and the third one in back also had four men inside. None got out, but Thick-neck stepped toward me.

"Nowhere to run this time, asshole," he said and pulled the back door open on the middle vehicle.

That was an understatement. "Thanks there, Butkus. Mind grabbing my luggage and picking me up a Pepsi from the FBO? I'm a little parched."

He stepped menacingly toward me, but the Mortician uttered a brief but effective command in their language and he stopped. If looks could kill, I'd be road schnitzel.

I climbed inside and dared a glance back at Big Mama where I saw Ray peering out from the cockpit, only his eyes and the top of his head showing. I didn't want these goons to grab him too.

"Can you guys hurry it up? I need to go potty, and I'm talking number two, so let's get on up to Berchtesgaden and get this over with, shall we?"

Thick-neck followed me into the back seat and crunched his shoulder into mine, with the not-so-subtle message that retribution would come sooner or later—and the odds favored sooner.

Once the Mortician sat in the passenger seat, the lead car set off swiftly and our vehicle followed closely after. Fortunately for Ray, the third one was right on our bumper, too. We drove for twenty minutes, away from Cortina and north up into the mountains toward Val

Gardena. As the road became steeper, and the lack of guardrails meant plunging to certain death if a driver became distracted, the thoughts of anything heroic were far from my mind.

Thick-neck leaned closer. "The cliffs are steep and deadly here, Reilly. Would be a shame if you fell off."

"Appreciate that, Schnorky. I'll keep my eye on you, too."

"I'm going to enjoy making you suffer," he said.

Based on the sadistic look in his eyes, I didn't think I'd enjoy it at all.

17

OUR PROCESSION CLIMBED DEEPER INTO THE MOUNTAINS, but to my amazement, we continued passing groups of cyclists riding up the vertical road. They were all headed up, none down. I estimated our altitude to be at least six thousand feet and thought these men and women must have legs of steel and lungs like scuba tanks as they pedaled steadily up the circuitous road, full of switchbacks and blind corners.

"Some stout people up here," I said.

The Mortician turned his head to peer at me over his shoulder. "There's a bike race that starts soon. If we don't get to the top before it commences, we'll be stuck on the side of the road."

Bike race down the mountain? Stout people indeed.

I still had no plan as I didn't know anything about the Promontory, but between the Mortician's statement about Harry being punished and Thick-neck's threats, a gnawing sensation was chewing a hole in my gut. These guys were very serious players—hell, the three G-Wagons cost a collective half million dollars. Did Harry name me in his contract knowing the Proprietor was demanding participation? Did he know they'd come for him? Or for me?

Anxiety shot through my limbs, and I stirred in the seat, causing Thick-neck to turn his cold eyes toward me.

"Where does the bike race start from?" I asked.

Thick-neck just glowered at me.

"Val Gardena," the Mortician said. "The road to the Promontory is before that, but our timing is unfortunate, thanks to the delays you have caused."

"Better late than never," I said.

I leaned down to look further ahead through the windshield. No town was evident in the mountains ahead. The craggy peaks and deep valleys were carved from sheer, light-gray rock, edges sharp, and small pines sprouted up from cracks where soil must have collected over time. The vista was incredible, but the constant passing of bikes on the shoulderless road caused us to veer into blind corners where oncoming traffic could hit us head-on or force us to plunge to our deaths below.

"What happens if the race starts and we get stuck down here?" I asked.

"Shut your mouth," Thick-neck snorted, then gave me a sharp elbow to the ribs.

"WHOOF!"

The air shot from my lungs.

When I was bent over, I saw steel cables extend up from the other side of the ridge to my right, not far away from the road. I glanced up and saw a cable car descending from a peak high above us.

The Mortician said something in German, and Thick-neck pulled a cell phone from his pocket and dialed a number. After a moment, he spoke to the man who answered. Thick-neck's statement seemed more like an order than a conversation, and when he disconnected, he said something else to the Mortician, who nodded.

I noticed the G-Wagon in front of us begin to accelerate faster up the hill, but suddenly its brake lights lit up and it came to a sudden stop.

"*Scheisse!*" our driver said.

The Mortician's phone rang, and he pressed it against his ear but said nothing. Seconds later he lowered it and made a brief statement to the driver and Thick-neck.

"What's going on?" I asked.

"The bloody bike race has started," the Mortician said.

We sat in silence for several minutes, each of us watching up the road past the line of cars, most of which had turned their engines off. The jitter in my gut had turned into somersaults. The realization that I was in way over my head caused a burst of perspiration to bloom under my arms and a sheen on my forehead. Would these guys really let Harry and me live if we didn't allow them into the deal? Or even if we did? And what amount of torture would they impose along the way?

The answer came to me through a voice in my head.

No, idiot, they won't let us live, and Thick-neck and his associates will relish battering us no matter what.

I gave Thick-neck a quick study. Solidly built, blonde crew cut, shoulders and arms of a power lifter. His clothes were still damp from getting knocked into Lake Como, and he had a soggy smell about him.

My gut registered that we were in deep trouble, and my gut was never wrong.

"I have to pee," I said.

Thick-neck shook his head, and nobody said anything.

Another five minutes passed, and my anxiety was climbing like a barometer due to a coming hurricane.

"Seriously, guys, I need to pee."

"Quiet, Herr Reilly," the Mortician said.

Thick-neck leaned menacingly against me, the fetid smell of his sodden clothes made worse by proximity. The steel cables off to my right shook and I saw the silver cable car now appear over the rise on its way up to the mountain peak. The sight of the cable car disappearing suddenly caused the anxiety to accelerate in my circulatory system. When I looked forward, I saw a wave of bicycles filling the left lane of the road above us, pouring steadily down with no end in sight.

"Seriously, guys, I'll pee my pants, right in this fancy German SUV."

Thick-neck turned to face me, his scowl now a sneer.

"I had asparagus for lunch too. It'll be nasty."

The Mortician turned in the front passenger seat and studied me, and I did my best to squirm in my seat, which wasn't hard given the feeling of wildebeests stampeding through my midsection.

"I'll take him outside," Thick-neck said.

I tried the doorhandle, but it was locked. A second later there was a click as the driver unlocked the doors. Thick-neck and I simultaneously opened our doors. I slid out on wobbly legs, my mind a jumble of foolish ideas.

Thick-neck came around the back of the car and pushed me toward the low ridge of chalky gray rocks. I started up the short hill, him on my ass.

"Can a guy get a little privacy here?" I said.

"Shut up, asshole."

My feet slid in the loose gravel, as did his, but I arrived at the top and ventured a quick glance up to see the cable car nestled in the mountaintop shed. Passengers would be disembarking while others waited to board. My eyes followed the cables down to the station, a quarter mile below us.

"Move it, Reilly."

Thick-neck shoved me, and I realized the small hill dropped off suddenly and sharply for a good fifty feet before the ground disappeared into the valley below.

"Sorry about you falling in the lake back there," I said.

He shoved me again, and as I slid a few feet down the gravel, my legs buckled. I dropped my right hand to catch myself from falling further as I skidded.

His voice was a low growl. "I'd kill you now if we didn't need to leverage you against the old man."

Anxiety caused a stormy mist to fill my head, and lightning struck in my brain. Their intentions were to eliminate us as soon as possible. Adrenalin pulsed and I stood up straight, bit my lip, and turned back to face Thick-neck. A roll of the dice was necessary, as this could be my only chance.

"Quit pushing me, fat fuck. At least that swim washed off some of your stench. The bosses don't give you time to bathe, or what?"

I turned back around and heard gravel rushing forward behind me.

Thick-neck's shadow appeared behind me. His arm raised quickly and I bent hard to the right just as it came swinging down like a sledgehammer. With nothing now to hit, he stumbled forward off balance and slid past me. I lunged toward him and crashed into his back, sending him airborne downward. Then I fell onto my knees and dug my hands into the gravel that ripped at my fingers as I tumbled in a power slide.

Thick-neck looked as if he were a giant bird swooping down toward prey, his arms flapping. He hit the hill on his side, but the momentum carried him down further: rolling, bouncing off boulders, leaving a trail of dust in his wake.

My left hand caught hold of a rock and my body extended until straight, my fingers stretched to the point of slipping. But I held on, and my progress suddenly stopped. Without delay I started pulling with my hands and crawling on my knees toward a flat spot, gravel dropping below like an avalanche threatening to sweep me away.

I made it to the slight plateau, then stopped and slowly stood.

Down the hill, twenty or so feet, Thick-neck had come to a stop on his back. Blood coated his shiny forehead, but he stared up at me, his eyes catching the sun and glowing like fireballs.

I faced back up the hill and determined a fall line to my left where erosion had caused a crease in the gravel. Without delay, I hurried up it, the sight of the third G-Wagon that had been behind us now above me to the right.

Dull cheering sounded. Had people been watching our struggle and now urged me on? Horns honked, bringing my attention back to the road getting closer above me, and I realized the peloton of bikes had arrived and was sweeping past. The cheering was from those in cars, their windows down.

I reached the road, three cars behind the rear G-Wagon, just as I heard Thick-neck bellowing from the canyon like an enraged grizzly bear. A door popped open on the middle G-Wagon, and the Mortician climbed out.

Shit!

I jumped between the cars, the older man driving the car to my left watching me with wide eyes. There was no place to run, and the cars were all frozen in place as bikes flew by like flashcards.

"Reilly!" the Mortician shouted.

With a glance to my right, I saw a break in the peloton and crouched. The next bike was coming fast. All I could see was a red helmet and blue sunglasses on the cyclist leaning down over the handlebars.

I timed my lunge perfectly and jumped in front of the rider with just enough room for him to jam on his breaks and nearly crash into me— he stopped in shock—I pulled him off and flung him to the side as gingerly as I could. He was screaming in Italian but didn't put up much of a fight.

Other racers swerved around me—bikes and riders flew past like projectiles—dodging me and each other on both sides of the road.

Several riders shouted at me creating a cacophony of protest, until I jumped onto the bike I'd commandeered—

"Reilly, stop!" the Mortician's voice sounded over the din, and not wanting to waste the time to look back, I mounted the racing bike, then kicked the tiny pedal—it was designed for clip-in shoes—forward, hard.

I was wobbly at first, and footsteps sounded behind me—whether from the biker I'd pulled off or the crooks, it didn't matter. I pointed the bike down the mountain road and immediately gained speed, hunkered down over the handlebars, expecting the sound of gunfire to follow.

Holy shit. Within seconds I was flying, the wind in my face causing my eyes to water. Other bikes whizzed past me—I tried the brakes—too hard—and nearly flew over the handlebars before releasing the grip. Off to my left a large presence loomed over my shoulder; I chanced a glance and realized it was the cable car descending.

It had been years since I'd ridden any bike more complicated than my island cruiser back in Key West, but I rode it a lot so I had my balance under control, at least. My adrenalin and anxiety had fused to center my focus on self-preservation. I knew the G-Wagons would be coming my way as soon as the road was clear, not that they'd hesitate to drive over riders like squirrels in their way.

I rapidly approached the cable car station and saw a vast parking lot, a few souvenir shops, and most importantly, the cable car come to a stop inside the shed at the bottom. There was a gap between cars parked in the road due to the race; I glanced over my shoulder to time a opening between riders and then sharply steered the bike through the cars and into the lot, peddling hard toward the ticket station. Once there, I jumped off and let the bike drop between two parked cars, now in a sprint toward the ticket machine, pulling out my money clip as I ran.

Before turning down the wood-planked path that led to the cable car station, I took a quick glance back up the road. Sure enough, two G-Wagons were racing down, weaving between racers, and I heard the shriek of brakes by the parking lot entrance. The cars I'd slipped past were too close together for a G-Wagon to pass through, but it wouldn't slow them down for long.

I jammed a twenty-Euro note into the ticket machine and started pushing buttons. Instructions appeared on the screen—in Italian. I pushed a green button and a question appeared. I stabbed my finger onto the green button again and a moment later a ticket popped out. I ran down the wood planking to the entry and saw that the couple waiting passengers had already boarded the cable car and the attendant was sliding the door closed.

"Wait!"

The door continued to draw shut as I closed the distance and lunged for it just before it latched shut, jamming my fingers between the door and the frame. The attendant's eyes went wide, and he released a latch and slid the door open, yelling at me—again in Italian.

I held up my ticket and offered a timid smile. "*Scusa.*"

The operator—in his early seventies, I guessed, and dressed in Tyrolean clothing—plucked the ticket from my grasp, then shoved a handle forward. The cable car jumped out of the gate. As we rose above the parking lot, I hazarded a glance down and saw one G-Wagon still on the road, parked, its doors open, then to my left, another continuing down the steep alpine road past the parking area.

They must not have seen me but were checking the parking lot anyway.

Would they find the bike between the parked cars?

No doubt.

Would they come after me?

No doubt.

Would they kill me if they found me?

No doubt.

I spun away and found two elderly couples in the cable car staring at me as if I were an apparition.

"*Buongiorno,*" I said.

They grumbled and turned to stare out the windows at the beauty of the Dolomites, the station diminishing in size below us but the peak growing closer above.

Now what, Buck?

18

ONCE TO THE TOP, I EXITED AHEAD OF THE OTHER
PASSENGERS and followed the walkway around the station, which
held little more than restrooms. Once clear of the building, I spotted
another larger structure up a steep hill. Pointing toward it, a small sign
with an arrow read *Rifugio Lagazuoi*. I was surrounded by treeless, jagged
gray peaks where clouds floated within reach, and I felt the change in
temperature at this elevation accentuated by a stiff breeze. Here I was in
tropical-weight attire, the cold now tearing through me.

As did my concern for Harry, given my foolish attempts to persuade
them to release him in exchange for me. It was increasingly clear that
Himmelman and his crew would dispose of us once they got what they
wanted. So even though I'd failed with my naïve efforts, the reality of the
situation had simultaneously crystalized and galvanized my resolve.

I had to save Harry, or at least get eyes on the Promontory to advise
Jones with intel.

But how?

The cable car embarked for the bottom of the valley, its station so
far below it appeared like a dot at the end of the dangling steel cables.

I turned and climbed the gravel path straight into the breeze. Once
I reached the top, my lungs burned, and I felt the gravel embedded in
the wide tread of my tennis shoes. A large sundeck filled with wooden
picnic tables faced out over the valley, which took what was left of my
breath away. The Dolomites were an old mountain range, compared to
the Alps or Rockies, as mountain dating goes, and the lack of trees struck
me. There were very few flat surfaces in the range, and the peaks
appeared to be hewn by chisel and hammer like a massive unfinished
Renaissance sculpture.

The Rifugio itself was made of wood and white plaster. Guests were visible inside, appropriately dressed in sweaters and jackets, dining at tables and enjoying this respite among their journeys. I pulled the heavy door open and found a bar straight ahead with shelves stocked with all types of liquor and other beverages, but more importantly, croissants and sandwiches under a glass counter and maps, jackets, and sweatshirts for sale. People were seated at the bar with beers and orange Aperol spritzes in front of them. The bartender approached me, his eyes wide.

"Can I buy a trail map?" I asked. "And a ham sandwich and bottle of water."

The bartender appeared to be in his early twenties; he had a thin beard on his cheeks and thick, dark tattoos on his arms.

"*Sì, dieci Euros, per favor,*" he said.

I handed him a twenty and received the change and map in return. I unfolded it quickly. "Can you show me where we are?"

"*Sì.*" His index finger stabbed the map at Val Gardena and ran across the ridge to the right, stopping on a peak a few over from the edge of town.

I studied it and saw the red line that depicted the cable car. There were dashed lines for trails heading in multiple directions from the top of the line, where the symbol of a knife and fork indicated the bar I was in now. In other locations in various directions were crude hut images with beds. I spotted one to the north.

"How far—" I stopped myself midsentence. If the Mortician and his henchman came up here looking for me, which they no doubt would, then the less the bartender knew the better.

"This is great," I said with a hollow smile. "I'm going to head back down on the gondola and over to Val Gardena before it gets dark." I hesitated and glanced back to the jackets folded up under the glass countertop. "Can I see that black Patagonia shell?"

He retrieved the jacket, which wasn't lined but had a hood; it would help cut the wind as well as keep me dry if rained rolled in. And it was my size. I saw the price and counted Euros off my money clip. The bartender smiled. Maybe he made commissions.

"We have room at the Rifugio here, if you'd like to spend the night," the young man said.

"Nah, think I'll head back down and get to Val Gardena before dark, but thanks."

He glanced out the window at the sky taking on the increasing hues of sunset. "You have maybe thirty minutes of daylight left, and there's only a couple more gondola trips down," he said.

I gave him a smile and thumbs-up and left with the new jacket on, the water and sandwich filling its pockets, and the map clutched in my hand. Once outside, I jogged up to an overlook beyond the Rifugio where three trails merged. One went down to the east, one descended to the west, and the other followed the ridgeline toward another peak to the north. I could now see that the mountain range I was atop of formed a horseshoe shape, which the map confirmed. I was at the bottom-left corner on the curve of the horseshoe. Across the horseshoe's opening lay a vast series of crevasses and trails—they looked like the palm of a hand, but in gray rock with lifelines and sparse tufts of green—that led to an even higher series of peaks on the far side. The range was desolate, barren, and unwelcoming. Small groups of people appeared like ants traversing trails in the palm, approaching from the north.

I consulted the map that fluttered in my hands due to the stiff winds. The trail off to the right would take me to the valley in the middle of the horseshoe, which would leave me exposed and vulnerable. Down to the left, the trail would ultimately take me back to the road I'd fled from, and once there, I'd have no place to hide from the black-clad kidnappers. The only other option was to traverse the ridgeline straight ahead toward the end of the horseshoe on the side I was on now. On the map was an icon for another rifugio at the end, down at a lower elevation—Rifugio Scotoni—that the ridgeline trail led toward.

It looked to be a few miles away, and given the setting sun and challenging terrain, I wouldn't make it by dark. But I needed a safe place to gather my thoughts and come up with a plan, and the rifugio was the closest option still in the direction of Val Gardena and the location of the Promontory. The Mortician had said Himmelman's impenetrable fortress was just before Val Gardena, so I hoped it might be visible from Rifugio Scotoni.

The temperature was dropping with the sun, and even with the Gortex shell, my lightweight clothing underneath would provide little warmth here in the mountains. Behind me, I saw the cable car again ascending from the valley below, so I folded the map and continued quickly along the ridge, passing defensive fortifications dating back to World War I, according to small plaques mounted on the stone walls. Tunnels led to vantage points where marksmen could pick off invading infantrymen, and I tried to imagine the scene as it would appear in the winter, covered with snow and ice. As inhospitable as it felt now, this was nothing compared to what winter would be like.

The trail was clearly visible in daylight, but as darkness came quickly, it became much more difficult to discern the well-worn trail, and one wrong step could lead to a life-ending fall into the valleys on either side of the ridge trail. I'd thought of asking the bartender at the rifugio if he had a flashlight for sale, but that wouldn't mesh with my story about taking the cable car back down, so I needed to rely on the light on my phone.

I pulled it from my pants pocket and saw that I had no bars—*and* the battery was at 48 percent. Great. I imagined what the Mortician, Thick-neck, and their goons would be doing to find me, and what they'd do if they did. That realization hastened my pace. After an hour of slow progress in the dark, my trail began to angle downward. Based on the topographic details on the map, that indicated I was about halfway to Rifugio Scotoni. My neck hurt from staring toward the ground, so I stopped to stretch, and my eyes grew wide at the panorama of stars in the heavens.

With no city lights for tens of miles, the night sky was brilliant and clear, except for a swirling haze to the north that I realized was the Milky Way. Shooting stars carved sudden paths of brilliant light, disappearing just as quickly, while satellites cut slowly through the night brilliance, steady and on a continuous journey to bounce television into living rooms, cell signals to social media surfers, or clandestine photos to huddled analysts in dark rooms around the world.

With my battery now at 17 percent, my phone's light grew fainter. The descent continued until a flat, dark area appeared below me to the right. Was it water? No stars were reflected in it. Could it be the valley floor, or the palm of the hand I'd envisioned earlier?

I walked on.

A lone light appeared further ahead at the end of the dark valley area. I stopped to turn off my phone light to make sure it wasn't a reflection off a star, but the pin light continued to burn in the distance. Standing still made me realize I was shaking. Under the jacket, my clothes were wet with sweat. Standing here now, exposed to the wind, that had me shivering with cold. I turned the phone light back on and saw that my battery was down to 7 percent. I picked up the pace.

The light ahead drew me forward like a bat to a bonfire, my mind shuffling different scenarios of what I might find when I got there. Then my foot slipped in loose gravel and I fell hard to my right. As I slid down, clutching my phone close to my chest in one hand, I waved the other to try and grab hold of something as I tumbled.

When I finally came to a stop, I still had my phone, but my other hand was scraped and bloody, fingernails torn, and my jacket and fishing pants frayed. The bottle of water was no longer in my pocket, and the second half of the sandwich I hadn't yet eaten was flattened.

When I stood and shined my light around, however, I realized I was now on the flat valley floor, and more importantly, the lone light ahead was now accompanied by dim lights around it. I squinted and realized the light came from windows.

Rifugio Scotoni was just ahead.

The wind whipped me in the face, and now chilled to the bone, I leaned into it and trod across a grassy field. When I noticed dark smudges ahead and around me, it donned on me that I was in a pasture. The familiar silhouettes of cows registered, but there were taller, skinnier creatures too. Curiosity helped me overcome the cold, and when I got close to one of the other animals in the pasture, I recognized its silhouette as a llama. My foot sank in a mud bog—no—the smell informed me otherwise.

Make that a cow pie.

Just then the light on my phone went out, my battery totally expended. My blessings were as plentiful as the stars overhead, as I'd made it nearly to the front door of the rifugio—but then a terrifying idea hit me harder than the oncoming wind.

What if it was closed?

But why would the lights be on?

I closed the remaining distance, oblivious to rocks, cow pies, and llama pellets. Once to the door, I said a quick prayer. I grabbed the handle and pulled, but it didn't budge.

"No!"

I knocked on the thick wood, but the sound of knocking was lost in the wind.

"Shit."

I moved to the side and stared in a window. There was a large dining room inside but no people seated there, and the tables were stripped down to the wood.

"No, no, no ..."

I walked back to the other side of the door and saw no sign of life inside this end of the room, either. A faint glow of light came from a stairway that led down, so I continued around the end of the building, where the ground sloped gradually away, and followed the foundation to the back of the structure. A gurgling sound emanated from what I realized was a balcony, and a lone lightbulb shone where I figured a door might be, but I couldn't see past the webbed slats of the railing. Mist hovered in the air, and I guessed it was from the exhaust on the heating system.

A shiver rattled me as I stood trying to understand the gurgling sound. It seemed familiar, but my powers of deduction were worn to the quick at this point.

"Hello? Is anyone up there?"

The gurgling continued.

"Hello? Hel—lo!?" My voice cracked I shouted so loudly.

The gurgling ended abruptly. Could it be a guard dog that had been snoring?

"Hello, is anyone there?" I said again.

A moment later, a head rose above the banister.

"Hello?" a woman's voice answered.

"Hi, I'm ah, down here and need to get warm. I ... ah, got lost ... and hiked here from Rifugio Lagazuoi."

The next sound I heard was that of splashing water, and I suddenly realized the gurgling was a hot tub. It wasn't mist from the heating system I'd seen upstairs but steam off the hot water.

"*Un minuto!*" the woman shouted.

Thank God.

Should I go back out front? I glanced around, but then a spotlight popped on from the balcony, blinding me. I shielded my face, then realized the woman was likely assessing me to see if I was a deranged lunatic here to harm her. I lowered my hand and attempted to appear normal, whatever that meant, but my chattering teeth sounded like a ticking time bomb, even to me.

Another light turned on, this one on the lower part of the building below the balcony, and I saw it was next to a door. Other lights lit up inside, and I shuffled over to the entry. I was afraid to try the handle so just stood waiting.

The woman came rushing to the door, and with the corridor lit inside, I saw through the glass door that she wore a white robe. She gave me a quick glance, then I heard the click of a lock and the door pushed open.

"Come inside—you look frozen," she said.

She stepped back and I followed her in, rubbing my arms as I walked, trying to get my circulation going. The warmth inside caused a sudden tingling on my skin—it almost felt as if it were burning, a sensation I hadn't felt since skiing in the Poconos when I was a teenager.

"Thank you, er, *grazie, grazie,*" I said.

"The rifugio is closed, I'm so sorry—" She must have seen the terror I could feel in my eyes, because she stopped midsentence. "You said you were lost? Are they expecting you back at Lagazuoi?"

"Yes—I mean, no—they're not expecting me." I cleared my throat. Pull it together, Buck, or you'll be back out in the cold. "I had taken the cable car up when traffic was stopped due to the bike race—"

"*Sì, sì*, the Falzarego race was today!" she said.

A shiver rattled me. "And I, ah, went hiking, but, ah, lost my way. Next thing it was dark, and the only light I could see was here—this is Rifugio Scotini, isn't it?"

"*Sì, sì!*" she said.

Now warming up, I realized my savior was a young woman, probably late twenties or early thirties, with wet brown hair, long, down past her shoulders, and large brown eyes. Her eyes grew wide and she smiled, her teeth white and mostly straight. Either I was delirious, dead from the fall earlier, or dreaming, but the woman appeared very beautiful in the yellow light of the hallway.

I cleared my throat. "My name's Buck Reilly," I said.

She placed her hand on her chest. "Bianca Bianchi, I'm please to meet you."

"I'm sorry you're closed, but my phone died, I have no food or water, and this jacket isn't—"

"Yes, you're freezing, of course. Come inside, please, I'll take you upstairs and make you some hot tea."

She turned away and continued down the corridor. I followed her to a staircase, and I couldn't help but notice her muscular calves as I followed her up the steps. I recognized the dining area from peering in the windows, but she flipped switches, and all the lights came on. Inside, the rifugio was decorated like you would expect a desolate mountain chalet to be: wood walls, thick animal furs draped over chairs, deer horns and other smaller horns on the walls, along with old black-and-white photos of men and women wearing skis with snowy mountains behind them.

"Sit here and wrap yourself in this blanket."

She pointed to a chair and one of the animal furs. Once seated, and beneath the furry hide, I felt instantly warmer. Bianca had disappeared into what I assumed to be the kitchen, and I leaned my head back against the chair. Either I dozed off or she boiled water in record time, because in what seemed like only moments, she placed a tall mug on a saucer on the table in front of me, then dashed back into the kitchen and brought one back for herself, followed by a tray of cheese and sausages.

"The inn is closed this time of year, but the restaurant is open during the daytime," she said. "I'm the manager for the season, so I stay here all the time."

I sipped the tea and could think of nothing to say that wouldn't end in her apologizing and sending me on my way. Finally, I placed the mug back on the saucer. I pointed toward the food. "May I?"

"*Sì*, help yourself."

With a mouthful of food, I studied Bianca to see if my initial observation was borne of exhaustion, but again I concluded she was beautiful, and caring to boot. I shrugged.

"Is the trail up the ridge the shortest way back toward Lagazuoi, or is there a better option?" I asked.

She swung her arm to the right. "There's a trail down from here that would be much easier to follow, and there's a road near here too, but it's private—I would not recommend going there."

Private road? I sat forward in the chair, adjusting the furry blanket as I did so.

"I was told by a friend to avoid a place near here called the Promontory," I said.

Her eyes suddenly went wide. "That was good advice. The road I mentioned leads to that place, maybe a kilometer away, but they don't welcome strangers there." She wagged her finger to emphasize her point.

A glow lit within me, but I bit my tongue rather than asking too many questions. I couldn't risk worrying Bianca, or I'd find myself back out in the cold.

"Would you like some wine?" she asked.

Was that a glint I saw in her eye? "No thanks, I'm loving this tea. And the blanket, my God, it's amazing."

She giggled, and I thought of Heather to keep my mind on track.

Heather. She and Ray would be beside themselves with worry.

"Do you happen to have a phone charger? I really should let my friends know I'm safe."

She jumped up. "I'll be right back."

She disappeared back down the stairs and was gone longer than I expected. Suddenly ravenous, I ate more cheese and sausage. When she returned, she was wearing jeans and a thick sweater, and her hair was tied up in a ponytail. Her olive skin glowed in the light and her brown eyes glistened.

"I made a bed in one of the rooms for you. You can stay here tonight."

Then she held up a phone charger and I nearly could have kissed her—out of gratitude—regardless of the fact that she was the epitome of raw Italian beauty.

She gave me a half smile as if she could read my mind.

"Thank you so much," I said.

We talked for another twenty minutes, but when I started nodding off, she stood and said, "Come, I will take you downstairs. We can save the talk for the morning."

I pushed my arms wide to shove the animal hide off my back and stood slowly. My feet and legs were sore, and as I followed her, the sound of a rock stuck in my shoe scraped against the floor. At the bottom of the stairs, she pointed to a door cracked open on her left. "Here is my room," she said.

The raise of her eyebrows and part of her lips made it clear she had more than slumber on her mind. Alone here in the middle of nowhere, who could blame her?

My mouth had gone dry.

"Ah, I'm in a relationship."

When was the last time I had said that?

Her brows dropped. "In that case, there's another one there." She pointed to the door across from hers.

My eyes followed her pointing finger to an opened door with a soft light glowing inside and a pair of single beds covered with more animal furs against each side of the room.

"And there's a shared bathroom at the end of the hall." She nodded to her left and her ponytail swung back and forth in the most charming manner.

Her hesitation caused me to clear my throat again. "Thank you so much, Bianca. I would have likely died out in the mountains tonight had I not found you. And if you hadn't taken me in."

"Can be very cold and lonely in the mountains, Buck." Her pronunciation of my name made it sound like *book*. She smiled. "At least I got to practice my English, which will help when I get back to school."

"School?" I nearly choked.

"Graduate school in Milano."

Jeez, for a minute I thought my estimate of her age had been way off, but graduate school could put her in the range I'd guessed.

She was watching me, waiting.

I gave her a salute of two fingers brushing off my forehead. "I'll see you in the morning."

With that, I pivoted on my sore toes, entered the room, and pushed the door closed without looking back. I inhaled a deep breath and blew it out fast.

"Let me know if you have trouble getting warm," she said through the door.

Get to bed, Buck.

19

MORNING ARRIVED WITH BRIGHT LIGHT SHINING THROUGH THE SHEER CURTAINS. I lay in the single bed for a moment, gathering my thoughts. What day was it? Saturday. There was another Formula 1 practice today followed by the qualifying round that would set the starting order for tomorrow's race. I had little more than twenty-four hours to figure out this situation and save Harry.

Still in bed, I studied the topographic trail map. I found Rifugio Scotoni and thought back to what Bianca had said last night. There were two trails that led away from the rifugio, one zigging down to the left, the other, not far from here, leading to a dotted road that dead-ended at the crest of an adjacent peak.

That must be the Promontory.

I jumped out of bed and pulled my clothes on. My feet hurt from hiking in tennis shoes that just yesterday had been fresh and white but were now brown and scarred. I pulled a pale gray pebble from between the treads and placed it on the bedside table.

When I opened the door out into the hallway, the smell of coffee hit me and pulled me up the stairs as if in a trance. Kind of Bianca to rise early to make me—the sound of voices penetrated my thoughts. I hesitated on the steps.

What if the Mortician and Thick-neck were here?

The sudden sound of a woman laughing set my mind at ease. I continued the remaining steps and found people seated at a few tables in the restaurant, drinking coffee and having breakfast. I spotted Bianca behind the counter near the cash register, and when she saw me, her eyes lit up and she waved me over.

"*Buongiorno*, Buck." Her smile was radiant. "Did you sleep well?"

"I did, thank you again. You saved me last night."

She nodded slowly, her eyes still fixed on mine. "You must have been warm enough." Her lip curled. "I waited for you in case you weren't."

I felt my face flush. "I fell asleep so fast, but I appreciate all you did for me."

"Of course. Come, I'll seat you for breakfast."

I pointed to a corner table by the window where I could see the pasture and the trail down as well as the front door. The thought of my adversaries finding me here had me anxious, not only for myself, but also for Bianca and the hikers. She took my order and said the server would bring coffee soon.

I studied the trail map as my stomach growled in need of food. Based on the topography, if the peak the road led to was the Promontory, it did appear impenetrable as reported. Bianca had warned me to stay away, but I had no choice but to ignore that advice. My breakfast came: a hearty American meal of eggs, toast, and sausage. The coffee was hot and the water cold, fresh from a mountain spring.

My ancient Rolex Submariner indicated it was 8:15, and I again thought of Heather and Ray, who would be worried sick by now. Would they have called the police to report both me and Harry as missing? I hoped not, as that was against Harry's wishes, which I'd be forced to break if the situation left me no choice—but I still had to assess the circumstances before making that call.

Back at the register, Bianca was now more businesslike given that her tables were three-quarters full of early morning hikers, and likely since I'd ignored her generous overtures.

I counted out the Euros for the meal and lodging and included a fifty percent tip. "Thank you again, Bianca. I owe you."

"Come back and make it up to me sometime." There was more disappointment than flirting in her voice.

"I'll do that." My wink caused her to purse her lips in a small frown.

Back outside, the sun hit my black shell and warmed me. Last night's winds had died down, and as I pulled the trail map from my pocket, I glanced around the green pasture. There were a half dozen black cows with white faces and a pair of llamas off in the distance from the direction I'd come. Seeing the ascent to that ridge from here, it appeared steep and inhospitable, to which the bruises and scrapes on my limbs and hip could attest.

I couldn't see past the first summit but knew the path to be long and arduous as it led back to Lagazuoi.

Had the kidnappers come looking for me?

Had they concluded I'd gotten away, or had they given me up for dead?

My eyes shifted to the trail map, and from there off to my left where the two roads down intersected. Himmelman and his goons would not expect me to come to them, but that's exactly what I planned to do.

I started down the gravel road that led to the forking trails, and once there, took the road less traveled toward the Promontory. The trail led up to a ridge then dropped back down again, which I'd anticipated thanks to the topographic map.

I checked my phone and saw that it had two bars of cell strength. I pushed the number one, which I'd recently reprogrammed to direct-dial Heather's cell phone.

"I've been worried to death about you," she said.

Her answer didn't surprise me. "Sorry, Heather. It's a long story and I don't have time or cell strength to get into details, but I'm safe, high in the Dolomites, approaching Himmelman's lair, aka the Promontory."

"Brilliant, Buck. The prey pursuing the hunter?"

I swallowed. "Yeah, something like that."

"What kind of fool shit is that, man?" a voice sounded from Heather's end of the line.

Wait … was that …?

"That sounded like Lenny Jackson," I said. But what would be friend, Pastor Lenny Jackson from Key West be doing here?

"Damn straight," Lenny said. "Your lady flew my ass over here to help out. You clearly determined to get yourself and your money-man killed over this shit."

"Heather, what the hell's going on?" I asked.

"Like he said—I'm sitting here clueless, and everyone's worried sick about you. Ray said they hauled you off from the airport. He's still waiting at Cortina, hoping and praying you return."

"Tell him I'm fine, and Lenny, well, thanks for coming. Please keep Heather company—"

"Screw that, Buck!" Heather said. "We want to help."

"Like she said," Lenny added. "What the hell else we supposed to do? Sit around here drinking champagne and mingling with the rich and famous?"

"That's exactly what you need to do for now. Himmelman no doubt has spies all over the paddock, and we can't sound the alarm—at least not yet. I'm hoping to find the Promontory to scout out the situation, then we'll decide on the next move."

"What if we don't hear back from you?" Heather asked.

"Give me until this afternoon. If you haven't heard from me by then, go ahead and tell Jones—not the police—what's going on. The Promontory is on a peak near a place called Rifugio Scotoni."

"Qualifying ends at five today, and the race is at three tomorrow," she said. "If Harry hasn't given Himmelman what he wants by then, what will happen?"

I bit my lip.

Our connection dropped and I saw that my two cell bars had been replaced with "SOS."

How appropriate.

Once at the road, gravel turned to pavement. It led up around a serpentine path, and high above, I saw the exposed stone walls of what appeared like a medieval fortress on the precipice. I started in that direction. There would no doubt be a sophisticated security system that could bring black-clad forces down upon me at any moment, but I didn't have the time, equipment, or training to attempt a more discreet approach. Plus I just wanted to get close enough to observe its access points and defenses.

Off to my left, I could see the ridgeline back south toward Lagazuoi, which was at a far higher elevation than that of the Promontory, but the isolation of this mountain was what provided its inaccessibility and, therefore, security.

After several switchbacks up the single-lane road, I rounded a sharp corner to find a ten-foot-high metal fence rimmed with barbed wire, and two black-clad guards pointing automatic weapons at me from behind the gate. A G-Wagon was parked on the other side of the fence.

Shocked at the abrupt discovery, I froze and slowly raised my hands.

The door to the G-Wagon opened and the Mortician stepped out. He said something incomprehensible, at least to me, and the gate slid slowly open. From fifty feet away, one of the two guards rested his gun against the fence and waved me forward.

Shit.

The Mortician stood waiting, but as I reached the gate, the still armed guard stepped forward, his rifle pointed at my chest.

"Stop there! Arms up!"

The other one frisked me and, finding nothing but my cell phone—which he returned to me, he retrieved his weapon and let me pass.

"We have been watching you ever since you stepped foot on the road leading here," the Mortician said. "Fleeing from our vehicle, stealing the bike, then your long walk from the cable car to Rifugio Scotoni all led to increased … discomfort for Herr Greenbaum."

I bunched my fists.

"Your stooge told me he was going to kill me, so I ran."

"Bruno, yes, he has developed a special fondness for you. If you humiliate him again, I may no longer be able to control him." He scrutinized my face a moment, then a hint of a smile bent the corners of his lips. "Yet you came here anyway?"

I swallowed. I couldn't say I was here to scout an attack. "I'm still hoping to swap places with Harry. The Williams people are even more concerned that he's vanished."

"Such a considerate business partner, but now that we have you both, why should we let either of you go?"

"If either I don't report in or I go silent, they'll send the cavalry."

"Report to whom? Ray Floyd sitting in the antique plane at Cortina?" he asked. "Or your ex-wife back at Monza?"

I advertently cleared my throat. "Not them. Others are waiting—the security team Harry hired."

"Ahh, yes, they were most effective." Again with the smirk.

He waved to the G-Wagon, which I realized he had driven here himself. I climbed into the passenger seat and he behind the wheel.

"We're glad you have come," he said.

"Why's that?"

"Even after using our most aggressive techniques, your partner is not cooperating. It would be a shame for him not to see his cars race at Monza," he said.

I tried to digest the Mortician's statement as we drove up the remaining steep road toward the gray, stone edifice. I also tried to absorb details along the route, as I might need to describe it to the aforementioned cavalry. The Promontory was indeed impenetrable.

The Mortician glanced at me and noted my studying of the tall stone structure ahead of us.

"The Promontory is a thousand years old. It has been used to defend the valley between it and Val Gardena through many wars and sieges since then." He gave me a sidelong glance as he drove. "It has never been breached in all those campaigns."

"Impressive."

We came to a stop in front of a large wooden gate constructed of massive beams, and then, as if reading my mind that explosives could blow these timbers apart, he said, "The gate is reinforced with military-grade steel designed to repel even the most destructive tank round."

"Quite the ski chalet Himmelman has here."

When the gate had opened, the Mortician hit the gas pedal, which pushed me into the back of my seat. Inside was a large courtyard with four other G-Wagons. A half dozen men in black tactical uniforms carrying guns came out from a side door. What appeared to be the main entrance was in the center of the stone structure, which stood four stories high. Turrets were visible on the roof with large black tubes protruding from them: gun barrels. More like artillery barrels, that is. If I wasn't mistaken, I also spotted the blade of a helicopter near the edge of the roof, indicating there must be a helipad up there too.

In juxtaposition to the exterior shell, the interior of the Promontory was decorated with modern furniture and contemporary art. The Mortician led me to a large conference room equipped with a large table and multiple television screens—two of which showed race cars driving around a track.

"Make yourself comfortable, Herr Reilly. The Principal will be here shortly."

The Mortician walked out, his left foot scraping against the stone flooring, and he closed the door behind him. The thud of a lock falling into place made it clear I did not have free rein. I poured a glass of water from the pitcher, took a large mouthful, turned around—and spit the water out in surprise at what I saw.

Himmelman stood there with Thick-neck at his side.

They both frowned.

"Where did you come from?" I asked.

"The Promontory has many secrets." Himmelman waved toward the conference table in front of him at the same computer he'd had at the hotel at Lake Garda. "Come, be seated."

I glanced quickly at Thick-neck, who looked as if he were chewing razorblades. His face was red and his neck muscles rippling, and he kept opening then bunching his fists. He looked like a horse in the starting gate at Churchill Downs, chomping at the bit to leap into action.

Himmelman spotted my gaze. "Stand down, Bruno."

The man I'd dubbed Thick-neck placed his hands behind his back, spread his feet wider, and adopted a position a notch off "ready to kill."

"Now, Mr. Reilly, let's discuss what you can do to prevent the increasingly inevitable death of your partner—and, sorry to say, you as well."

"I want to see Harry."

"In due time, Mr. Reilly."

MISTY MOUNTAIN HOP

20

"THE FINAL PRACTICE HAS ENDED," Himmelman said, pointing to one of the televisions.

Commentators filled the screen, which then shifted to a list of drivers in order of the fastest time on the practice lap on the top, down to the slowest on the bottom.

"Alas," the Principal said. "Williams is in the bottom two spots again."

I studied him, dressed in black slacks and a black long-sleeved shirt, both of which were pressed and wrinkle-free. "Big racing fan, are you?" I asked.

"No interest whatsoever aside from the investment potential, thanks to the increased popularity now." He squinted. "It is virtually impossible to break into the ownership on an F1 team. Some of the biggest names in motor racing in the US, Asia, Europe, and Russia have applied and offered hundreds of millions of dollars but been rejected."

Finally in front of the Principal, I exhaled hard. "I'll trade myself for Harry," I said. "Matt Sterling has deduced something's awry and is second-guessing the entire transaction. Only Harry can smooth this over. You can hold me as collateral."

"But I have you both."

"That won't fly, Himmelman."

"If you want Mr. Greenbaum to be set free, you need to make it work, Mr. Reilly."

His smug face showed no sign of doubt or vacillation. The man was used to negotiating from a position of strength, and compromise was not in his lexicon.

"I want to see Harry," I said.

He continued to stare at me, no doubt calculating whether I was capitulating or conspiring against him.

"And you will, shortly." He took a sip of water and sat forward. "But first you'd better call the lovely Heather Drake and tell her all is fine here. We wouldn't want any unfortunate interruptions expediting fatal injuries to our guests."

I sat staring at him, my own jaw quivering out of anger at his persistent threats.

Slap! Himmelman whacked his palm hard down on the table. "*Now,* Mr. Reilly. Time is running short. And put it on speaker so I can hear what is being said."

I fished my cell phone from my pocket and held it flat, staring at the screen. My index finger visibly shook as I lowered it onto speed-dial button number one. It rang twice and Heather answered.

"Buck, are you okay?"

"Be careful what you say." Himmelman's admonition was a sharp whisper.

"Yes, hello dear. I'm fine, but our Austrian friends invited me up to their mountaintop hideaway. We're, ah, getting to know each other."

Heather was quiet for a beat, then said, "Well, practice three is over and qualifying starts in an hour. How's Harry?"

Himmelman nodded once.

"I haven't seen him yet."

Another beat passed. "Check back in after you see him."

Himmelman nodded.

"I will, Heather. Is Sterling still asking questions about Harry's whereabouts?"

There was a long pause and Heather must have recognized I was attempting to telegraph something.

"He's very nervous about Harry being MIA."

Himmelman waved to me and mouthed, "MIA?"

"Missing in action," I said.

He pursed his lips.

"Lenny behaving?" I asked.

A hollow laugh sounded from the receiver. "Lenny has decamped to the Mercedes paddock where he's hoping to see Lewis Hamilton."

"Aah, gotcha. My money is on Jones to win this one in the end, but it looked like Red Bull and Ferrari have the best times so far."

"There's no—" Heather stopped midsentence.

She must have realized I was giving her yet another code about having Jones and Tactical International at the ready, even though from what I'd seen here, a rescue mission was impractical.

Himmelman waved his index finger in a circle.

"Okay, Heather. They're going to take me to see Harry now."

"Check back in when you're done."

We disconnected and I turned to face Himmelman.

"You hard what she said. The Williams team is nervous that Harry has gone quiet." I paused. "I need to talk to my partner."

I might as well go along with whatever ruse Harry had been using.

"Bruno will take you. Our team should be finished with him by now."

"Finished with—" I took a step toward Himmelman. "If you've hurt him, I swear I'll rip your smug head off!"

Himmelman smiled as Thick-neck stepped between us. "I warned you, Mr. Reilly. I sought to approach this as a businessman negotiating a transaction, but you and your partner have been obstructive."

Thick-neck grabbed my bicep with his vice-grip hand and turned me toward another door, different than the one I'd entered from. There was a wide staircase outside the room, and Thick-neck shoved me toward it from behind.

"Move it, asshole."

His accent reminded me of Arnold Schwarzenegger and his famous line, "I'll be back."

I picked up my pace to prevent getting shoved any further and glanced around to survey the interior. No other security forces were visible, but I noted the windows had bars on them.

A cage is a cage, refuge or not.

Once to the second floor, I hesitated.

"Go to your left," Thick-neck said from behind me. "Then enter the first door to your right."

I did as I was told, and when I opened the door, I was hit in the face with a blast of distinct smells. Was that urine? I stopped in my tracks.

155

A subtle sound of whining swirled through the air.

A large, blond-haired, muscular man in a tight-fitting black t-shirt and spandex pants emerged from a doorway inside the room. The brute gave me a stern stare and nodded back behind him.

"Herr Greenbaum is in there." He looked as if he could twist steel with his bare hands.

"What have you done to him?"

I pushed past the man into the room. The door closed behind me. Inside, the small room was dark, and I heard slow, ragged breathing.

"Harry, are you in here? Are you okay?"

I brushed my hands on the wall to the side of the door I'd entered through. My hand grazed a switch and the room lit up.

Harry lay face up on a slab, and he suddenly raised his hand to shield his face. He appeared to be naked, only partially covered by a sheet over his waist.

I rushed forward. "What have they done to you?"

His eyelids blinked slowly and it suddenly hit me that he'd been asleep. The smell was even stronger in here—not urine, eucalyptus.

"Buck, is that you?" He tried to sit up, but his girth was too great, so he slid an elbow down and peered over at me. "I must have fallen asleep. That Klaus has incredibly strong hands."

My jaw fell open. "Were you getting a massage?"

"Yes, every day before lunch, Klaus works me over. It's marvelous."

"What the fuck, Harry? Everyone thinks you've been kidnapped, and the Mortician convinced me you've been getting tortured."

"Is such coarse language necessary, dear boy?"

He cleared his throat, dropped his left leg over the side of the table, then spun slowly into a sitting position with his toes touching the ground. Harry's ample belly held a white towel in place. He slid forward until he was standing on shaky legs, turned around and I saw red welts on his back.

"It's not all been wine and roses."

"Are you kidding me?"

He looked up at me, wiped his eyes with one hand, and held the towel in place with the other. "I have no doubt, they will kill me—us—if we don't give them what they want."

"Jesus, this is crazy." I stood towering over Harry and staring him in the eyes. Even amid the desperation of the situation, a questioned gnawed at me.

Harry walked away and through another door; I followed. There was a shower and dressing area in the next room—this was a full-scale massage suite.

"What's the news at Monza?" he asked. "Does anyone know about this situation?"

I assumed Himmelman had the room bugged. "Matt Sterling senses that something's up. I've tried to keep the truth on the down-low, but we're running out of time. He's anxious about you disappearing. Either you or I sign the documents electronically at the ceremony after the race ends, or it automatically goes to the next highest bidder."

"The next bidder, indeed," Harry said. "Himmelman informed me that the syndicate in second position is backed by a hedge fund that will seek to gain control in order to sell the entire team—history be damned."

"Really, Harry, why does it matter? Is your life—or mine, for that matter—less important than a car-racing team?"

"I understand how you must feel, dear boy, but I swore an oath to people I respect deeply—some of the most important people in England—to protect this team. Frank Williams was knighted, just as I was, and while other teams may be based in the UK, Williams is special. My desire is to help the team be restored to the top of the racing business."

"I offered Himmelman to swap positions with you so you can settle down the Williams team."

Harry frowned. "I will not allow that."

"What am I supposed to do, then?" I asked.

"Go back to Monza and prepare to go forward. Good chance I may die here, as I have no intention of cooperating—"

"I can sign the agreement with Himmelman, Harry. That's how you set it up and I refuse to let you die."

Harry shook his head quickly while holding a finger up to his lips. His stern glare and watery blue eyes burned through the haze of the poorly lit room. "You will honor my wishes, young man. If you don't, I will see to it that information I have about you warning your parents to sell their stock in e-Antiquity before the SEC and FBI closed you down is delivered to that dreadful FBI agent who has hounded you all these years."

My jaw fell open.

"I don't want to do that, but if you defy me, I promise you that will be the result."

Speechless, I finally closed my open mouth and stood taller. The dilemma now was whether I would sacrifice myself to save Harry's life. The FBI agent he was referring to was my nemesis of the last decade, T. Edward Booth, who had forced me into doing his out-of-jurisdiction dirty work under the threat that he had evidence related to e-Antiquity that could land me in jail. He never proved that he did, and as many times as I'd pissed him off, I'd been surprised he hadn't already used it against me, so Harry's threat to give evidence about insider trading could indeed give Booth the ammo he needed to put me away, once and for all.

Would he really do it?

His zeal to protect the English royalty behind Williams was clear. This knighthood he'd recently received had changed him. Once a pure capitalist, he now held honor and country over transactions and profit. There was no doubt in my mind he'd throw me under the bus if I screwed that up for him.

"Then why the hell did you put me in the contract?"

"Because even if I die, you can sign the Williams contract. There are funds escrowed to automatically support the transaction, whether I'm alive or dead. My solicitor has instructions to take care of you, but I will need you to interface with Sterling to ensure my monies are used to best enhance the development of new engineering that will restore the once-great team to its previous championship form."

"What do I know about—"

"You're a smart lad. You'll learn."

In all the years I'd known Harry, he had never spoken to me in this tone.

"But—"

"But nothing. Time for you to grow up, Buck. You've squandered enough time on that little island and narrowly averted incarceration more times than I care to recall."

My jaw would have fallen open again if my teeth weren't clenched so tight. I took a couple breaths to settle the blood racing through my veins.

"There are ten Formula 1 teams, each with two cars in the competition," I said. "Can't Himmelman buy into another one?"

"The others are owned by major constructors and the line is long of large automobile companies like Cadillac, Audi, and Porsche who desire to enter the sport, but beyond the ante price of two hundred million, the full price tag to add a team is over a billion dollars. Himmelman is looking for a bargain-entry price and a management team he can manipulate with threats and violence. He believes Williams to be the perfect quarry."

That was consistent with what Himmelman had just said downstairs.

KNOCK, KNOCK, KNOCK.

The sudden pounding on the door surprised me, and Harry suddenly stepped toward me.

"Follow my lead." His voice was a harsh whisper.

The door opened a moment later and Thick-neck peered inside. He looked us up and down, then stepped back. Himmelman appeared behind him and entered the room.

"Are you gentlemen having a nice reunion?"

"Quite," Harry said.

I bit the side of my mouth and held my breath.

"What have you decided?" Himmelman asked.

"We will return to Monza and finalize the transaction," Harry said.

"And our contract?"

"Provided that we are allowed safe passage, yes."

I fought to maintain a poker face in light of Harry's ploy.

The smug smile I'd already come to hate reappeared on Himmelman's face. "Splendid. I knew you would come to your senses." Then his eyes hardened. "Reilly will be returned to Monza, but you will stay here as our insurance until all documents are fully executed, Mr. Greenbaum."

Harry held his stare.

It had been worth a try, but Himmelman was too shrewd to be suckered.

"I'm not going without Harry—"

"Silence!" Himmelman turned his steely gaze toward me.

Harry winked so only I could see.

"I'll have the pilot start the helicopter," Himmelman said. He then leaned in to look up into my eyes. "If you fail, or you try any other foolish maneuver, then Mr. Greenbaum will suffer from a massive coronary."

He left the room.

Harry and I stood staring at each other.

"Jesus, Harry."

"Play along, Buck. Play along."

21

THE VIEW OF THE PROMONTORY AS WE TOOK OFF provided me the opportunity to assess the mountaintop stronghold. The rear of the fortress backed up to the gray rock of a steep outcrop, and the sides of the structure had been erected to the width of the plateau. The only entry from the ground was through the massive timber-and-steel-backed gate at the front, which the Mortician had bragged could withstand a tank round.

I shook my head as the chopper veered hard toward the valley. As I'd deemed from the ground, an assault would be impossible.

Rifugio Scotoni appeared below on the side of the cow-dotted pasture. I should have listened to Bianca when she'd told me to stay away from the road that led to the Promontory. It had been harebrained to think I might exchange myself for Harry, and the ensuing discussions had him threatening to throw me under the bus to the FBI if I didn't follow his instructions. He had all but signed his own death warrant and refused any potential for a pardon.

The helicopter was a sleek, black craft with a soft gray leather interior and an instrument panel containing the latest technological hardware and technology, though in my haste I'd failed to notice the manufacturer. Now I was strapped into the backseat. Seated next to the pilot and directly in front of me was Thick-neck. Given all the humiliation I'd dished out to him these past couple of days, I'd be lucky if he didn't throw me out of the craft at a thousand feet. The snowcapped peaks, gray jagged stone outcroppings, and green valleys would have been a tourist's dream to view from this altitude as we wound through canyons toward the southeast. But my mind was on Harry, his instructions, and his likely fate if he double-crossed Himmelman.

There was no way to change his mind now, and from what he'd said, his attorney had the money locked and loaded for tomorrow's closing. The contract required all assignments or addition of any proposed partners to be approved by Williams, but they trusted Harry implicitly. If I warned Matt Sterling now, then all hell would break loose, which placed me squarely between the proverbial rock and hard place.

"Thanks, Harry."

The circuits in my brain fired as I tried to think how we could turn the tables on Himmelman and get ahead of the curve. The ceremony would be tomorrow afternoon, but it was largely just a photo op. As Harry had said, the transaction would happen electronically.

That's it!

Sudden inspiration hit and the view of the mountains was lost as my brain raced as if down the straightaway at Monza.

I pulled my phone from my pocket and texted Ray. My idea was simple yet would require him to repurpose his gaming skills into a darker arena. It would likely require the cooperation of Williams, which would risk Harry's ire, but it felt like the only possible option for us to get out of this situation alive. At least temporarily. I finished the text to Ray and dubbed the idea "Operation Trojan Horse."

Next I wrote to Heather to say I was okay and headed for Monza, then texted Matt Sterling to keep Harry's commitment on track and position myself to seek help with Trojan Horse.

Sterling responded seconds later saying he'd meet me at the Hotel de la Ville that evening. Heather texted me a moment later to say she'd left a bicycle marked with the hotel's name at the autodromo in the parking lot where Percy had been earlier. The hotel was situated on the southeast corner of Monza Park and was accessible through trails that ran from there to the track.

Ray also responded that he'd leave Cortina immediately for Linate and had reached out to his gaming buddies for help with my idea. He didn't whine or complain that it was impossible and even noted that he loved the flourish of creativity.

Perfect.

Twenty minutes later, we'd flown through the mountains, past Lake Garda, and the chunky vastness of Milan was visible on the horizon. The

162

pilot began to descend, and I looked down to my left to see the gourd-shaped track of Monza, where the stands and grounds were jam-packed with Tifosi and dots of cars sped around the narrow pavement. Qualifying was on, which was the last official milestone before tomorrow's race. The helicopter kept dropping lower and I wasn't sure where we were landing; I glanced out the right side and saw a field with a half dozen other helicopters tied down there. We touched softly down a moment later.

Thick-neck peered back at me, then waved his hand as if to shoo me out. I popped open the door, gave him a hard glimpse, and hopped outside, keeping my head down as I hurried away from the still rotating blade. The chopper lifted quickly and banked hard to the right, speeding away at treetop level.

As the sound of the receding helicopter diminished, the roar of the race cars storming around the track was punctuated by the cheering crowd. I hoofed it down the access road that led from the field down a hill and under a bridge, until I saw the familiar sight of the VIP entrance in the distance. Just before that was the parking lot Heather had referred to, and there by the entrance I found a black bicycle with "Hotel de la Ville" painted in gold letters on the frame. A lock was draped over it but wasn't closed.

Using the map app on my phone, I zoomed out until all of Monza Park was visible on a satellite image. Light-brown lines crisscrossed through the eight-thousand-acre park. I zoomed in on the southeast corner and saw what had to be the hotel at a major intersection. I climbed aboard the bike and retraced my path back toward where the helicopter had dropped me, then turned right on a broad pedestrian path flanked on each side by concession stands. The track was to my right but blocked by low grandstands full of fans cheering as cars blew past. The wide path continued up a hill and I had to stand to pedal the single-speed bike up its slope. At the top was a security gate and just past that were rolling fields of green grass with narrow dirt trails leading in multiple directions.

I meandered through the fields that were largely free of fans while qualifying was still going—or maybe had just ended because the growl of F1 cars had quieted. Fifteen minutes later I came to a road that led out of the park a block away from the intersection I'd seen on the satellite image on my phone where the hotel should be situated. I took the road and was pleased to find I was correct. What I hadn't expected was to find hordes of people gathered around the hotel, mostly dressed in red, with Ferrari flags waving. As I got closer, I realized that a decorative metal fence atop a brick foundation separated the fans—or Tifosi—from the hotel grounds.

Heather had said many of the drivers and team principals stayed at the Hotel, so it made sense that their most ardent fans would be here waiting for them to arrive once qualifying had ended. Only problem was, I had no idea how to get in as I stood behind them looking for an entrance.

"Buck!"

I heard my name shouted over the din and happened to look into the courtyard on the corner. There, above what I presumed to be the main entry past the secure courtyard, was a second-floor balcony. I saw the waving hand just before I spotted the long blonde hair.

It was Heather.

I waved back to her, and she pointed down toward the left side of the fence where it curved at the front corner. I followed her pointed finger to a gate there hidden behind fans, three deep.

"Excuse me," I said.

People looked back at me with incredulous stares as if I were trying to butt in line. A man in a tuxedo appeared on the inside of the fence and unlocked the gate, waving people aside. I rolled the bicycle through the narrow human corridor that had opened in front of me, and the faces I passed stared at me with jealous contempt. Once I was inside, the man in the tuxedo, a happy-faced fellow with his short dark hair slicked back, gave me a generous smile.

"Welcome to Hotel de la Ville. My name is Riccardo. I'm the general manager. Ms. Drake asked me to let you in."

His charming smile was a life ring of calm among the raucous sea on the other side of the fence, where hundreds of people stared at us: some talking while others jeered or yelled in Italian, causing others to laugh. I had no idea what they were saying, but Riccardo gently rolled his eyes as if amused by the scene.

"Allow me to take the bicycle," he said. "Ms. Drake will be waiting in the lobby."

"*Grazie*," I mustered.

I hurried through the courtyard and noticed outdoor patio seating to a ground-level restaurant ten feet from the perimeter fence, which extended all the way to the gate and private parking area at the end. The hotel's dining area was to the left of the patio. People were seated on the outdoor area with orange Aperol spritzes on their tables along with charcuterie boards and smoldering ashtrays.

I jogged up the few steps and into the lobby where an old-world allure awaited. My eyes were drawn to the dark wood paneling with classic oil paintings and numerous antique clocks on the walls.

"Thank God!"

Heather's voice alerted me to look up as she dove into my arms. Hers were wrapped around my neck, squeezing me for all I was worth.

"I thought I'd seen the last of you." Her mouth was so close to my ear, the sound of her words was muffled.

I squeezed her back, though my mind shot back to my last sight of Harry draped in the towel in the little treatment room at the Promontory.

"There he is, 'James Bond' Reilly, agent double-oh-oh."

I opened my eyes to see Lenny Jackson standing behind Heather, his thousand-watt smile lighting the otherwise muted room. Even with the weight of Harry's life and threats against me on my shoulders, seeing Lenny and hearing his sarcasm made me smile. I held up my palm and he slapped me a high-five.

"Damn, boy, you really upped your game this time," he said.

"Yeah, well, we have Harry to thank for that."

Heather curled her lip ever so slightly.

"And Heather for getting us into this hotel." I winked at her. "What a scene out front."

"Bunch of these F1 drivers are staying here, man. Team owners and even the boss man from Ferrari." Lenny's eyes widened with each addition to his statement.

"How do you know all that?" I asked.

Lenny held both palms up, bowed, then pointed them toward Heather. "Your girl knows everybody, man. Shit. I've just been hanging here in the lobby. When the crowd out front starts cheering, I step outside and see some young-ass driver signing autographs, posing for selfies, and shaking hands with the crowd. Unreal, man."

"Don't let him fool you," Heather said. "Lenny's taken about a dozen selfies inside the lobby with drivers, too."

"I don't even know who these cats are, man, but they're cool customers," Lenny said. "This racing shit's the bomb."

Heather's mouth was pursed and there was no joy in her eyes. "Did you see Harry?"

"Yeah, I saw him." I glanced around the room as Heather and Lenny drew closer. "He's prepared to die to prevent Himmelman from forcing his way into the agreement, and if I do anything contrary to his wishes, he has evidence from the e-Antiquity days that will be forwarded to the FBI."

"What?" Heather asked. "Harry said that? To you?"

"Damn, boy," Lenny said. "Thought you all were tight?"

"The Crown's his passion now. That and restoring Britain to greatness through this bloody racing team."

I noticed the slight wrinkles deepen on Heather's temples.

"Speak of the devil," she said.

I turned to see that Matt Sterling had entered the lobby with a woman I presumed to be his wife. He saw us off to the side and walked straight toward me.

"Buck, Heather said you went to find Sir Harry in the Dolomites," he said.

I shifted my gaze to Heather, but she dropped her attention toward the floor. I smiled—and in a flash knew Trojan Horse was the only way to proceed.

"That's right," I said. "Do you have a minute to talk?"

Sterling gave me a curt nod and turned toward the restaurant entrance. I started to follow, then turned halfway around and saw that Heather and Lenny were following me. I held up my hand and shook my head once. Heather's mouth curved into a frown, but she stopped, and Lenny bumped into her.

I trailed Sterling into a small bar area, then turned right into the restaurant, which was only three tables deep and ran the length of the outdoor verandah. Sterling exchanged waves with a couple of other men along the way as he walked to a two-seat table in the far-left corner and sat facing the room. No doubt his concern was over both Harry's well-being and whether the closing would occur without incident tomorrow, but knowing there was an alternate contract in position should Harry or I fail to sign, I concluded it was Harry on his mind. Plus, he must not be aware that the backup was a hedge fund intent on selling the team.

His face was serious: the wrinkles next to his eyes deepened and his short gray hair was askew from being outdoors much of the day.

"Will you please tell me what's going on?" he asked.

I bit my lip, which he appeared to notice, because he sat back with alarm curving his mouth into a frown. I then smiled and sped toward the mental intersection where the lights blinked red and the headlights of traffic came fast from all sides.

I placed my elbows on the table and leaned forward.

"Harry's in trouble, but I have a plan."

22

MORNING CAME EARLY IN THE SECOND FLOOR CORNER SUITE that Heather had arranged for us. At 7:22 local time, I parted the full-height mauve curtains to peer outside and check the weather and was surprised to see the crowd of people filling the sidewalk on the other side of the street.

Several gawked up at me standing in my underwear as I processed the momentary shock of the vast number of people who had either spent the night there or had come very early in the morning to hold vigil to see some of their favorite drivers.

One woman waved to me with a leer on her face and I slid the curtains shut and pivoted to face Heather in bed, staring at her phone.

"You won't believe the number of fans out here."

"Oh, I believe it. This is the Italian Grand Prix and Ferrari is on the pole today," she said.

Last night I didn't know what "on the pole" meant, but thanks to Charles Leclerc having the fastest time in qualifying yesterday, he and his Ferrari would start today's race at the front of the grid—which was the lineup of the twenty cars at today's race, all starting in pairs nearly side by side, from fastest time to slowest time.

I may have been the only person in Monza who felt sick about it finally being race day because it also meant the deadline for Harry to close on a portion of ownership with the Williams team came with the certainty of his death if he didn't also agree to cut in Himmelman's mob. But I also had the power to execute both agreements. Even though Harry had threatened me with certain incarceration over the now decade-old insider trading crime—warning my parents to sell their stock in my former company, e-Antiquity, when I realized the Feds would be shutting us down—if I interfered with

168

his potential martyrdom for the British monarchy, I was still wrestling with the dilemma of saving his life over sacrificing my freedom.

Heather must've been reading my mind. "Maybe Harry's been harboring a grudge all these years because you didn't warn him about e-Antiquity's collapse like you did your parents."

As our largest early-stage investor in e-Antiquity, Harry had lost over twenty-million dollars, but he'd made millions more from selling shares when our stock skyrocketed after I discovered the tomb of the Mayan Serpent King in Guatemala.

"Maybe," I said. "Or he was just acting in case Himmelman was spying on us."

Heather watched me over the top of her phone. I'd once again become accustomed to waking up beside her shocked at how naturally beautiful she was in the mornings, with no makeup or designer clothing and jewelry. To me, that's what made her the real deal as an internationally known fashion model. She truly was spectacularly beautiful but was also Harvard educated and brilliant to boot.

"Why won't you tell me what you and Ray have cooked up?" she asked.

"I don't want to put anyone else at risk, Heather. Sterling was shocked enough at what was going on but said he'd discuss my idea with his legal team."

"I'm sure he was more shocked to learn the next buyer in line was a shill backed by a hedge fund too. If anybody's motivated to help you help Harry, it's him."

My jaw hurt from a long night of grinding my teeth. "He'd better be based on the plan we perfected last night."

Heather lowered the phone and I saw she was still naked, her breasts exposed from sitting up with her back against the headboard. She must've seen the admiration on my face because a wry smile bent her lips, and she beckoned me forward by wagging her index finger toward her.

"Come here, baby. Let me take your mind off today's challenges."

I stood there, my mind in a spiral over the crazy plan I'd spontaneously hatched with Sterling last night, and no matter how seductive Heather looked in bed, I didn't think the distraction was a good idea ... until she slid out of bed and pranced over to me with the same exaggerated, runway strut

I'd seen her use at Paris Fashion Week many times before.

I inadvertently licked my lips.

She embraced me, her body still warm from the bed, and mine chilled from standing nearly naked in the middle of the room. Her hands felt hot on my skin, and she wasted no time sliding one down the front of my underwear where she began to knead my instantly responsive manhood.

"That's my man," she whispered in my ear. "Come to mama."

She literally took me in her grasp and forced me to follow her like a pull toy, giggling as she led the way.

We slid slowly onto the bed—me half worried about getting injured if she slipped—but the other half of me quickly became lost in her seductive powers. By the time I was flat, she'd continued her initiative by slowly climbing atop me, and my mind had become focused completely in the moment, or moments …

HEATHER, RAY, LENNY, AND I WERE SEATED in the middle of the restaurant, and Heather whispered the names of drivers seated around us. Carlos Sainz, the other driver for Ferrari, was huddled over a table near the buffet with his manager, no doubt discussing strategy; Kevin Magnussen, a driver for Haas, appeared stoic seated by himself, but Ray said he was likely imagining every corner of the track here in his head, which was typical for how F1 drivers prepared. George Russell, one of the Mercedes drivers, sat with a beautiful woman who Heather reported was his longtime girlfriend.

"Longtime," I said. "The guy's barely twenty-five years old."

"Relatively speaking," she said. "No need to be grumpy."

I scanned the room for Fernando, who we'd seen arrive last night via scooter—unlike the Ferrari boys who showed up in their own cars of the same make, which I figured were likely benefits of driving for the team—but he was nowhere to be seen. Seeing Heather here at the hotel had produced a sudden smile on the Spaniard, perhaps thinking she was here for him, but he maintained his cool when Heather re-introduced him to me. He was literally a foot shorter than me but had an electric charisma that made him seem larger than life. Plus, he was lined up third on the grid for today's race, behind Leclerc and Max Verstappen, the two-time defending champion from Red Bull, so had been in an ebullient mood last night.

Ray said something that caused Lenny to laugh, but my mind was back at the Promontory. Well, in the helicopter as we rose above the Promontory, anyway.

"I found a place where I can get what you asked for," Lenny said.

"Good," I said. "Do it this morning. But also make sure to attract a lot of attention at the autodromo."

He laughed. "That's like telling a lion to growl, man. Don't you worry about that," Lenny said. "Like that old cracker Mel Fisher used to say when he was searching for the Atocha, 'today's the day.'"

I turned my attention to Ray. Once again, I was relying on him to provide the technical wizardry that would make Trojan Horse work, plus putting him in harm's way—again.

He held a hand up. "I've got the flyover covered too, Buck. Carmen Micciche from Aero Club Como is going to fly with me, so we're all set as far as anyone else will know."

"Good man."

Sterling entered the restaurant, again with his wife, and when he saw me, he nodded back toward the corner table where I had presented the plan last night. His wife stopped at our table to chat with Heather as I jumped up and moved over to where he was now situated. My nerves were frayed, having never been in the middle of a situation like this, and based on what the day would bring.

"What did your lawyers say?" I asked.

His expression was deadly serious. "They weren't happy about it, but in light of the circumstances, they agreed."

I pumped my fist then leaned closer. "*All* the pieces?"

He gave me a slight nod.

Nice.

"There'll be a lot going on at the autodromo today, which will be a good diversion," he said. He then paused and gave me a long look. "Are you sure this will work?"

I again ran my discussion with Harry at the Promontory through my head. I saw no other way to ensure his safety—well, at least try to ensure it—and if successful, then Harry would be at the ceremony to close the transaction himself.

"You know I can't answer that, but I think it's our best chance for success. What's the schedule?" I asked.

"We need to leave shortly. You'll come with me."

"I'm ready when you are."

We both stood. So much for breakfast. Heather, Lenny, and Ray watched me approach. I gnashed my teeth as I debated what to tell them but figured it best to stay close to the truth, leaving the finer details to omission.

"I'm heading to the track with Sterling." I said. "Ray, go straight to Linate from here and await orders. Lenny, work your magic."

"What about me?" Heather asked.

"You're the center of the operation. If you can't convince the world all is well, then Himmelman will suspect something's afoot."

"The flyover formation leaves at two-thirty," Ray said.

Heather stood and took me in a tight embrace. "Be careful, Buck." She shuddered, then glanced up into my eyes. "I love you."

The shock of those words caused me to freeze. I felt the eyes of Sterling, Lenny, and Ray boring into me. I pulled her back in close and squeezed her hard.

"I'll see you at the Williams suite."

With that I followed Sterling out to the dining patio, and we turned left toward the private parking area. Guilt chafed me for not telling Heather I loved her too, but my mind was on the mission, and she'd caught me off guard.

Sterling had a large Mercedes waiting and we both climbed in the backseat, me behind the driver. It was a short ride to the track, and we didn't speak as the driver was a contract employee. Traffic was already getting thick and we probably could've biked to the track faster, but that wasn't Sterling's style. After twenty minutes we pulled into the same parking lot where I'd found the bike yesterday afternoon, where the racing drivers parked their cars, and across from the VIP entrance.

"Ready to make a show of it?" he asked.

"Let's roll," I said.

We cruised through security and found that the VIP tent already had a lot of people inside. Once through there, we made our way to the paddock. Up ahead we saw a group of three people—television commentators—and a cameraman waiting near the press tent. They spotted us—or at least Sterling —and waved.

The commentators were all British, two men and a woman. They introduced themselves and we shook hands. The lead person was an attractive black woman named Naomi. There was a younger man of Indian or Pakistani decent named Karun, and another man named Damon, dressed in blue jeans and a pale-blue pullover shirt.

"Are we ready to film?" Naomi asked the cameraman, who merely nodded.

She turned to face us and put on a big smile. "Big day for you and Team Williams today, Mr. Sterling."

"Every race day is important to us, Naomi."

"Of course, but isn't your transaction to sell an undisclosed portion of the team also scheduled to occur today?"

"That's right." He paused then gripped my bicep. "This is Buck Reilly. He and his partner, Sir Harry Greenbaum, will be purchasing a stake of Williams Racing Team today."

"How exciting for you." Her gaze was directed toward me.

I hesitated but felt a nudge from Sterling. "Sir Harry and I are thrilled to both invest and help contribute to restore Williams Racing to its former glory."

"Given the competitive process that Williams ran, there's been a lot of speculation in the news about this transaction," Damon said. "Are you headed to your lounge to finalize it now?"

"Not quite yet," Sterling said. "We have a few more things to do, and while Sir Harry is a very busy man, we're hoping he'll join us for the signing, even though Mr. Reilly can sign it too."

I smiled. "Traffic's tough out there. If Harry gets stuck, I brought my signing pen."

"Fantastic news for Williams Racing, and all of Formula 1, I would say," Karun said. "Let us know when it's going to happen, and we'll televise it live on Sky Sports."

Sterling laughed. "All right. We're off to get the team ready."

I bit my tongue and feigned smiles for the camera before they cut the interview. We thanked them then made our way slowly through the paddock, talking to other team executives that Sterling knew, each wishing the other well for the race, but I was too tense to utter a word.

Finally, we arrived at the Williams tire-storage trailer and walked through the middle of it, across an open aisle, and into the actual pit area where the two cars were in separate yet adjacent garage stalls—all of which were marked with the blue-and-white Williams logos and the drivers' names.

"Right, that went well," Sterling said.

"Did it? Felt like torture to me," I said.

He cleared his throat and without a word we passed by one of the jacked-up cars, a team of engineers all over and under it, tightening bolts and adjusting torque and various fittings. Outside were dozens of people in pit lane, many of them spectators, being cautioned by security to stay behind a yellow line with the word *Aramaco* spelled out in large letters.

"You'll now take a tour of the track on that flatbed trailer out there," Sterling said.

I followed the direction of his pointed finger and saw three large flatbeds, all situated with protective railings on their perimeters and attached to large matching trucks.

"Which one?" I asked.

"The one in back."

I scrutinized that one and saw a familiar face aboard, which explained the rationale.

"Right."

We stood eye to eye—Sterling the same height—and exchanged steely stares.

"Good luck then," he said.

Nothing like the British sense of laconic speech. I walked away without shaking hands or drawing attention to myself. I was just another VIP about to take a tour of the track. At least that was my cover.

I walked up the pit and around the large jersey barrier that separated it from the actual grid and racetrack, then backtracked down to where the trucks and flatbeds were collecting passengers. I continued past the first two and made eye contact with a familiar face on the third one, where I walked to the back of the flatbed, showed my credentials to a guide by the steps, then climbed aboard.

From the back-right corner, Jones ignored me. I stayed in the back-left corner of the flatbed. Moments later, our vehicle lurched forward to follow the others. The guide immediately started talking, his voice carried over a loudspeaker so all aboard could hear him as he explained the details of each corner, track history of previous races, famous crashes, and drivers who had won here. I kept my eye on Jones, waiting for a sign as we drove slowly around the track. Fans cheered us from the stands as we passed, and I assumed this must be a standard routine here, or maybe at all circuits.

Finally, when we were a little more than halfway around the track, I saw the familiar sight of the parking lot and VIP entrance. As we passed under the pedestrian bridge that crossed over the track, our vehicle came to a brief stop—and my eyes bulged as Jones stepped off the right-rear corner. I hesitated, my heart in my throat, until a flash of adrenalin hit me, and I jumped off the rear as well.

The guide said nothing about us making what had to be a highly irregular exit, and I assumed Sterling and Jones had made all the arrangements for the unique jumping-off spot. Jones walked quickly toward a gate that was open from the track to the viewing area adjacent to the bridge, and I hurried after him. No words were spoken, and as we passed through the gate, another man dressed in black closed it and followed us. He was average height but muscular and had the cold eyes of a professional accustomed to breaking rules—and probably heads. I checked my Rolex Submariner; two hours had passed since we'd left the hotel. I hoped Lenny had had enough time to do his part.

I kept my mouth closed as we hurried up a flight of steps that took us out to the main pedestrian path, where another man dressed similarly to the first one had a second gate open. Once we were all through, he closed that one and joined our merry band. Together, the four of us pushed our way through the Tifosi, several of whom already reeked of beer but were jovial, laughing, and wearing their favorite teams' colors.

Once across the pedestrian path and past the concession stand, the familiar sight of the helicopter landing field was ahead. Three helicopters were parked there; only one, a silver one, had its engine running and its rotor blades spinning slowly. The W on the door confirmed it was our destination.

Jones had slowed down and was waiting for me to pull up the rear. My heart was racing at not only the jaunt to get here, but in anticipation of what was to come.

"We need to go, Reilly," Jones said.

I paused and glanced around but didn't see—

A burgundy blur suddenly roared up the service road. I'd never seen an old Rolls Royce move that fast. The epitome of all luxury automobiles jumped the curb and landed on the grass, fishtailed, then righted itself as it sped toward us.

Jones reached under his shirt. "Is this a problem?"

"No, a solution," I said.

Percy slid to a stop in front of the helicopter and Lenny jumped out carrying a small brown bag. He jogged up to me, his eyes glancing from me to Jones to the others in the chopper, no hint of his trademark smile.

"Got you covered, brother," he said.

I took the bag and peered inside.

"Good luck, man."

I held out my fist, we bumped, and he dashed back to the Rolls. Percy drove off at a more measured pace.

"You ready now, mate?" Jones said.

I glanced into the chopper. "Is it just the four of us?"

He smiled.

"Climb aboard, we'll brief you on the way."

23

THE HELICOPTER LIFTED STRAIGHT UP as I studied the two men with Jones, both of whom had serious expressions of weary, yet keen eyes and appeared very comfortable in rapid deployment situations. Once I had Sterling's tentative approval last night, I'd called Jones to set him in motion, but we hadn't communicated any further, so I didn't know anything about what he'd planned.

Jones looked from me to the two men and spoke up.

"Buck Reilly, meet Operators Two and Three."

The men stared back at me, not acknowledging which was which, nor extending their hands to say, "Pleased to meet you."

"Thanks for being here, guys. Are they part of your team, Jones?"

"Call me Operator One," Jones said. "Yes, former Royal Marines, battle hardened in multiple shitholes in the Middle East and Africa."

As I suspected. I studied them a minute longer while the autodromo came into view as we ascended. "Does that make me Operator Four?" I asked.

Jones smiled. "No, you're Buck Reilly, a known commodity. We're here to rescue your partner from an impenetrable mountain retreat called the Promontory. Let's keep it simple."

Simple. Right.

My eyes searched the cabin of the helicopter. I saw no guns or other assault weapons. "Are we going to fist fight our way into the Promontory?" I asked.

"Relax, Reilly. The briefing will occur on our next hop."

Next hop? What was that supposed to mean?

Having already flown from the Dolomites to Monza, I was familiar with the course and visual references along the way. We were headed in a completely different direction, southwest instead of northeast. Either they knew something I didn't or had different logistics beyond just Operators One through Three and me.

A pang of anxiety shot through me.

I couldn't even remember the last time I'd shot a gun, so even though I'd set this plan in action, if our next hop included getting armed, I'd need a refresher.

The helicopter's course didn't vary, and we made a beeline to the south until I started seeing planes in a pattern to land and others taking off.

"Linate airport?" I asked.

Jones gave me a long stare and a short nod. His body language indicated questions were not welcome, so I pressed my lips tight and adopted the same bored demeanor as Two and Three. Five minutes later we circled in at Linate Airport, and when I saw where we were going to land, my heart skipped a beat. I again pressed my lips closed as Jones, er, One, didn't appreciate any questions.

The pilot set the chopper down on the flight line next to Big Mama, where I saw Ray pacing in a circle as if he needed a restroom.

"What the hell?" I asked.

The door on the chopper flew open and Two and Three jumped out, followed by Jones. I grabbed my orange Last Resort Charter and Salvage hat from the bag Lenny had brought and followed them out. I walked straight to Ray Floyd.

"What the hell's going on?" I asked. "You're supposed to be readying Trojan Horse—"

"You telling me? Big Mama's full of fire and brimstone, which is all supposedly under your orders."

I spun to find Jones standing behind me. "What's going on here, Jones?"

"That's One to you—"

"Okay, I'm not military, and we're in this mess because you let Harry slip through your fingers, so get to the damn point."

Jones bit his lip. "We have a team of ten men, including you, ready to assault the Promontory. But we need a quick-strike opportunity that can deliver all of us and our gear."

I looked around the tarmac. "What gear? I don't see any gear—"

"The men and the gear are already loaded on the plane," Ray said.

"*Our* plane?" I asked.

"Sir Harry's your partner," Jones said.

"Your *partner*?" Ray's brow creased into deep wrinkles.

"In the racing team, not Last Resort," I said. "What about Trojan Horse?"

"In process," Ray said.

I turned back to Jones. "The airport at Cortina's an hour away from the Promontory—"

"They loaded parachutes onboard," Ray said.

"*Parachutes*?" My stomach flipped.

"And a shitload of guns," Ray said. "Am I going to get arrested for this?"

"Based on your intel and our satellite data, it's the only way in," Jones said. He spun away from our conversation and turned to Two and Three. "Load up, the others are already on board."

Two and Three followed orders.

"You ride up front with the pilot, Reilly, so you can show him where we're going."

"It's my plane, Jones—"

"Our plane," Ray said.

I shook my head, climbed the ladder, and peeked inside when I got to the top. The cabin was packed tight with weapons, and the seats were full of men in black battle gear wearing parachutes. The new arrivals would have to stand. My jaw hung open as I surveyed the scene.

"Move it, Reilly!" Jones urged from behind me. "We need to get to the jump zone and free up this bird so the pilot can return to Linate in time for the flyover before the race starts. If we don't, their spies at the track will know something's amiss."

I climbed aboard and struggled to maneuver through the arsenal-packed cabin. Big Mama had been converted to a warbird. An active warbird. When I arrived at the flight deck, I found the right seat piled high with a parachute and black assault clothing.

Son of a bitch.

I stopped at the bulkhead, then turned and looked back. The scene was the result of my idea flying back from the Promontory yesterday. I smiled.

If I was going to die over this damn deal Harry wanted so bad, at least it would be on my terms.

And for this would Harry throw me under the bus with Special Agent Booth of the FBI?

Would Himmelman kill Harry the moment he knew he was under attack?

My teeth clenched as I recalled the layout of the Promontory. I'd need to provide these men as many details as I could to help ensure success. There was no choice but to don the parachute, but I did that over my tropical fishing pants and blue linen shirt. Based on the assault, I knew Himmelman's men would have orders to shoot me unless Harry was already dead.

Hell, I would've rather signed their damn contract to save our lives than commence this operation, but inaction wasn't an option. And I'm not an Anglophile or a racing fan, and I couldn't care less about the British monarchy, but those were the reasons Harry was risking both of our skins.

Then I thought of Matt Sterling and his Williams Racing Team family. He'd been instrumental in agreeing to Trojan Horse and organizing my exit from the track to facilitate the rescue attempt, both to save Harry and to ensure the Williams team had a chance to return to its former greatness. His intentions were pure—capitalistic to a degree because it was a business—but there were plenty of people out there who'd be happy to lend money or invest in what was the hottest growth sport in the world. He and his syndicate had chosen Harry for the same reasons that Harry wanted to be a part of it.

But damn it, I launched this effort to save my friend. I didn't give a damn about the rest.

I cinched the parachute straps tight.

Let's do it.

I'd only parachuted once in my life and that was over Sugarloaf Key strapped to an instructor. It'd scared the crap out of me and I swore I'd never do it again. I couldn't even imagine how we'd pinpoint a landing on the precipice of a mountaintop, either.

Lost in my own thoughts, I jumped when the left engine started. I hadn't even noticed Ray enter the cockpit or do the preflight check, as abbreviated as it may have been. I edged awkwardly into the right seat, the parachute harness making me sit higher and pushing me closer to the instrument panel.

Ray pointed to my headset, which I pulled on over my Last Resort hat and clicked on.

"You didn't tell me about all of this," he said.

"We don't really have a choice. Plus, if it all goes according to my plan, they'll have no choice but to release Harry."

Ray shook his head. "And we're supposed to have two pilots onboard Big Mama."

I just stared at him but held my tongue. Harry hadn't shared any of the risk or issues with me when he invited us to fly five thousand miles in our ancient aircraft to participate in a flyover at a bloody Formula 1 race, so I was equally numb as Ray, but at least he'd fly away—alone on the flight deck or not—once we all jumped out of the plane into the oblivion of the frigid Dolomites.

"No radio chatter," came another voice in my headset.

I glanced behind me to see Jones, er, One, wearing a headset and waving his finger from side to side.

"Christ," I said.

"At your service," Jones replied.

I didn't give him the pleasure of recognition by looking back again.

"Can you enter the destination in the GPS while I taxi to the runway?" Ray asked.

I reached down into my rear pocket—I had to loosen and reach under my parachute harness—and pulled out the trail map I'd used when navigating from the Falzarego Pass up to Lagazuoi then over to Rifugio Scotoni. The map was titled "Alta Badia," the name of the region.

I didn't speak Italian, but in my mind that translated to "high bad."

With the map unfolded, I found Lagazuoi in the upper-left-hand corner. The altitude was listed as 2,778 meters, which roughly translated to 9,100 feet above sea level. Scotoni was due south and labeled 1,985 meters, or 6,500 feet—so nearly a three-thousand-foot drop. The peak where the Promontory was located was unlabeled, but it appeared to thrust straight up out of the San Cassiano Valley floor. There were no compass headings, latitude, or longitude on the trail map, but I found the location of the valley on the GPS, zoomed in, found the peak, and marked it as our location.

Ray alternately watched me and navigated Big Mama through the taxi area while communicating with air traffic control. Once I'd entered the destination, I pointed out the location to Ray, and his jaw dropped open. I knew why but had an answer.

Access to the Promontory could only be from the south, through the valley, because behind it were even higher mountains with elevations ranging from 10,300 to 10,500 feet. Big Mama was a workhorse, not a fighter plane, so her maneuvering capabilities were not fit for the dexterity needed to navigate precisely between tight mountain peaks.

I pointed to the valley, ran my finger up through it to the location of the Promontory, and tapped the screen there. Ray gave me a disgusted glare, then reached down and zoomed in on the mountains behind the drop zone. He then used his hand to mimic the plane flying through the valley, held a thumb up at the drop point, and pointed toward the Civetta peak at 10,500 feet, flashed his fingers wide as if the plane hit the mountain, then pointed his index finger straight down.

I alternately studied the trail map and the GPS for another route to approach the area from the east: vectoring northwest over Colfosco then Corvara, then following what appeared to be a ski area straight to the Promontory where we could drop in. Then Ray could maneuver out to the west through a smaller valley where the mountains were much lower.

He grimaced but ultimately gave me a thumbs-up, so I plotted the course through there. It was still tight, but it provided a safer escape for him.

God only knew what would happen to the rest of us while he was making his getaway, though.

Air traffic control directed us to the head of runway 36, and a moment later, Big Mama was hurtling up the 8,012-foot asphalt strip. It was plenty long, but given our heavy load, it took far longer than usual for us to achieve liftoff. Big Mama lumbered into the sky. Since Ray and I had already flown to Cortina d'Ampezzo a couple days ago, I knew it would be a fast trip.

"Radar shows precipitation in the Dolomites where we're headed,"

Ray said.

I clicked the mic. "Twenty minutes to the destination. And it may be wet when we arrive there."

"Roger," Jones said.

I glanced back and the men were already moving into the aft section of the cabin. Small machine guns hung from straps wrapped around their chests, and I saw what looked like grenades attached to their belts.

This is happening.

"You'll have to put her on autopilot after we're gone and go back to close the hatch," I said to Ray.

He nodded. But then he surprised me by genuflecting and giving me a thumbs-up. I smiled. I hadn't had time to process what seemed to be happening at the speed of light, at least for a battle virgin like me— much less the insane risks of this mission.

The biggest question that had been rattling quietly around my skull was how the hell we'd get out of there if successful, or even if we were not.

There had been four or five Mercedes G-Wagons parked inside or outside the fortified gate when I'd been there, but we'd need all of them for what I hoped would be eleven of us departing.

One step at a time, Buck.

I had to survive the jump first.

24

LOW CLOUDS MADE VISUAL FLIGHT RULES IMPOSSIBLE, so Ray flew using instruments for our approach. The clouds were just above five thousand feet so we tried to stay just under them, and what Ray had reported as precipitation turned out to be light snow, the valley below was smudged with white. I thought for maybe the hundredth time that this was an insane mission that would likely get Harry and all of us killed.

But I wasn't entrusting his rescue to anyone, not even Jones and his men, without me along for the ride. And if my plan worked, it might just save his life.

"We're above Colfosco—get ready to jump!" Ray shouted through the cabin.

Ray had already slowed our airspeed to a few knots above stalling, and Jones had everyone standing in the aisle and in the aft part of the cabin, ready to go.

I'd briefed the men, One (Jones) through Nine, on what I'd seen of the Promontory on the hike in, after I was captured, inside, then from the helicopter ride out.

"As I observed then, the only way in is through the front gate, and it's heavily fortified," I said.

"You're wrong, Reilly," Jones said.

"What are you talking about?"

"You said there was an open-air courtyard inside the gate where cars park, and that's how you get inside the house."

"Yeah, so?"

He smiled. "That's where we need to aim our jump."

"Oh, sure. That's like threading a needle with your eyes closed," I said.

Jones checked an app on his phone. "Winds are light and out of the east, the same direction we're approaching the site. Given the small target, we need to hit it right. Reilly and I will jump tandem."

Jones must've seen my wide eyes. I'd only jumped that one time and it too had been tandem, so I was slightly relieved, but I still had my ass cheeks pinched together.

"You good, mate?" he asked.

I nodded quickly.

The men lined up; no words were spoken.

"Open the hatch," Jones said.

The man closest to the hatch popped it open, and even at the slow speed, the lightweight door panel fluttered hard in the wind, not built to be opened during flight.

"Hurry up!" Ray shouted. "That hatch will rip off its hinges!"

"Where are we?" Jones asked.

"Just passing Corvara," Ray said.

"Get ready!"

I was looking out one of the right windows and saw the cable car climbing up Lagazuoi to the right. "Almost there!"

My eyes followed the valley to where Rifugio Scotoni was—there, I saw it! The peak with the gray stone fortress on top was just past it. I pointed it out to Jones, who shouted the location to the men.

"Reilly and I will jump third—now go! Go! Go!"

The first two men jumped in quick succession, as I choked trying to prevent myself from hyperventilating. I grabbed the Last Resort hat off my head and stuffed it inside my shirt. Jones grabbed me and spun me toward the door and clipped us together. It was probably fortunate that my jellied legs gave out when he pushed me forward.

The sound of wind whistling past my face—my eyes watering—face cold and wet with snow—freezing!

I fought against the harness—Jones behind me—the ground was coming at us fast!

RIP—WHIP!

Jones pulled the cord and we slowed immediately, then he pulled the levers on each side of the square blue chute. Through the light snow we could see the Promontory below, but further west—

"Lower your head!" he said. "Point your arms down straight so I can steer us!"

I did as I was told, and when he leaned us forward, we increased in speed and accelerated toward the target below. I spotted the other two men who'd jumped before us: the first landed short of the peak into trees, sending snow flying off their branches, and the second was headed toward a grouping of G-Wagons—

"We're going to hit the wall!" I said.

"Quiet!"

Jones expertly steered us—the top of the wall closing fast—we'd land on top of it—

"Lift your legs!" he said.

The soles of my shoes scraped at loose gravel on top of the wall—his ass must have scraped it because it pushed us forward, and like a bullseye, we drifted down inside the walled courtyard, also freshly powdered with snow. I pulled my hat back on, making sure Lenny had fitted his modification properly.

Miraculously, I saw nobody there, but I heard shouting outside the wall, then—

BOOM!

Gunfire!

BOOM!

BOOM!

Jones must have hit a quick-release clasp on our harnesses because we rolled free of each other, and he immediately popped up onto a knee with his machine gun at the ready.

"We have to open the gate!"

BOOM!

A shot came from the now open front door. Jones rolled to his right and returned fire.

BOOM! BOOM!

When I'd been here before I'd seen a guard next to a control panel in the corner of the courtyard. He must've been operating the gate. I glanced around and saw the gray box, though it closely matched the color of the stone wall.

BOOM! BOOM!

I sprinted for the box as Jones returned fire and the man inside the front door ducked for cover.

I opened the box and slapped a round red button. I heard the sound of a chain turning on a wheel, and the gate slowly lifted.

"Reilly!" A voice sounded from the front door.

I spun to see Thick-neck in a prone position, his weapon pointed at me. My heart jumped, and I knew this was it—

BOOM, BOOM, BOOM!

A sharp pain tore at my cheek as chunks of stone splintered from bullets. I fell to the ground.

My hand clenched, my eyes closed tight, and a *pop* sounded in my ears. The hot red liquid of life poured down my cheek and over my eyes, skewing my vision.

"Reilly's been hit!"

Was that Jones?

He returned fire into the front door of the promontory, but Thick-neck had disappeared into the mansion.

There was more gunfire outside the wall.

Jones rushed forward, his weapon raised.

BOOM!

Silence followed his single shot.

He stepped outside and waved his arms.

I lay there, covered in the red elixir that had poured out from under my hat.

"It's clear, Reilly," Jones said.

I sat up, removed the Last Resort hat from my head, and pulled the bullet hit squib from inside my hat where Lenny had mounted it. The film industry used the same special-effects device on actors to simulate being shot. Lenny had obtained it from a studio friend of Heather's this morning, and with any luck, the charade would have the desired effect.

The first two teams came forward, one from the woods, their black outfits standing out against the snow. The other pair emerged from behind the grouping of G-Wagons, the closest one peppered with bullet holes, the side windows shot out. The men approached cautiously, scanning in all directions as they proceeded.

Jones and I kept our focus on the front door and windows looking into the courtyard, but there was no movement and no further gunfire.

That caused my heart to double-pump.

I had to stay out of sight, but the sense of urgency supercharged adrenalin through my veins. "We need to get inside, fast!" I said. "It's too quiet."

Jones replaced the clip on his weapon with a fresh one, and when the others arrived, he stepped forward. "Spread out and follow me."

I had no weapon and was trying to stay out of sight, so I stayed behind Jones in the center of the assault force. We made it all the way to the front steps without encountering any other resistance.

"Harry was on the second floor," I said. "Let's go—"

"Not until we secure the ground floor," Jones responded.

I bit my lip as the men fanned out inside the fortress to check the different rooms.

I rushed to the conference room where I'd met with Himmelman. I found plated food, half eaten, and glasses of water, ice still floating in them.

"They can't have gone far," I said. "Get upstairs!"

Cautious to stay out of sight, I hung back as Jones hurried out the door that Thick-neck had taken me through previously, then up the stairs with the team following two at a time. A couple of men surrounded me as I led them to the treatment room where I'd last seen Harry.

Fear flooded my mind, and my breathing became ragged.

What if he's dead in here?

Himmelman would not take kindly to us storming his impenetrable fortress, especially since we proved that is was penetrable after all. But when Thick-neck reported that he'd shot me in the head, it would force Himmelman's hand to keep Harry safe or there'd be no transaction for him to force his way into.

The massage suite was empty, and inside the locker area was—my reflection stopped me in my tracks. The fake blood on my face looked real—wait, what's this?

Someone had used soap to write "Gigi" on the mirror.

"Gigi," I said.

"Is that supposed to be a clue?" Jones asked.

What the heck is that? It was familiar, but—mental lightning struck.

"Gigi is the owner of the Hotel de la Ville in Monza where we're staying."

Jones's face remained inscrutable for a second, then his brow furrowed. "Do you think that's where they're going?"

"Possibly," I said.

A loud humming sound stopped our conversation.

My mouth dropped open. "The helicopter pad on the roof!" I said.

We rushed back into the hallway and started up another flight of stairs when we heard the unmistakable sound of a helicopter taking off.

"I have a rocket," one of the men shouted.

"No, Harry must be onboard!" I said.

Just then we heard another sound, this one of vehicles speeding in—or away; I couldn't be sure from where we were.

"Downstairs, quick," Jones said.

We followed him, again taking two steps at a time, but by the time we arrived at the front door, several of the vehicles were gone.

"Two of the G-Wagons are missing," one of the men said.

"Damn, he's right. There were three, now there's only one," I said. "What if they saw me alive and told Himmelman?"

The remaining G-Wagon was the one that had been shot up, most of its windows shattered.

Jones yelled. "Reilly, me, Three, and Four will take that G-Wagon. The rest of you search the property and wait for instructions."

I ran to the vehicle and climbed inside the passenger seat. Tempered glass from the driver's window was all over the seats and floor, but mine was intact. What if it wouldn't start? I glanced down and there were—

The driver's side door was pulled open, and Jones jumped in as two more men climbed in the back.

"No keys!" I said.

Jones grunted, climbed back out, then crawled down under the steering wheel and started to pull wires. In less than a minute I noted a slight smell of smoke, glanced down, and saw a spark as Jones touched some wires together. The G-Wagon roared to life. He jumped back into the driver's seat and jammed the vehicle into gear.

I wiped the fake blood off my face with my hands and rubbed them on the dashboard. It was a mess but hopefully had accomplished the goal.

Tire tracks from the vehicles that departed before us had left a trail in the thin layer of snow, and it was just enough to see where they'd gone. Jones accelerated forward and cold air whistled through the vehicle's interior. The gate on the edge of the property was closed and there was no longer any guard. Jones floored the accelerator and crashed through the gate, sending shards of wood and metal up over our windshield. It only took moments to retrace the distance that I'd walked just yesterday when I first came here.

At the bottom of the hill, I saw that the trail toward Rifugio Scotoni was clear of any tire tracks, so at least Bianca would not be placed in the middle of this mess. Jones continued to follow the fresh tire tracks on the main road, and we began to descend, zig-zagging our way through switchbacks as we got out of the forest and into open country.

Our vehicle slipped and fishtailed through corners due to the wet, slick conditions, and I feared Jones might kill us all. My heart skipped as I saw the road ahead curve back at a steep angle due to a switchback. As we hurtled toward the apex of the sharp curve, someone yelled out from the backseat.

"There! I spotted two G-Wagons a couple of curves ahead."

I peered over, and sure enough, two of the black vehicles disappeared behind the next rock outcroppings. Jones pressed down on the accelerator and our vehicle became even less stable on the slick road.

"You'll kill us before we catch them," I said. "They're too far ahead."

The GPS map on the dashboard showed a series of maybe six switchbacks ahead as the road carved through the mountains. We came out into the open and could again see Himmelman's fleet down below us, with multiple more switchbacks ahead.

"I have an idea," Jones said.

"What's that—"

Before I could finish my question, Jones turned sharply to the left, hurtling over the edge of the road and launching down through snow-covered gravel and low shrubbery, straight down the hill toward the next switchback.

"Joooonnnneeeessss!" I shouted.

SLAM!

We crashed into the shoulder of the road below and bounced up onto the paved surface, skidding and sliding, but Jones was able to get the vehicle under control.

"You crazy bastard!" I said.

I checked the GPS: only three more switchbacks ahead until the road straightened. The two G-Wagons appeared below us, now one level closer, and I knew Jones would repeat the insane maneuver. Sure enough, once we got to the apex, he again jumped the edge of the road— this one was steeper—we went airborne—*crash!*

The front of the vehicle dug into gravel and the shriek of metal caused me to wince. The front bumper spun to the side and slapped against my door, shattering the passenger-side window—the only one that hadn't been shot out earlier.

"There they are!" Jones yelled.

I glanced up just as he rocketed over the lip of the shoulder, again launching free of the ground right toward—

CRASH!

We slammed into the side of the lead vehicle, airbags blasting out, smashing me and Jones into the backs of our seats and momentarily blinding us.

We had come to a stop, but we were tilted up at a sharp angle, held up by the vehicle we'd crashed into. I heard the rear doors open as our two other men jumped out to approach the other vehicle.

My head was ringing, and my chest felt as if an elephant had jumped on it. Fortunately I'd put on my seat belt when Jones started driving like a man possessed.

BOOM!

A gunshot sounded.

BOOM! BOOM!

I scrambled for my door handle, fighting to free myself from the airbag, and I could sense Jones next to me doing the same. The door would only open a third of the way, no doubt crumpled from the impact with the other vehicle. I squirmed through it and landed in the gravel.

"Reilly?" A voice called.

My heart stopped for fear of what would come next.

25

ONCE I GOT ON MY FEET AND PEERED OVER THE HOOD
of the G-Wagon, I saw that careening into the side of their lead vehicle
had pinned and killed two of Himmelman's guards on the passenger side
and seriously injured the driver.

"Reilly, back here," Jones said.

I walked around the back of our vehicle, which looked as if it had
been dropped from a plane and crumpled like a beer can on impact. It
was a miracle none of us had been seriously injured.

What I saw next caused my eyes to bug wide.

One of our troops had a gun pressed against the temple of one of
Himmelman's men, who was on his knees with his hands up. I noted
two bullet holes through the windshield on the passenger side of the rear
G-Wagon and could see a man slumped over inside. I glanced back at
the man I recognized as Three.

"Why'd you kill him?"

He pointed to his leg, and I saw blood soaking his pants. "Bastard
almost blew me balls off."

Jones and I hurried over to where our other man held the remaining
black-clad guard at gunpoint.

"Where's Himmelman and Harry?" I asked the guard.

The guard glanced up, his face bunched into a mask of defiance. He
didn't respond. Jones stepped forward and kicked him in the face, wiping
off the insolence like it was milk on a child's upper lip.

"Where the hell are they?" he asked.

The man tried to rub away the blood that now poured from his
nose, but there was too much. Jones must've shattered it.

"Gone," the man said. He then leaned forward and spat a wad of
blood on the gravel in front of him, then looked up at the fake blood on

my shirt, staining my face and neck, and still matting my hair. "I was told you were dead."

"Resurrection came fast," I said. "Now where are they?"

"Flew away on the helicopter."

"Where were they going?" I asked.

The man glared up at me, lips tight.

I stepped forward, reached down, took his neck in my hands, and started squeezing it. The man wriggled below me as I squeezed tighter. The anger, frustration, fear, and anxiety his boss had caused me, along with Harry's threats of betrayal, bubbled over. Tunnel vision narrowed my focus to the raw emotion that consumed me.

"Buck—hey!"

Jones grabbed my arms and shook free my grasp from the man's throat.

"We need him alive, Reilly," he said. Then, to the now terrified soldier, "Where'd they go, mate?"

The man, still crouched on his knees, rubbed his throat with his right hand. He cleared his throat a couple of times then nodded once. "He said they were going back to Monza."

I stepped forward again. "Monza as in the town? Or to the autodromo?"

The man nodded slowly. "He'll kill me if he knows I told you."

"And we'd have killed you if you didn't," Jones said.

"Something about a hotel to wait for the end of the race," the man said.

"And the prisoner, Harry Greenbaum, was still alive?" I asked.

The man held up his hand to block his face as if I were going to hit him. "Yes, very much alive. Jolly, even."

"Jolly, huh? Hmm."

The man's report was questionable, but we also had not found a body or evidence of foul play, so maybe he was telling the truth. I hoped so for everyone's sake. I checked my watch and felt a fresh surge of concern shoot through my system.

"The race starts in two hours. We need to get back to Monza ASAP," I said.

The chopper was deployed to Cortina," Jones said. "We can take the remaining G-Wagon to get there."

I imagined Ray at Linate with the others getting ready for their flyover at the start of the race. It felt like a month ago that we'd arrived for what I thought was that specific purpose. Why hadn't Harry been truthful with me from the outset? Everything would have gone so much smoother.

"What about this mess? These dead men, and this guy?" I pointed to the man on his knees.

"We'll explain to the Carabinieri later. For now we need to go." Jones said. "Take his phone and throw him in the back. We can't allow him to call his boss or talk to the cops."

Traffic had begun to queue on both sides of what looked like a horrendous automobile accident. The wail of a distant siren sprung me into action.

"Right, let's go."

We mounted up in the remaining G-Wagon, and true to form, Jones pointed it downhill and bypassed the backed-up traffic by once again skipping the next switchback but, thankfully, more slowly this time. We cautiously crossed over the road's shoulder and were able to slip between two cars that had parked as they awaited the resolution of the traffic situation up the hill.

If they only knew.

When Jones steered onto the road again, he continued like a normal driver—albeit with half the windows shot out of the vehicle—toward Cortina d'Ampezzo, fifteen minutes away. I unbuttoned my breast pocket, pulled out my cell phone, and held down the number one until the ring began on the other end.

"Hello, Buck? Is that you?"

"Yes, Heather, it's me."

"Did you get Harry?"

I bit the side of my lip. "Unfortunately not. The operation went, ah, okay, but they got away in the helicopter before we could reach them."

"Damn," she said. "I'm so glad you're safe."

If she saw the fake blood on me, she might feel differently. "Our ruse seemed to work, at least so far. We caught up to some of Himmelman's men, and one of them shared their next steps."

"Voluntarily?"

"Kind of."

"Um, Lenny and Matt Sterling are here too … let me put you on speaker."

I waited a few seconds, then continued. "From what we've learned, it sounds like Himmelman is taking Harry back to Hotel de la Ville. The guard said Harry was in good spirits, so maybe they think Harry capitulated. But I'm not sure."

"I certainly hope not," Sterling said. "We'll have no choice but to default his contract if Sir Harry has agreed to partner with the likes of Himmelman."

"I'll check with Ray on Trojan Horse, so don't give up yet."

I just hoped this whole plan wouldn't blow up in my face.

A click sounded in my ear and I looked at the phone; a call from Ray was coming through.

"Guys, Ray's calling me, I'll call you back—but don't mention my name to anyone or this whole thing could blow up."

I hit end then answered his call.

"Ray?" I said.

"You're alive." A loud exhale caused distortion on the line.

"The stage is set. Himmelman thinks I'm dead. Tell me some good news."

"Trojan Horse is in the paddock, heading for the starting gate."

I pumped my fist twice.

"Good man. Thank your gaming buddies for me—but not until later. We need to have everyone else think I'm dead."

Jones glanced over from behind the wheel. "What was all that about?"

"All the pieces are in place. Now it's up to Harry."

"So what do we do?"

"Focus on getting us to that chopper. Time for the next phase of the plan."

26

RATHER THAN GOING TO THE *AUTODROMO*, I guided the pilot to a destination further south: the Royal Villa of Monza, across the street from the Hotel de la Ville. He set the chopper down on the grass behind the Royal Villa, which attracted the attention of tourists wandering the formal grounds. When we jumped out, with most of the men dressed in black battle gear and carrying automatic weapons, these same gawkers fled down the walking paths away from the Villa.

The text I was hoping and praying for finally came through. It was from Harry.

"I'm free and here to do the deal."

"Thank God," was my response. "Gigi still on?"

"For H, yes."

I sent a thumbs-up emoji.

"Leave the guns in the helicopter, guys," I said. "The hotel is surrounded by Tifosi and there are Carabinieri everywhere."

"But Reilly—"

"No butts about it, Jones. We have no official authority to be vigilante-ing our way around Italy, so as powerful as you're feeling right now, we don't want to get into a firefight with the authorities."

Jones grimaced, then turned to his men. "Leave the longarms in the chopper. Sidearms only—and keep them concealed."

I bit my lip. I wanted to say no guns at all, but I let it slide. The hotel would not be happy, but hopefully Himmelman had already arrived and was holed up in some suite to await the news that the deal had been consummated.

The four of us hustled around to the south of the Royal Villa, cut through a metal gate, and walked over the manicured lawn toward the

Viale Brianza, the main road that intersected with Via Giuseppe Sacconi. The Hotel de la Ville was right there on the corner, and we could see a smaller crowd of Tifosi there waiting. Most people would either be at the race or at the equivalent of an Italian sports bar to watch the contest, but these few die-hard fans didn't want to give up their position on the wall, hoping to catch a glimpse of their heroes once they returned from the autodromo.

A loud roar sounded overhead, and I glanced up in time to see Big Mama flying lead, two smaller planes on each side of her, as they headed toward the autodromo to commence the festivities. A moment later, they simultaneously released colored smoke from cannisters mounted to each plane's wings, with red coming from the two planes on the left side of Big Mama, white from our plane, and green from the two on the right side.

I couldn't help but smile.

"Good job, Ray."

When I glanced down, I realized people were staring at us, not the planes, with me in tropical attire surrounded by the men in black tactical gear. It gave me an idea.

"Guys, pretend I'm a celebrity and you're my bodyguards so we don't freak people out."

Jones nodded, and given that their real jobs were as bodyguards, they fell into place around me. I donned my sunglasses and strutted across the road when the traffic signal changed, and every single Tifosi there watched us approach. I heard different names mentioned as some speculated incorrectly who I was, and I raised my hand to block my face and further confuse them—all in the interest of playing the part.

Cheering began, and I steered the men to the same gate where the general manager, Riccardo, had let me in earlier. Fortunately, it wasn't locked, and a moment later we were all inside.

Tifosi continued cheering and calling to me, holding autograph books and magic markers through the fence for my signature and waving cell phones to request selfies. I turned away and earned a few boos.

Rather than leading the private militia inside the elegant establishment, I turned right and entered the restaurant, where I told them to take a seat and wait so I could find Gigi or Riccardo and inquire about Himmelman.

The men sat at a table, appearing highly uncomfortable and out of place.

At the front desk I could hear the fevered pitch of an Italian television announcer and found Riccardo and another man, both in tuxedos, hunched over a laptop. I stood at the front desk a moment and finally cleared my throat.

Riccardo glanced up quickly, and the gentle smile I'd grown accustomed to immediately bent his lips.

"Ahh, Mr. Reilly, forgive me. The race is about to start, and Ferrari is on pole."

"Don't let me interrupt you," I said. "Just a quick question. Has Hans Himmelman arrived yet?"

"No, sir, but Mr. Himmelman called a moment ago to have the attendant open the gate for his car."

I stood up straight, a rush of adrenalin blasting into my veins. I wanted to hurry away but felt the need to warn him.

"Um, Riccardo, ah, there's a bit of a problem with Mr. Himmelman. He's been holding Sir Harry against his will, and I have a group of security people here in the restaurant to ensure the latter gentleman's safety."

Riccardo's smile faded like an ice cream cone under a heat lamp.

"There won't be any trouble," I said. "At least I don't think there will, but ah, it would be a good idea to keep staff and guests away from the parking area for the moment."

Now his face was all business. "I will call the Carabinieri—"

No!" I held my hand up, startling him. "That won't be necessary."

A bell sounded and he turned his attention to another closed-circuit monitor, then looked back up at me. "That's his car now."

"Okay, great. Sorry about this, but I, ah, promise there won't be any trouble—at least I hope not."

His eyebrows raised higher, and with nothing more I could say, I hurried back toward the restaurant. Ever vigilant, Jones saw me enter in a hurry and jumped up. I pointed toward the far end of the restaurant where a door led to the private parking area. From the window, I could see the gate open and a throng of people blocking the car's entry—no doubt Tifosi hoping to see a celebrity—but anyone here for the race would be there at the event now.

I led the way out the back door and watched as a large black Mercedes pulled into the parking area. The elderly man in a red windbreaker who was working the gate waved off people who sought to follow it in, then closed the gate.

Jones and his men took up positions on both sides of the Mercedes, and I walked in front of it trying to peer in the windshield, but it was darkly tinted. I walked to the passenger side of the car and stood waiting. None of our men had brandished weapons, but all had their hands poised to do so.

I had the sudden feeling of Clint Eastwood in a spaghetti western, albeit in a tropical linen shirt and lightweight khaki slacks.

The rear passenger door popped open, and my man standing near the rear quarter panel assumed a battle position. A white handkerchief suddenly appeared out the slit of the door, and whoever held it waved it back and forth across the top.

"At ease, men," I said.

The door pushed open further and the Mortician exited from the back of the vehicle.

"Mr. Reilly, what a surprise to find you here," he said.

"The reports of my death have been greatly exaggerated," I said.

I bent at the waist to peer inside and didn't like what I saw—or didn't see.

Himmelman slid out the same door and stood. He wasn't smiling. He was attired in a blue-and-white Williams-branded shirt with dark slacks and leather shoes. His broad smile caused my stomach to flip-flop.

"Fake blood, is it?" he asked. "Impressive."

"And Harry's safely at the track."

"Don't be so sure—"

"Time for you to back off, asshole," I said. "You now hold no cards."

Himmelman smiled, which after a second caused my gut to flop. "Sir Harry has already executed our electronic documents, Mr. Reilly. We're just in town to enjoy the Italian Grand Prix now, just like the other hundred and fifty thousand people here for the race."

My mouth fell open. "What do you mean the documents are executed?"

"I'm not a fool, Mr. Reilly. Before I returned Sir Harry to the autodromo to assuage Mr. Sterling's concerns and finalize everything at this afternoon's ceremony, we had our own ceremony. Once the other documents are executed electronically, our agreement will automatically amend yours, and we will be partners."

"Williams and the FIA will never allow it," I said.

I had no authority to speak on behalf of the Fédération Internationale de l'Automobile, but I assumed that would be the case.

"They'll never know. And if it's leaked, well, you, Sir Harry, Ms. Drake, Mr. Floyd, and everyone close to you will be looking over your shoulders for a very long time."

His eyes all but twinkled at the sight of me standing with my mouth hanging agape. He leaned closer.

"I could have you and your illegal band of mercenaries arrested with one phone call, Reilly." He paused, the smile turning cold. "You clearly have no idea who you're dealing with, do you?"

"What's your game here, Himmelman? Why do you care so much about being part of an F1 team?"

He licked his lips. "I'm surprised you haven't figured it out." He paused as if he were deliberating. "As an insider on one of the teams, we'll be in a position to change the outcome of races—"

"By helping them improve their engineering?" I asked.

He scowled. "Don't be a fool. By betting and using our cars to defy the odds."

"What?"

"When it comes to racing, there are numerous options to place bets—not just on who wins, but also who is on pole, who will be on the podium, or head-to-head betting on the order, say, in which two drivers will finish. Or whether a safety car will appear—all these lines of betting we can manipulate from the inside."

"You can't control the drivers or team principals."

"We will have the existing ones replaced by others we can control."

I stood staring at him, my mouth hanging open again.

As he said, I should've figured this out on my own. Of course an organized crime player like Himmelman would seek to manipulate races, even in small ways to control betting, and would then make a fortune doing so.

"Un-fucking-believable."

Himmelman then smiled and took a step toward me. "And we'll make you rich in the process." His eyes narrowed. "But if you interfere further, and my transaction is derailed for any reason whatsoever, then I will create mayhem for all."

His matter of fact statement caused my mouth to drop open.

The Mortician stepped forward. "We should go soon, sir. This is no longer a safe place to await the end of the race. We should go to the autodromo or we may have difficulty getting into the VIP suite before the appropriate time."

Himmelman's blue eyes shimmered in the afternoon light, and a slight breeze tousled a wisp of his blond hair. "We wouldn't want to miss that, now would we?" He then turned back to me. "Would you like a ride, *partner*?"

I stepped back as if from the strike of a rattlesnake.

"No thanks, Himmelman."

He bowed slightly. "Suit yourself." He then glanced at the Mortician, and all his fake geniality faded away. "Let's go."

The Mortician limped to the other side of the car and got in.

"Buck?" Jones asked.

His arms were spread wide as if to ask if we were just going to let them drive away. I shook my head, implying that he should stand down. We watched as the large Mercedes backed up toward the gate and the old man in the suit and red windbreaker stood up off his stool and ambled in an unbalanced posture to unlatch it.

"What the hell's going on here?" Jones asked.

"We've got to get to the track, ASAP," I said.

Everything now rode on Trojan Horse.

THE RACE IS ON

27

BACK INSIDE THE HOTEL RESTAURANT, I CALLED HEATHER ON MY PHONE and put it on speaker. It rang several times before she answered. When she did, the noise in the background caused me to pull the phone away from my ear.

"Buck, are you there?" she asked.

"Crazy noisy over there," I said.

"The crowd's going wild. They just pushed the cars out onto the grid to prepare for the start. Only about thirty minutes away now, and with Leclerc's Ferrari on the front row, the Tifosi are beside themselves with excitement."

"I'm at the hotel and just talked to Himmelman—"

"Harry just arrived here at the track." Her voice raised a couple octaves. "He looks a mess and doesn't seem happy. But I'm guessing the plan worked?"

"Depends on Trojan Horse. Harry was forced to sign Himmelman's deal."

She was silent, but the noise in the background filled the void.

"Where is Harry?" I asked.

"He and Sterling hurried up to the conference room and wouldn't let anyone else join them. The head of security here at the track—what's his name?"

"Mazza," I said.

"He's furious about being kept in the dark. He has the Carabinieri wound up too." She paused when the crowd roared loudly. "What did Himmelman say?" she asked when the noise quieted down.

"He said Harry was there to do what they had discussed in order to protect me—us all, really."

"Dear God."

"This whole thing is about being able to manipulate gambling from inside a team." I paused. "He said something else, too, something about creating mayhem if we double-cross him, but I don't have any idea what he meant about that."

"Mayhem?" she asked. "Well, there's thousands of people here, so if they plan to create mayhem, it could be a serious mess."

Jones and I stared each other in the eyes as my conversation with Heather played out. His grimace was serious, and when he pinched his lips together, he pointed outside and mouthed the words, "Let's go."

"Okay, Heather. Can you and Lenny stay close to Harry? Jones and I are going to ride over on bikes; it's the fastest way to beat the crowds."

She grunted. "Lenny's doing what you told him and being very visible to throw off Himmelman's spies. He's off in the paddock chasing after celebrities and drivers and is now the newest and most ardent Formula 1 fan."

"That game's over. Find him and remind him we brought him here for a reason. I'll see you shortly."

When I disconnected, Jones and I jumped up and hurried into the lobby. Riccardo was behind the reception desk, an older man with him. It was Gigi, the owner. He spotted me and stepped forward.

"Mr. Reilly, is everything all right?" His normal genial smile was gone and his eyes were serious.

"Too soon to say, Gigi, but Harry, ah, *Sir* Harry is okay. That was my initial concern."

"Riccardo said that Mr. Himmelman had been holding him against his will? What did he say in the parking lot? He never came inside."

I pursed my lips. Spreading the word on Himmelman's plans to force his way into Harry's deal wouldn't help the situation. "He drives a hard bargain, that guy." I glanced back toward Jones behind me. "We want to get over to the track. Can we use bicycles again?"

"Of course, of course. It's about to start so there shouldn't be too much pedestrian traffic in the park."

Riccardo looked up and waved to Gigi. "They're starting the formation lap."

My lack of knowledge about the sport must have registered on my face as I had no idea what that meant. Gigi's smile returned.

"The drivers do a single lap around the track at slow speed to warm their tires just before the start. Should be only five minutes to light's out—the start of the race."

"We're out of here," I said. "Thank you."

Gigi bowed slightly as I ran toward the front door with Jones in tow.

"We're riding bikes?" he asked. "The helicopter is just over there—"

"It's faster, trust me."

We found two bikes on the right side of the hotel, and when we wheeled them toward the gate near the corner, I realized only a handful of Tifosi remained. Once outside, we mounted up, dodged traffic at the intersection, rode on the sidewalk for a block, then cut through a gate there to enter the park.

What had been beautiful grass fields yesterday were now filled with rows of cars. I rode as fast as I could through them, then down the dirt trails through the grasslands up to the main gate. We flashed our credentials then rode down the paved road, weaving around late groups of pedestrians on their way to the *Autodromo*. We flew past the concession stands toward the field on the right where the helicopters were parked, then left down the hill and under the tunnel that led to the VIP entrance. As we'd gotten closer, the roar of the cars storming past had grown to an ear-shattering decibel level.

We left the bikes leaning against the inside of the fence where I'd recovered one yesterday, then jogged through the VIP entrance, using our credentials on the electronic turnstiles. Sweat poured down my back and my face was soaked, as was my shirt and my ass from sitting on the bike seat. My vision swirled as I hurried through the VIP tent where TVs showed the cars racing around the track. The bars were three deep with patrons, and waitstaff circulated with trays of hors d'oeuvres. I didn't think I'd eaten a bite all day, but now wasn't the time.

Outside we navigated the labyrinth to get into the paddock, where, thankfully, the crowd was minimal. The teams were busy in the pits, the commentators were in their booths, team managers were in their trackside stalls, and I presumed ownership groups were entertaining family, friends, and business associates in their private condos. We hurried down toward the end where the three-story, gray Williams condo reflected the afternoon sun.

"Jones, Reilly!" A voice shouted from between team buildings.

We stopped and turned to find Director of Security Mazza rushing toward us with his cadre of Carabinieri. He appeared to literally chew his lower lip as he came our way. None of the group smiled. By the time he arrived he was breathing heavily.

"You two have been bloody busy!" Spittle shot out of Mazza's mouth as he shouted.

"Let me handle this," Jones said. He stepped forward. "What are you talking about?"

"There are all kinds of rumors about the missing British knight, attacks on mountaintop castles, and all types of malfeasance."

I didn't trust Jones to field this without causing more trouble, so I interjected, "Impressive word choice there, Mazza."

He shifted his attention to me, the corners of his mouth angled down in a decided sneer.

"My understanding is that Sir Harry Greenbaum is here at the race," I said. "Doesn't the security system confirm badge swipes?"

He leaned back and narrowed his eyes. "Here? Where?"

"Pretty sure he's in a trackside VIP suite sipping champagne and watching the cars drive in circles," I said.

"The track isn't circular," he replied. "When you see him, I need to talk to him."

It was my turn to appear confused. "What do you need him for?"

Mazza turned and looked at the pair of Carabinieri, who exchanged a glance, and the uniformed woman shook her head slightly from side to side. That did arouse my curiosity. Was the word out on Himmelman's threats?

"As you were told, Sir Harry and I will become part owners of the Williams team at the end of the race, so if there's a security issue, we have the right to know."

Uncertainty bent Mazza's brow.

I was a proponent of taking the high road when it came to throwing law enforcement off unwanted trails of inquiry.

"There's nothing specific," Mazza said.

He then cleared his throat and, as if answerable to a higher authority than the Carabinieri, shuffled his feet a moment, but then stood firmly, crossed his arms, glanced from the police officers back to me, and licked his lips.

He leaned closer to us. "However, there are rumors of potential foul play here during the race."

"During the race?" I asked.

Himmelman threatening me and Harry was high on my list of concerns, but Mazza's information felt broader. Could it be the mayhem Himmelman had alluded to?

"What kind of foul play?" Jones asked.

Mazza wouldn't look Jones in the eye. "I'm not entirely sure, but there's an elevated security concern as we try to get to the bottom of the rumors."

"But who—"

I squeezed Jones's shoulder from behind him as he stepped toward Mazza.

"Good to know, Director," I said. "If we learn anything about that, we'll be in immediate contact."

His eyes narrowed again as he looked from me to Jones and back. "You do that, Reilly." He chewed his lip a second, then said, "You said Sir Harry's in one of the VIP suites? Williams's, I presume, given your news about the investment into their team."

"That would be logical," I said.

Mazza hesitated a moment, then pivoted partially on his heel toward his bookend colleagues. He nodded them forward toward the pits, the VIP suites above them with a clear view of the start / finish line.

"Let's go," he said.

The threesome hurried off as Jones and I watched.

"What do you think he was referring to?" Jones asked.

"I don't know, but I don't like the sound of it. You know what they say, 'Hell hath no fury like a criminal scorned.'"

"Thought it was woman scorned."

"That too. Let's get to the Williams condo and see if Harry's there."

His brow furrowed. "But you said—"

"Let's go, Jones."

28

THE CROWD IN THE PADDOCK WAS MINIMAL, EXCEPT FOR A—What's that ahead?

I paused, and Jones, who had been following close behind me to fight through the crowd, crashed into my back.

"What are you stopping for?" he asked.

I couldn't believe my eyes, but a television interview filming in front of us had caused a small horde ahead. There was Lenny, standing inside the circle with Sylvester Stallone and will.i.am while the latter two gave interviews.

"What the hell?" I said.

"I didn't realize your friend was a celebrity," Jones said.

"He isn't."

I pushed my way forward, but security for the stars stepped in our path and shouted that we need to stop. Stallone looked unphased, and when Lenny looked over and saw us, he stepped forward.

"Hey, yo!" Lenny said.

The security guard glanced back toward him.

"It's okay, brother, those two are with me," Lenny said.

The guards let us pass. The crowd pressed me close to Lenny. "I'm with *you*?" I asked.

"Yeah man, well, you know, I kind have these guys eating out of the palm of my hand," he said. "Just doing what you told me to do."

"Enough stargazing, Lenny. We need to get to the Williams suite," I said.

"Aww, man, Sly was taking me to meet some of his friends—"

"*Sly?*" I said. I grabbed him by the arm. "I need your help, Lenny. Now let's go."

His open mouth clamped shut and he glanced back once, but then he nodded and stepped forward.

Good grief. Only Conch Man could show up a couple of days earlier and parlay his paddock access into rubbing shoulders with the stars. After I literally pulled him by the arm for fifteen feet, he tugged free and I stopped to face him.

"Your moneyman, Harry, is back, man," Lenny said. "What's all the urgency about?"

Jones rolled his eyes.

I clamped my jaw tight for a moment, deliberating what to say. "He may be back, but he's not out of danger, and neither am I—or any of us for that matter. Himmelman can get us anytime—and if Trojan Horse works, he'll be plenty pissed, and the proverbial excrement will hit the fan."

"Excrement, huh? You getting all fancy over here in Italy. In Key West you'd just say shit."

"Where's Heather?"

"In that big gray box over there." He nodded toward the Williams three-story condo building. "Away from all the action. Hell, you gotta watch the race from the TV in there—you can't even see the track."

"That's where we're headed," I said. "Now, c'mon."

No sense debating the situation further with Lenny, who, as a former bartender turned politician turned preacher, was more adept at verbal sparring than I was. My strength, though rustier, was actual sparring, going all the way back to my Golden Gloves boxing days.

We arrived at the door to the Williams building and Jones stepped forward. The guard stationed there recognized him and practically saluted.

"Is the subject here?" Jones asked.

"Yes sir, upstairs meeting with the team owner."

"Sterling?" I asked.

The guard, who was cut from the same cloth as the rest of the Tactical International team had been—no doubt also a former Royal Marine—nodded his head. I didn't bother to correct him to say he was the chief executive but not the owner.

We walked past the guard and Jones told him to remain on duty and keep an eye out for Himmelman or any of his men. We stepped inside the air-conditioned reception area where the lone receptionist gave us a broad smile, but I ignored it and hurried up the staircase past the second floor and onto the third.

Upstairs was full, with people seated at the bar—

"Buck!"

I turned to find Heather jump up from a corner table with Claire Robbins, the woman we'd met here before. Dressed in blue heels, a white pencil skirt, and a blue silk blouse buttoned halfway, Heather ran over and grabbed me in an embrace.

"Finally, everyone's back," she whispered in my ear.

"This isn't over, Heather," I said.

She pulled back to gaze up into my eyes, hers now narrowed in confusion, then wide with recognition. "That explains the urgency to Harry's and Sterling's meeting—they're totally ignoring the race."

"We ran into the head of security for the track on the way over here," I said. "He mentioned something about rumors of potential foul play afoot."

"Here? At the race?"

"That's what he implied."

"From Himmelman, if you guys don't play ball with him?"

"I assume so, but remember, the next team in line after Harry is a hedge fund looking to gut the team, so who knows."

Her complexion lost some of its tanned color. "Are we in danger here?"

"I don't know, Heather, but we need to get to the bottom of it."

Jones stepped over to us. "What's the status?"

I nodded toward the closed conference room door. "Harry and Sterling must be in there."

"Ray, too. They left instructions for nobody to disturb them," Heather said.

"Screw that," I said.

I walked to the door, hesitated, and knocked once. I heard no sound, so opened the door to find Ray, Harry, and Sterling hunched over a laptop. Their initial expressions were serious and maybe annoyed until they saw it was me.

"Buck, good to have you back," Harry said.

"Join us, Reilly," Sterling said.

Jones, Heather, and Lenny hesitated in the doorway. Sterling waved them inside too.

"Mazza briefed me on rumors of foul play," I said. "What's the latest?"

Sterling stood tall and crossed his arms. "Let's just say it was a good thing you advised me of Himmelman's plot to infiltrate our ownership through threatening Sir Harry's and your lives." Then he nodded to Ray. "And your colleague here has proven to be quite adept at hacking the electronic system that controls our contract and the one Sir Harry signed with Himmelman."

"Under duress," Harry said.

My stomach clenched as I looked past Sterling to Ray, who appeared as nervous as I'd ever seen him, and Harry, who remained inscrutable. Was he angry with me? Would he release the evidence on insider trading to the FBI as he'd threatened if I interfered with his plans? My eyes locked onto his, but he gave me nothing.

"Ray, you said your team was successful, right?" I asked, my eyes still watching Harry.

"We were able to modify the electronic document to create an instantaneous trap door," he said, "which changes your entity to a series of accounts in different countries that will be impossible to track, much less hack."

Ray's description of what they had done was over my head—techno-logically speaking.

Harry now had a fresh smile pulling at the corners of his mouth. "Thanks to Ray Floyd, once we sign our documents with Williams, then Himmelman—along with the backup investor who stood to benefit if we were unable to proceed—will be notified immediately that all has been finalized. And as soon as he attempts to synch his contract with ours, it will malfunction."

"Congrats on the success of your operation in the Dolomites," Sterling said to me and Jones.

"I thought you'd failed at first," Harry said. "Seeing how they whisked me away, and then I learned you'd been killed and ..." Harry paused. "... "I was crushed. Himmelman said Heather and your friends would be next, so I signed the bloody document not knowing that had been your plan all along."

"Operation Trojan Horse," I said.

"Turnabout is fair play, after all," Harry said. "Not only will the contract I signed evaporate, but it's also booby-trapped. Brilliant, Raymond."

I'd never heard anyone use his full name before. Ray beamed.

"What about your nasty threats back in the Dolomites about turning me in to the FBI?"

"Sorry about that, lad, but I knew they were listening, and we had to make a good show of it."

My heart skipped and I let out a long exhale. "You certainly had me fooled."

With that, Sterling opened the laptop in front of him on the table.

With a satisfied grin, he slid the computer in front of Harry. "After all this, I'd rather not wait for the silly ceremony at the end of the race. Sir, Harry, can we conclude this transaction, once and for all?"

Aside from Harry participating in deals to back e-Antiquity, I'd never seen him in action before. The warm smile that bent his lips turned his cheeks rosy too.

"With pleasure, Matthew."

Harry pulled the computer closer to him, scanned through the document one last time, no doubt confirming it was the latest version, then used his index finger to provide his electronic signature. I couldn't help but smile seeing the joy this gave Harry, even though it had nearly got us both killed.

"All done?" I asked.

"Not quite, dear boy."

To my surprise, Harry then used both hands to push the laptop in my direction. I glanced down and saw a blank signature block with my full name under it: Charles B. Reilly, III. I hadn't seen my name typed out in full since the last time I'd been arrested.

I glanced toward Sterling, who gave me a polite nod, so I sat down and scanned to the top of the document.

"What am I signing?" I asked.

"The partnership agreement to participate in the Williams Racing ownership syndicate," Sterling said. He cleared his throat. "You'll be a non-voting member and a backup to Sir Harry, should anything happen to him."

I looked up and gazed at Harry over the back of the computer screen. His smile remained, and after a few seconds of seeing my mouth hang open, he waved his hand at me with a quick impatience.

"Do get it over with, Buck. We've had enough barriers to conclude this transaction."

I swallowed, but my mouth had gone dry. The investment amount of €100,000,000 caught my eye, and I gave Harry another sidelong glance before paging to the end. That price was approximately ten percent of the value of a typical Formula 1 team, so it wasn't like Harry was buying a controlling interest, but still, it was a ton of money, and I was a part of the deal.

My hand shook as I lowered my index finger to the screen and swirled a nearly unrecognizable signature above my name. I let out a long exhale then smiled at the two men in front of me.

"My solicitors will send you wiring instructions this afternoon." Harry was speaking directly to me.

"What?" I mustered.

His smile faded. "For your pro rata share of the investment. Fifty percent, my dear boy."

I choked and both men started laughing.

Harry turned to Sterling. "He believed me!"

"Very funny, gentlemen."

Sterling reached over and pulled the laptop back toward him, busily pressed a number of keys, then closed the lid.

"*Now* we're all done."

Neither man moved as I squirmed in my Recaro seat. "What's next?" I asked.

"We'll get a notification through the Trojan Horse when Himmelman signs," Ray said.

"Shouldn't be long, I suspect," Harry added.

"Until what?"

"Until Himmelman either threatens retaliation or seeks to exact revenge."

I swallowed. Ray appeared pale.

"When I saw him at the hotel, he said he would cause mayhem if we double-crossed him." I paused. "They'll come after us."

Ray's eyes narrowed. "I certainly hope so. In booby-trapping his document we coordinated with Tactical International to set a phishing snare that will be embedded in his personal computer. Through that we will monitor all communications and detail whatever records or communications for his criminal activities he has stored on there."

Just then, the familiar *ping* of a text sounded. Ray lifted his cell phone off the table and read the screen.

"That's my notification that Himmelman has signed his version of the document."

"Which also means our phishing attack has commenced." Harry leaned back in his chair, which creaked under his girth. "I think I can hear the Austrian bastard screaming from here," he said.

"Why did he want in so badly?" Ray asked.

"Gambling," I said. "He bragged about how he could manipulate all aspects of outcomes associated with races by planting people inside the organization."

"Appalling," Sterling said.

Harry and Sterling sat back in their chairs, but my elbows remained on the table and my palms gushed perspiration. As self-satisfied as Harry looked right now, I wondered if he realized the intensity with which a man like Himmelman could come at us.

Trojan Horse or not, violence would just be another form of negotiation for our adversary. Harry would be well protected, but what about me?

Or Heather?

Or Ray or Lenny?

29

DIRECTOR OF TRACK SECURITY MAZZA had joined us in the third-floor conference room, along with Heather, Lenny, and Jones. Jones was in direct contact with Tactical International's data security team, which was monitoring the electronic traffic from Himmelman's computer. So far it had been minimal, but they were simultaneously copying all his files and seeking opportunities to expose his operations to the proper law enforcement agencies.

"Himmelman's here at the track, according to his electronic credentials," Mazza said.

"Do you know where exactly?" I asked.

He held up the pair of colorful badges on a lanyard around his neck. "These credentials do not have tracking capabilities, but he last swiped into the second-floor VIP level, which runs the full length above the pits."

That was a very expansive area in front of the paddock, next to pit lane, that provided the best view of the starting grid, the longest straightaway, and the finish line. Thousands of people had access to the VIP floor, and they were constantly moving around between different hospitality suites from various promoters as well as the different Formula 1 teams.

"We have people there searching for him," Jones said.

The race was on a large television screen mounted to the conference room wall, but the sound was muted. The lap counter in the top-left corner showed only ten of the fifty-three laps left to run.

"Why're the cars moving so slow?" Lenny asked.

We looked up at the screen, and the cars were indeed moving slowly around the track, following behind a Mercedes coupe with yellow flashing lights on its roof.

"There's a yellow flag," Sterling said. "There must have been a crash, or a car has broken down and is impeding the safe continuation of the race."

Just then the shrill sound of a phone ringing startled me.

Everyone reflexively checked their phones.

Harry held his up in the air. "Unidentified caller."

"Probably spam," Lenny said. "I get that shit all the time—"

Jones plugged a small black electronic device into the charging port on Harry's phone, then said, "Answer it, but don't put it on speaker. That may spook him."

Harry cleared his throat, swiped the slider across the bottom of his phone screen, and held the phone up to his ear.

"Hello?"

His aristocratic British manner of speech made the single word last nearly three seconds.

Harry's eyes went wide and he nodded his head quickly.

Jones had in an earplug that was also connected to the small device, and he gave everyone a thumbs-up that the conversation was being recorded. Harry's mouth puckered as he listened to what was said on the other end of the line, which had the rest of us on pins and needles.

"Sorry, old man, but it's not in the cards," Harry said.

There must have been a brief yet strong response because Harry's eyes opened wider, then he lowered the phone. The caller had hung up.

"It was Himmelman," Harry said.

"Here, I can replay the conversation," Jones said.

He placed the black device in the center of the table, and we all gathered around to hear the recording. He pressed a green arrow on top of the device.

"That was a foolish decision on your part, Mr. Greenbaum," Himmelman said. "I will give you one last chance to cooperate, or you will soon regret this decision."

Harry's voice sounded. "Sorry, old man, but it's not in the cards."

There was a slight pause.

"Then the blood is on your hands."

Himmelman's statement sent a chill up my spine.

The recording ended.

"What's that supposed to mean?" Heather asked.

We all looked from one face to the next, but of course none of us had a clue as to what the parting statement might have meant. In my mind, though, if the blood were on Harry's hands, that meant somebody else's blood, and another rush of chills curled my fingers. That could be any of us sitting around the table, or someone else close to Harry.

Harry turned to Mazza. "Would that be considered a threat punishable under law?"

Mazza grimaced. "I'm not a prosecutor, sir, but I would say no."

"Jones, anything from your team searching for Himmelman?" I asked.

He checked his phone and shook his head.

"He can huff and puff all he wants," Harry said. "After kidnapping me and treating me like a prisoner of war, he can rot in hell."

"You mean the massage at the Promontory, or the suite at il Sereno at Lake Como?" I said.

"Against my will, all of it." He curled his lip. "Don't forget the beatings."

A knock on the door caused everyone to jump. Jones rushed over, and with a hand over the bulge under his shirt—which I presumed to be a gun—he spoke loudly. "Who is it?"

"Alex Johnston," the voice behind the door said.

Jones glanced back at the table to scan our faces.

"Johnston is the head of the FIA, which is the governing body for world motor sports that enforces the rules for Formula 1," Sterling said. "Let him in."

Jones grimaced but opened the door abruptly. The tall, gray-haired man in a white button-down shirt with FIA on the breast pocket stood there alone and flinched at the sudden movement.

"Hello, Alex," Sterling said from across the table. "How may I help you?"

Johnston licked his thin blue lips and stepped into the room. He wore black jeans and tennis shoes, which made sense given the amount of walking around at a race, even though he held such an important role.

He cleared his throat. "Sorry for the, um, interruption."

Based on his voice, I immediately knew he was British.

"I just wanted to come congratulate you for the new partner." His eyes shifted to Harry. "And to you, Sir Harry, for entering the sport."

Sterling gave him a wry smile and nodded.

Harry donned what I considered a business-friendly smile, one I'd seen him use to charm potential takeover targets in the past. "Very kind of you, Alex. I'm pleased to support the Williams team."

"Yes, quite," Johnston said.

The man appeared somewhat distracted, even though it was he who had come here. Harry seemed to sense that as well, because he tilted his head forward and narrowed his eyes. "Is everything all right, old man?"

The man licked his lips repeatedly. "Well, I'm not sure, but apparently there is a heightened security issue here at the track."

Mazza stepped forward.

"We heard a similar rumor earlier. Do you have any more details, Alex?"

Johnston's eyes narrowed as he turned toward Mazza at the far end of the table. "I didn't see you there, Luigi, but you should check in with your office."

Mazza walked toward Johnston. "We have been dealing with another security matter."

Johnston's eyes sharpened. "Such as?"

Mazza hesitated and glanced toward Sterling, then Harry.

Harry sat forward. "I've been the victim of coercion by an Austrian mobster by the name of Hans Himmelman who sought to force his way into my arrangement with the Williams organization."

Johnston's mouth dropped open so wide I could see that old silver fillings covered all his molars. "Hans Himmelman? Dear God, that man has been a constant nuisance for the last five years."

I stepped forward. "How so?"

Johnston gave me a sidelong sneer. "And who are you?"

"Buck Reilly," I said. "I'm, ah—"

"Ah, the mystery partner in Sir Harry's syndicate," he said. "We researched you to approve his bid—"

Harry stirred in his seat, a grumble emanating from his throat.

"I'm sorry, Sir Harry, standard protocol for any changes in team ownership—even non-controlling interests—but there was hesitation over Mr. Reilly here."

I swallowed and felt blood rush to my cheeks but knew to keep my mouth closed.

"His history with e-Antiquity—"

"Where I was the lead investor," Harry said.

"Indeed," Johnston said. "And subsequently his, um, issues with Last Resort Charter and Salvage are well documented." He hesitated. "To be honest, it did cause us to pause—"

Harry pushed back from the table and the legs of his chair screeched across the floor. "Dear God, man."

"No offense to you, Sir Harry, but it is the likes of Hans Himmelman who has forced the FIA to increase its scrutiny on all forms of investment into the sport."

With a deep breath filling my lungs, I leaned closer to the man. "Again, how so?"

"Himmelman has made numerous threats to other team owners demanding that they allow him to invest, and when one succumbed—we think due to some form of blackmail—the FIA rejected the proposal on the grounds that more time was needed to study Himmelman's enterprise."

"How did he take that?" I asked.

"Not well, but it did defuse a tricky situation. The other team owner later confided in me that Himmelman had threatened violence if he was blackballed from future investment and that he would expose whatever, um, dirt he had on this poor man—his name I cannot reveal."

"Himmelman bloody well kidnapped me," Harry said as he lumbered to his feet.

Johnston turned sharply toward Mazza. "Why were we not informed?"

Mazza held up his hands. "Nobody told me either."

The FIA boss's stare rotated to Sterling, who had deer-in-the-headlights wide eyes.

"It's my fault," I said. "I was threatened by his men to keep it quiet, or they'd kill Harry if he didn't cooperate."

Johnston's eyebrows lifted higher. "And did you cooperate, Sir Harry?"

"We staged a double-cross, Johnston, fear not," Harry said. "Buck and my man Jones here—he's an operative with a private security firm, Tactical International—staged a daring rescue effort on Himmelman's mountaintop lair which flushed him back into the open, and he dropped me here to conclude the transaction. Buck's associate Ray Floyd there took appropriate measures to foil Himmelman's efforts by modifying the electronic documents, thereby rendering his subversive addendum useless."

Ray bowed.

Johnston's mouth sagged, and he sat quickly in one of the side chairs. "When did all this play out?" His voice was now a whisper.

"Moments ago," Harry said. "Himmelman called to appeal my decision, but I said it was final. Damn the torpedoes and all that."

Johnston looked up into Harry's eyes. "And his response?"

Harry now licked his lips. "Not good, I'm afraid. He said the blood will be on my hands."

"Bloody hell," Johnston said. "That brings us back to the security threat I mentioned at the outset."

"What's the source of the threat?" I asked.

"Anonymous, again, moments ago."

"What specifically was said?" Sterling asked.

"A veiled threat of violence here at Monza."

I glanced up at the silent television and saw that the lap counter was down to one lap left in the race.

"The race is almost over," I said.

Just then, Mazza let out a shriek.

All eyes turned to him, and his face suddenly turned ashen white as he stared at the phone in his trembling hands.

"What's wrong?" I asked.

"There's a bomb threat here at the *Autodromo*."

"Bomb?"

30

"I MUST RUN!" MAZZA SAID.

"Details, man!" Johnston said, up on his feet.

Mazza had a death grip on the doorknob, but he turned to look back at the FIA director. "There was an anonymous phone call stating that a bomb had been placed in a highly populated area here at the track."

It was as if the oxygen had been sucked out of the room.

"What did the caller demand?" I asked.

"The caller demanded nothing. He said it was for revenge."

Jones immediately pressed buttons on his phone and moved to the rear corner of the room.

"That's not all," Mazza said.

"That's not enough?" Lenny blurted.

"One of the teams reported that a man dressed in FIA clothing was seen making inappropriate inspections on a race car that had just entered pit lane a moment ago."

I again glanced at the TV and saw that the race was over. The top three cars were Red Bull, Ferrari, and Aston Martin, in that order. The screen showed bedlam in the stands and people swarming the track.

"We do inspect cars on a random basis as part of our purview," Johnston said.

"All your people are well known by the teams," Mazza said. "This man was a stranger and acting suspicious. He was carrying a package and fled into the crowd when one of the pit crew asked what he was doing." He pulled the door open. "I have to get down there."

Jones hurried back over. "My team is searching for Himmelman but hasn't found him yet. Let's stay in touch!"

"Are you going to sound the alarm to warn the crowd?" Sterling asked.

Mazza hesitated, his jaw now quivering. "The Carabinieri fear it will cause widespread panic. We need to find this man immediately and put an end to the situation."

With that, he turned and ran toward the stairs where he disappeared in a flash.

The rest of us stared at each other with open mouths and wide eyes.

"What are we going to do?" I asked.

"I feel responsible," Harry said.

"Nonsense," Sterling said. "You heard Alex, Himmelman's a serial psychopath. Others have rejected his overtures before."

"But none have led to the sick bastard bombing innocent people," Harry said.

"Do we have access to pit lane and the victory ceremony?" I asked.

Sterling spun toward me. "Yes, ownership has all-access privileges. What do you have in mind?"

Jones started toward the door. I followed.

"I'm not sure, but my name's in the damn contract, too, and we can't allow our double-cross of Himmelman to cost innocent lives."

I glanced around and nobody argued against my point.

"Come on, Lenny, let's go!" I said.

"I ain't going down there!"

"I'm coming!" Heather said.

Lenny rolled his eyes, no doubt realizing he couldn't allow Heather to show more courage than him.

"Ray, you stay with Harry," I said.

"I'll lead the way," Sterling said.

THE PADDOCK WAS AGAIN A MASS OF PEOPLE—PIT CREWS MOVING TIRE RACKS, television interviews and hordes of people all moving in one direction: toward pit lane. The most famous podium in Formula 1 was situated at the far end, suspended over pit lane and out to the track itself, where the three top drivers would collect their trophies in the winner's circle— actually constructed as a circle—and the winner's national anthem would play.

"That way," Sterling said. "Team members have a shortcut."

224

Given the location of the Williams condo where we'd met, we were now at the opposite end of the paddock from the podium and subsequently the far end of the pits. We were caught up in a crazed wave of people rushing to get as close to the ceremony as they could, but it was quite a hike. Jones was on point for our group of five, literally pushing between people and earning multiple angry admonitions and stares.

I stayed close behind Jones as we were jostled around, with Heather hanging onto my belt and Lenny and Sterling bringing up the rear.

I whacked Jones on the back, and he spun around to face me.

"Any news from your team?" I shouted.

We had hurried through a narrow corridor in the garage building in which the teams all had two service bays each, one for each car; they made more in-depth modifications there than in pit lane, where typically only tires and front nose sections were replaced during the race. Once we were outside into pit lane, the cheering Tifosi became more deafening than the race had been; even with an earbud in, Jones spun a finger next to his ear indicating he couldn't hear anything. He stopped suddenly to read texts on his phone. Under the circumstances, making calls was impossible.

The rest of us circled around him to try and make a sound barrier.

Just beyond the outer pit wall was the track itself, the long straightaway where the starting grid and finish line were situated. As far as my eyes could see, Ferrari's Tifosi, along with fans of all teams filled the track, waving flags and banners and cheering as they awaited the ceremony. Pit lane was crowded too, but more toward the far end, down by the elevated podium.

Jones scanned texts and finally looked up at us. "Our teams are going suite to suite searching for Himmelman, but some are private and unwelcoming to non-guests," he said.

"They have to get into every suite," I said.

"Oh, they are, by force in some cases," he said.

Jones suddenly placed a hand over his ear, cupping it to try to capture whatever someone was saying in his earbud. His eyes grew wide then narrow like a hawk's.

"One of the men has spotted an anomaly," he said.

"What's that mean?" I asked.

"Thousands of people are pushing forward in a throng down pit lane, but he's spotted one man in a white shirt fighting his way in this direction, away from the celebration."

"Is he wearing a white FIA shirt?" I asked.

"He didn't say, but sounds likely—"

He cupped his ear again, then glanced over to the garage building and stood on tiptoe to scan in that direction.

"He's just approaching the Alfa Romeo garage right now."

Taller than Jones, I could read the names of the teams stenciled above each service bay.

"Alfa Romeo is right there," I pointed.

It was the next bay down from where we stood.

"Fan out!" Jones said. "If you see him, grab him!"

I glanced quickly at Heather with the intent of telling her to stay back, but like us, she had fire in her eyes and no way would she accept being told to back off.

Jones shoved his way closest to the building, and I was behind him with Heather, then Lenny and Sterling, making a loose line across the oil-streaked pit lane. The smell of burning brakes and engines that had been running at two hundred miles an hour for a couple of hundred miles gave off the unmistakable smell of automobiles run hard and put away hot. I tried to look through the crowd for any inconsistency. I spotted someone coming toward us, rather than going with the steady flow forward—there!

A white blur hurried in our direction, bouncing off people and getting yelled at but offering no apologies nor looking back with any sense of regret.

"Jones!"

He immediately looked my way, then toward the center of pit lane where the man had broken into clear air and now jogged in a direction that would hit our invisible line, somewhere between me and Heather. Jones pivoted and hurried toward us, his eyes fixed on the white-clad target like a hammerhead shark zeroed in on a wounded fish.

I glanced at Heather, who also saw him, but beyond her, it appeared that Lenny and Sterling were focused on the outside perimeter and therefore oblivious.

White-shirt was approaching fast, reading the crowd as he went. I recognized him as one of Himmelman's men I'd seen at Lake Garda, the one who'd accompanied Thick-neck to retrieve me from my plane. Beak-nose.

I'd altered my course, now near Heather, the man coming right for us. I saw his eyes light up as he spotted Jones slashing across the crowd toward him, and he cut to his left toward the Jersey barrier that separated pit lane from the track.

If he was able to jump the fencing erected atop the barrier, he'd be lost in a sea of tens of thousands of cheering fans and we'd never find him, much less be able to hurry through the mass of bodies to search.

I cut to my right and sprinted toward the man, who was short but fit and looked young enough to be able to run as long and far as he'd need to—and to scale the pit fence like an agile monkey.

The sound of Jones's feet slapped the asphalt behind me. The man dove for the fence, held on, and started to scale it quickly as I closed the remaining distance—just in time to grab his foot as he neared the top.

He kicked at me, breaking free, but I jumped up and got hold of his foot and leg with both hands this time, then jerked him off the fence like a pesky vine growing up the side of a tree.

The man clattered to the ground—landing on his left shoulder with a clunk—then immediately rolled to his left and got on his knees, ready to spring, a knife now in his hand. I dove onto him and crushed him to the ground just as Jones arrived and stepped on the man's knife-wielding arm, pinning it.

Heather arrived and twisted the man's pinned wrist until the knife fell free. Lenny scooped it up and held out in front of him as if the man might break free and come at him.

Jones spun the smaller man around, face down in the rubber refuse from the degraded tires that had been shed by the cars over the course of the race. He bent the man's arm at an angle I thought might shear it from his shoulder.

"Aaaaaaagh!" the man shrieked.

"Where's Himmelman?" Jones shouted directly into the man's ear, inches away.

The thug struggled and Jones torqued his arm even further, causing another, higher-pitched shriek to spring from his mouth.

"I … we need … to get … farther … away!" the man said. His face was pressed sideways into the rubber and asphalt, but the fear in the one eye I could see was profound.

I bent down to look in his eye. "What's the hurry, Fritz?"

"It … will blow … soon!"

Jones bent the man's arm more sharply and I heard a tendon pop, followed by a pained shriek.

"What will blow soon?" I asked.

"The … bomb …"

"Bomb!" Lenny yelled.

"Where's Himmelman?" Jones persisted.

"Forget Himmelman, where's the bomb?" I asked.

"Where is it?" Jones's voice had the shrill urgency of brakes screeching.

The man was crying now, his shoulder socket and possibly elbow ruined. A snot bubble erupted from his nostril as he heaved.

"Jones," I said, "let up a little."

He did so slightly, and the man lay in a slump, not going anywhere.

"Where'd you place the bomb?" I tried to control my voice.

Between tears and blubbering, the man nodded his head toward the far end of pit lane. "Down … there."

"Where down there?" I asked. The urgency was back in my voice.

"In the motor … buried in an orange … compartment."

"What motor? What team?" I asked.

He shook his head, half burying his face in the degraded rubber again. "I'm a bomb maker … not … a racing fan."

"Holy hell," Sterling said. "The only fully orange car would be a McLaren, but others, including ours, have orange details depending on sponsors."

We all stood, but the bomb maker remained on the ground, now curled up in agony.

"We've got to go," I said.

"Buck," Heather said. "Let the authorities handle—"

"What about him?" Jones asked. He kicked the bomb maker.

"I'll stay with this bastard," Sterling said. He suddenly pulled credentials over his head and tossed them to me. "You're an owner now, but nobody knows that, so use these. They'll open every door. Good luck!"

I pulled his credentials over my head.

"We'll need it."

I hurried into the crowd followed by Jones, Heather and Lenny. The number of people in pit lane had significantly increased in the time since we captured White-shirt, and the orange signs of McLaren were beacons over the crowd's heads, drawing us forward.

31

JONES WAS ABLE TO GET A CALL OUT TO MAZZA, who in turn had radioed McLaren's head of security, to let them know we were on the way and tell them to empty their garage. Against my better judgement, Mazza and his Carabinieri handlers refused to provide them with details for fear of widespread panic. We arrived at the McLaren garage, which like the others consisted of two stalls, each containing a car—but void of people, several of whom milled about in front of the garage instead due to the warning from Security.

A man in dark glasses and an orange McLaren polo shirt jumped in our path.

"Can I help you?" His accent was British.

"Did Mazza call you? I'm Reggie Jones here on his behalf to take a quick look at the cars."

"The FIA normally does that after the podium ceremony—"

"This has nothing to do with the race," I said. "Please, have your team stay back."

The man reluctantly stepped aside.

"Jones, you and Lenny check this first car, and Heather and I will go inspect the one next door."

If looks could kill, Lenny's stare would put me in my grave, but if we didn't hurry, many could indeed die. Heather followed me past a cart of giant slick tires and a couple of nose sections sitting on a rack. Inside the garage was tight, and a clicking sound from the car initially concerned me, but I recognized it as the noise of metal cooling rapidly.

"The thing's half orange," Heather said. "And so damned big."

In reality, the paint job was orange in places: on the side of the nose, on the width of the narrow front top of the engine cover, on the halo, on the sidepod that was an air-intake, over the engine compartment, and on the rear wing.

"You check that side and I'll check this one. The bomber said it was buried in an orange compartment, so search for anything he could have opened quickly then stashed the device and fled."

I worked my way down the side of the car. The heat off the brakes was palpable, and I used the light on my phone to search inside the air intake on the side. I had no idea what should be in there, but everything visible was bolted down and looked as if it belonged. The intake behind the halo was empty, so I unscrewed the small threaded Tridair fasteners that released the engine cover. A blast of heat washed over me—

There was no bomb.

Heather and I met at the back of the car where there were a series of lights and air channels that must have been designed for both aerodynamics and downforce.

I crawled under the back of the car but saw nothing but more channels for air and a metal strip running down the car's length in the middle.

Back on my feet, I shook my head.

"Nothing," I said.

Heather frowned. "Me either."

"Buck!"

I recognized Lenny's voice and saw him back outside the garage. Jones appeared in a hurry next to him.

"Find something?" I asked.

"Nothing!" Jones shouted.

Damn.

We stood under the scrutiny of the concerned faces of the McLaren pit crew and management. I looked both ways up and down pit lane. It suddenly donned on me that Mazza had reported someone challenging the bomber before we even arrived at pit lane and that McLaren was in the center, which was largely vacant of people trying to see the podium ceremony down at the far end. If the man had fled, he must've been caught up in the crowd, which had slowed his pace.

"It's got to be down at the end," I said. I bit my knuckle. "What cars were in the top three?"

"Red Bull, Ferrari, and Aston Martin," Heather said. "That's who Fernando drives for."

"Are any of those cars orange?" I asked.

"Ferraris are red, Aston Martins green, and the Red Bull is black and red," she said.

"Stallone and I were checking out the Red Bull earlier, and she's right, it's red—but part of the red is surrounded by yellow, man," Lenny said. "Kind of looks orangey together."

Shit.

I glanced around and saw the two-level tire cart I'd seen earlier.

"Help me up here!" I said.

Lenny and Jones boosted me up, and once precariously balanced on top, straddling tires that were as wide as two normal tires, I peered down the lane toward the multitude of people facing the elevated podium. Just past them, and right before the podium itself, I saw the backs of the three winning cars lined up side by side.

Green on one side, red on the other, and … son of a bitch!

I jumped off the top of the tire rack and landed squarely on my feet.

"What'd you see?" Jones asked.

"It's got to be in the Red Bull car," I said. "Lenny was right, from here the back portion looks orange. What's worse, there must be a thousand people crowded around it—"

The words froze in my mouth as I looked past my friends up to the viewing area one level up, where the VIP suites were situated. My eyes must've revealed my surprise, because Heather's face twisted, and she looked at me as if I was having a stroke.

"What is it, Buck?"

I pointed up to the viewing deck. "Himmelman's up there."

Everyone spun to see where I was pointing. A few garages away, above the Haas sign, stood Himmelman and the Mortician, the latter staring through binoculars down toward the podium.

"Son of a bitch!" I said.

Jones pulled out his phone and hit send on a number but kept staring at the glass screen for what seemed like an eternity. He finally swung his wrist down, the phone clenched tightly in it.

"I can't get a signal."

Lenny and Heather each looked at their phones. Same. There were more than one hundred and fifty thousand people here at the *Autodromo*, and every single one was carrying a cell phone and probably texting pictures to their friends.

My heart raced and I knew there was no time to waste.

"Jones, take Heather, get up to the condo level, and grab that bastard."

"I'm staying with you," Heather protested.

"What about the bomb?" Jones asked.

"I'm now a partial team owner. Lenny and I should be able to get down there and try to find it—"

"I ain't going down by no bomb!" Lenny said.

Heather grabbed my arm. "No, Buck—"

"There's no choice!" I stared her in the eye, mine unflinching. "Get to safety and get that son of a bitch Himmelman."

Jones's teeth were clenched tight, and I knew he wanted to argue, but between my fresh ownership privileges that allowed access and his ability to rally his crew to detain Himmelman, it was the only option.

"Buck, no!" Heather said.

Jones grabbed her by the arm and swung her around toward the McLaren garage where they could pass through to the paddock then take the stairs up to the VIP level. I turned toward Lenny who was slowly shaking his head. I grabbed him by the arm and pulled him after me.

"Let's go, Lenny!"

32

WE PUSHED OUR WAY THROUGH THE MASS OF HUMAN EXCITEMENT gathered to watch the podium ceremony, which would be ready to commence at any second. Time was clearly working against us, but we pressed forward with me on point, repeatedly shouting "Emergency!" as we carved our way through the thick crowd.

Miraculously, everyone was more civil than you'd expect at most sporting events, and they largely leaned away just enough for us to squeeze through. On our right were the management boxes where the team principals and the drivers' strategists and engineers huddled together during the races, monitoring data constantly flowing back from the cars, electronically fine-tuning different performance aspects, and communicating with the drivers to update them on everything from lap times to incidents on the track. Most of these boxes situated on the wall between pit lane and the track were empty, so Lenny and I navigated our way to them and I waved Matt Sterling's ownership credentials to any track official who sought to impede our progress.

Finally, after what had seemed an eternity but must have been only a handful of minutes, we arrived at the perimeter of the ceremony where the team members of the top three finishers stood with satisfied smiles, laughing and giving each other high fives at their good fortune to win such a major event.

Miraculously, I spotted Mazza standing between the Ferrari on the right and the Red Bull in the center, staring back at the crowd with intense scrutiny on his face.

Security was thicker between the crowd and the race cars than at a presidential rally. We'd never be able to penetrate that to reach the Red Bull.

Damn it!

I turned to Lenny. "You need to create a diversion."

"Diversion? How the hell am I s'posed to do that?"

"Think fast and get creative." I gave him a nod.

He looked to his right and dove into the line of security in front of him, screaming at the top of his lungs, "Help! Help!" He waved his arms over his head with a crazed look of desperation on his face.

All the security guards around us closed in on him, and I spotted Mazza hurrying in our direction. Finally, when he was about ten feet away, I lowered my shoulder and drove through the gap Lenny's diversion had created between the guards.

Hands grabbed at me, but too late to stop my momentum to break into the hallowed ground of the podium and *Parc Fermé* where the teams were not allowed to touch the cars until after they'd been inspected.

Startled, Mazza spun toward me as I waved my arm, which grew harder by the second as security guards wrapped theirs around me, but I saw the head of security's eyes open wide with recognition. He rushed over.

"*Fermare! Fermare!*" he yelled.

I had no idea what that meant, but the guards released their grip as Mazza grabbed me by the shirt and pulled me toward him.

"Reilly! What the hell are you doing?"

I fell forward, tripping over the guards who had descended on me. I glanced back at Lenny, who was still in the grips of several men.

"Lenny!"

I waved my hand for him to come forward, and Mazza stepped toward them, yelling in Italian until they let Lenny go and he stumbled toward us.

"What's going on?" Mazza said. His expression was both intense and stunned.

"We found the bomber—and Jones is on his way to apprehend Himmelman up above the Haas garage."

"Excellent, but what about—"

I leaned closer to him just as the crowd began to roar. Up above us, the music had started and the first of the three drivers, Heather's old friend, Fernando, was walking out from the main building across the bridge toward the podium, waving and blowing kisses.

"We think there's a bomb in the Red Bull car."

My voice was lost in the wail of the crowd. Mazza held up his hands then pointed a finger toward his right ear. Yelling was pointless, so I waved for him to follow me, and I ran under the elevated winner's circle to the back of the Red Bull, just twenty feet away, with Mazza and Lenny in tow. The combination of red and yellow on the rear cowling and engine compartment tricked the eye to make it appear orange.

Without further attempts to tell Mazza what I was doing, I stepped up to the Red Bull, simultaneous with the crowd's next eruption. The Ferrari driver, Charles Leclerc, was now crossing the bridge toward the victory circle, and it was as if de Gaulle was marching down the Champs-Élysées after repelling the Nazi horde, the celebration was so intense. I couldn't even imagine what it would have been like had he won the race.

Fortunately, the wild admiration of the Tifosi distracted everyone from me popping open the engine compartment on the Red Bull.

Well, almost everyone.

A Sky Sports television crew filming the celebration had spotted our inexplicable inspection of the winning car and hurried over to film me as the engine lid lifted open.

There was nothing there but a steaming motor.

Damn!

I looked up and saw confusion on the camera man's face. Mazza appeared ready to explode himself. Lenny's mouth dropped open, and he suddenly pointed behind me. I spun around to find an orange flatbed recovery vehicle parked just in front of the winning race cars.

I hurried over and noticed that the latches on the side of its engine compartment were unclipped. With a fast glance toward Lenny and Mazza who had followed me-and beyond them to the curious cameraman who stood behind them-I took hold of the engine lid and lifted it open

Inside, I found a shoebox-sized chunk of plastic explosive with a digital timer jammed in a tiny gap, with red numbers counting down the time—now 2:11. When I turned around, my face must have appeared like that of the man in Edvard Munch's famous painting, *The Scream*, because Mazza's jaw dropped open. He peered into the engine compartment, spotted the bomb, and began to point and shout uncontrollably.

"Bomb! Bomb! Bomb!"

Lenny's eyes were as wide as hard-boiled eggs, and the cameraman standing behind him either heard or saw Mazza pointing because he pointed his camera at the engine. A second later, the sound of the crowd shifted from wild admiration for Leclerc to extreme shrieking over the image now being transmitted from the Sky Sports television camera to every giant screen throughout the *Autodromo*—and the entire world, for that matter, as these races were broadcast globally.

The cameraman's jaw dropped open when he realized what he was filming, then he dropped his camera and fled along with everybody near us—thus creating a mass exodus that left several people trampled and writhing on the asphalt of pit lane.

Mazza was gone, but Lenny stood in shock, staring from me to the digital timer inside the bowels of the engine compartment. Shaking like a palm frond in a hurricane myself, I turned back to check the digital timer, which now read 1:37.

I studied what appeared to be a simple mechanism—two red wires leading from the timer directly into the plastic explosive—while a dozen similar, albeit fictional, scenes from movies and TV played through my head.

Which wire should I pull? If either.

And would that stop the counter, or would it blow me, Lenny, the three race cars, the podium, and everything around us to smithereens?

1:22.

A sudden inspiration hit me. I grabbed my cell phone and hit my speed dial for Heather. Fortunately, all the people fleeing must have freed up some cell capacity because the phone was ringing. While it rang, I yelled to Lenny.

"Grab that television camera and zoom in on the timer!"

"Hell you talking about, man?"

"Do it!"

Lenny scrambled to grab the camera, and up on the large screen facing the grandstands, I saw a shaky image of asphalt shift to the engine compartment, then to me holding the phone.

"Buck, is that you on TV?" Heather said. "Oh my, God—"

"Give Jones the phone!"

To her credit, she didn't argue, and the next thing I heard was the calm voice of battle-hardened experience.

"Reilly, get closer to the device," Jones said.

Lenny must have heard him, because he shuffled closer, hesitating slightly as if the extra couple of feet might make a difference in the .42 that remained on the timer.

"What do I do, Jones?" I asked.

The sound of my voice suddenly broadcast all over the *Autodromo*, and I realized the Sky Sports camera had a built-in microphone.

"Get closer!"

His voice also boomed over the track's speakers.

"There's two wires," I said.

I glanced back up at the megascreen and could clearly see the brick of plastic explosives, the timer now reading .31.

"Damn, that's bad luck," Jones said.

"No shit!" I replied.

Our voices echoed over the receding melee of scrambling race fans.

"Angle to the left a little."

Lenny was strangely calm, and I could hear him quietly reciting "The Lord's Prayer" under his breath.

"Now to the right."

Lenny scrambled behind me and zoomed in on the right side.

The image on the large screen showed: .18, .17, .16 …

"All right, Reilly, I have a pretty good idea what to do," Jones said, his voice calm.

"Yeah, what the hell's that?"

.12, .11, .10 …

"Run, you bloody bugger!"

"What the—"

A surreal laugh filled the *Autodromo*. "Just kidding, Reilly! Grab the red wire coming out of the left side of the timer and pull it off."

What an asshole!

My hand shook for all the world to see as I thrust it into the engine compartment, grabbed hold of the wire, my eyes fixated on the timer—

.05, .04, .03 …

"Pull it!" Lenny screamed.

I yanked it with all my might—

33

SILENCE FOLLOWED, AND THE DIGITAL TIMER FROZE ON .02.

"We still alive?" Lenny asked.

He was still watching me through the camera, and if the scene weren't already surreal enough, I saw the relief on my face broadcast onto the large screen facing the grandstands. With my light-blue linen shirt unbuttoned and open wide, the 1708 gold escudo coin on the fisherman's chain was bright against my tanned chest. A big smile bent my cheeks and I laughed aloud, which was broadcast worldwide.

"Yes, Lenny, we're alive and well."

"Hot damn!" he said.

He moved closer and pointed the camera at the bomb, focusing on the digital timer that read .02.

A slow roar began to fill the air. It took me a moment to realize it was the race fans who'd fled for safety but must be watching the drama unfold on the countless TV screens all over the *Autodromo*.

I pumped my fist for the camera and the distant roar grew louder.

I smiled one last time and looked past the camera to Lenny.

"Turn that damn thing off."

Behind Lenny, I saw a rush of activity—men in blue armored clothing moving toward us, led by another armored man aboard a four-wheeler towing a large cylinder.

"Bomb squad's on the way," I said.

Lenny had placed the camera on the ground and turned to see the group slowly approaching.

"Little late, aren't they?" he said.

The television screens now showed an aerial view of the tight group of men moving toward the podium, following the four-wheeler and round vault. I glanced up and noticed four helicopters hovering high over pit lane. The scene shifted to a mass of people standing silently somewhere on the track, watching a giant screen. When they saw themselves, they started cheering again, the sound arriving to us a few seconds later.

I glanced around and looked at the race cars. Damn impressive, low-slung but long and wide monsters of speed. I peered inside the cockpit of the Red Bull, amazed how tight it was. The cockpit of my smallest plane, Betty the Widgeon, was luxuriously spacious in comparison.

These cars could only be compared to fighter jets or rockets, given their sleekness and speed, and seeing them up close gave me true respect for the drivers who risked their lives inside them.

"You men move away from the vehicle," a voice sounded from a bullhorn.

Speaking of risking our lives, I'd felt such relief after the bomb didn't go off—but who knew if the heat from the still hot engine could ignite it accidentally. I waved to Lenny, and we moved away from the truck to the other side of the podium bridge. We were still in harm's way, but after what we'd been through and done, I felt magnetically connected to the scene. Some kind of Stockholm syndrome, maybe?

My cell phone rang, and Lenny jumped.

"Goddamn, that scared the hell out of me."

It was Heather.

"Hi, dear. How's everything up in the VIP section?" I said.

All I could hear was her crying and whimpering, the sound of which ignited my own emotion, and my chest heaved as the bomb squad arrived at the back of the Red Bull.

"You ... did ... it ..." she finally managed.

I rubbed my palm over my moist eyes.

Lenny was suddenly next to me, his arm around my shoulder.

I lowered the phone and hugged him.

Son of a bitch if we hadn't.

I caught my breath and raised the phone again.

"Did you and Jones find Himmelman?"

As I spoke, I watched a heavily armored man wearing a helmet, looking like something between a deep-sea diver and an astronaut, lower his thickly gloved hands down into the truck's engine compartment.

"We ... did." Heather's voice broke again. "He's ... in custody."

The bomb squad member lifted the slug of plastic explosive out of the compartment, then slowly turned and lowered it into the large metal vault.

"What about the bomber we intercepted?"

"Sterling held him until the police arrived."

"Good man."

With the lid closed on the vault, the man on the four-wheeler slowly drove toward us and past, followed by the half dozen heavily armored men, like a twist on some kind of medieval reenactment. They turned left through a gate that had opened just past the pit garages and led to a service road away from the track.

Lenny and I watched their procession recede, still in shock from the events we'd been forced into executing, the gravity of which now washed over me. By the sight of him seated on the front of the Aston Martin, it had hit Lenny too.

"You're a hero, Buck," Heather said.

I forgot I was holding the phone. I shook my head to shrug off the sense of paralysis that had hit me since pulling the wire.

"That's silly," I said. "All this happened because of our investment in Williams, so we were responsible. I don't run from my responsibilities."

She giggled on the other end of the line. "I hope not."

"Buck!"

Lenny called my name, and when I glanced over, he pointed up pit lane.

What I saw caused my eyes to open wide.

"I need to drop off, Heather," I said. "You should come down here if you can. I don't think we'll be going anywhere anytime soon."

I stood up and walked over to Lenny. We both watched as a wall of people walked—or in some cases ran—back down toward us. Numerous security guards hurried out of doors between the Ferrari and Red Bull garages to again establish perimeter control below the podium. Among them was Mazza, who walked slowly toward us, flanked by his usual pair of Carabinieri sidekicks.

"The hell's going on?" Lenny asked.

"Maybe they're going forward with the ceremony," I said.

Mazza arrived and we no longer had the area to ourselves. Everything was going back to normal, if that was even possible, but everything was also different.

"Great job, men," Mazza said. He extended his hand to me, then to Lenny.

I'd forgotten that he'd disappeared after squealing like a schoolgirl about the bomb in the Red Bull. That explained his contrite demeanor now. Behind him I saw a golf cart pulling up, driven by Matt Sterling, with Harry in the passenger seat and Ray in the back. With all decorum out the window, they parked next to Fernando's Aston Martin.

I'd never seen Harry smile at me so broadly before. It sent chills through my limbs. Sterling jumped out first, hustled over to us, and gave me a warm embrace—no handshakes this time—then did the same to Lenny.

"This has turned out to be the best investment I've ever been a part of," he said. "Well done, gentlemen."

Harry lumbered over and just smiled.

His cheeks were pink, and were those tears in his eyes?

He didn't say anything. He didn't need to.

Sterling interrupted the emotion that made my jaw quiver. "The FIA has a question for you that, well, frankly, I've never heard of before."

"What's ... that?" I asked.

I swallowed.

Pull it together, man.

Behind Sterling, I realized the pit was once again full, and the roar from the track meant the Tifosi had retaken their position and the party was back on.

"They've asked that you join the drivers on the podium for a quick ceremony upstairs."

"*What?*"

Harry reached over, gripped my bicep, and nodded, his cheeks pinched, and a tear shot out and skipped across his dappled skin. He cleared his throat and wiped his nose with the back of his starched blue sleeve.

"When all this is said and done—and as I mentioned when I asked for your help in the first place—I'd like you to come visit me at Hamphshire." His eyes sparkled and he brushed away another tear with his beefy mitt. "We have much to talk about."

Hampshire was Harry's country estate outside of London somewhere. He'd never invited me there before. I wasn't sure what he meant by much to talk about, but many strange things had surfaced during these past few days—not the least of which was that he'd included me in the Williams contract in the first place. I'd concluded it was because he wanted to ensure that he was able to perfect the investment, even if Himmelman killed him.

"Ray and I will need to fly Big Mama home, plus Heather and Lenny are—"

"Bring them with you. There's a small airport in Cotswold where you could leave the Albatross."

He still had my bicep in his hand, and he squeezed it again.

"I'd be honored to," I said.

THE WALK ACROSS THE BRIDGE OVER PIT LANE TOWARD the circular podium was more dreamlike than anything I'd ever experienced. Tens of thousands of people filled the track, and it seemed every one of them was screaming, whistling, or waving banners representing their favorite constructor—mostly Ferrari—which made sense given the location.

Above the crowd, the megascreen flashed video of me defusing the bomb in the truck's engine compartment, then smiling when I realized we'd succeeded; then the video flashed to a present-time shot of me walking across the bridge. The race winner was there, along with the drivers who had placed second and third, all watching as I approached. They too were clapping.

I had to pinch myself when "The Star-Spangled Banner" started playing over the music system that had just played the Dutch national anthem for Max Verstappen, the race winner. Fernando, whom I'd already met through Heather, was the first driver I came to, and he bowed to me. Then Charles Leclerc walked over and shook my hand, a trophy in his other—all the while, the cacophony of cheering nearly deafening. I looked up at Max who stood in the center on an elevated podium, and he waved me over. Whatever he said, I had no idea, the sound was so loud and raucous. When he extended his arm to pass me his trophy—a brilliant golden, twisted circle of thick metal on a base—my mouth fell open.

Numb, I accepted the trophy and the noise escalated to a level that became disorienting. I turned around to look out over the circular balcony and my jaw fell open at the sheer mass of people that stretched the entire length of the track, even as it disappeared around the first corner.

Next thing I knew, I was getting soaked with champagne. I spun around and all three drivers were aiming their celebratory bottles at me, laughing, and waving to the crowd.

Charles handed me his to share in the celebration, and I tipped and guzzled it.

EPILOGUE

WE'D FLOWN INTO COTSWALD AIRPORT, built at the outset of World War II and known then as RAF Kemble. Big Mama was right at home with a number of retired airliners and a RAF Spitfire from back in the day. The airport had been closed to private or commercial use for years, now used by clubs, flying schools, and industry—the latter was how Harry had access to fly in and out of there. It was nestled in the Cotswolds, further west of London than I'd expected.

Percy collected us in the Rolls Royce. The drive to Harry's estate passed through rolling hills that rose from the meadows of the upper Thames, which flows down to Oxford. The region predominantly consisted of rural landscape, dotted with small stone-built villages, towns, and more stately homes built of local rock. The entire area was protected, so Hampshire, Harry's estate, set on over four hundred acres, would never be impinged upon by any form of development.

"I love the Cotswolds," Heather proclaimed.

I didn't think she'd ever been here, but there was a lot to her I would never know—even though we'd previously been married and had recently rekindled our relationship after a decade of bitterness.

"This whole area just smells of money," Lenny said.

"Loved that little airport," Ray said.

From the front passenger seat, I saw the corner of Percy's lips curl up in a silent smile. Ever the professional, and having worked for Harry since the 1990s, Percy kept his thoughts and comments to himself. When he turned off the main road onto a tree-lined gravel entry that kept going and going and going, the butterflies in my stomach told me we were close.

Fall colors filled a small forest that evoked oohs and aahs from the backseat as we passed through. Once through there, we came to a huge lake that was so still and calm, the trees on its banks reflected clearly like a Rorschach test. When the drive curved around the head of the lake, my mouth fell open at the site of Hampshire at the far end of the water, its reflection appearing as tall as a six-story skyscraper. Even at three stories, the carved stone building was both massive and elegant. Various sculptures were placed evenly across the length of the roof, and the windows were so tall, I imagined the ceilings must be at least fifteen feet high.

"Goddamn!" Lenny said. "Looks like the freaking White House."

Percy piped in. "Hampshire is actually three times larger than the White House but was built around the same period, the late 1700s."

"Harry lives here alone?" I asked.

"Along with a staff of twelve, and another twenty who perform various tasks around the grounds."

Lenny laughed. "Grounds. The man has *grounds*."

"It is a beautiful estate," Heather said.

The way she phrased it made me wonder if she'd been there before. But why?

And when?

I swallowed away that thought, too amazed to think of anything beyond the grandeur of what we were seeing. As I recalled, Harry Greenbaum wasn't a billionaire when my parents had first met him through Dad's career at the State Department—or CIA, whichever account you cared to believe—but Harry's wealth had grown rapidly through the acquisition of more than a hundred companies since he had first invested in e-Antiquity. I had no idea what his net worth was today, as I didn't really care about those kinds of things, but I bet Heather had a good idea.

Harry greeted us in the first room we entered, which was even taller than I'd expected. An amazing floor of black and white tiles, set in an angle, led toward a massive center staircase at the end of the room.

"Welcome to Hampshire."

Dressed in a red smoking jacket, Harry looked the part of the landed gentry. As was clear in his desire to invest in Williams, he was very serious about contributing to the support of British history and helping it remain relevant.

With hugs all around, I paid extra attention to Heather's remarks about Hampshire and seeing Harry, but there was no clue as to whether she had been here before. In hindsight, it was more likely she had researched the home and grounds in great detail. Harry led us on a tour of the ground-floor rooms, which were decorated in full Elizabethan grandeur, with large windows; long galleries of important paintings; more tall, decorated chimneys than I could count; and ornamental wood and strapwork.

The table in the dining room sat twenty people, and it seemed we met another staff member in every room. It was all at once stunning and overwhelming. The tour ended in a sitting room as large as the restaurant at the best Ritz Carlton I'd ever visited. There were multiple large sofas—a mix of paisleys and leather—with matching chairs. Trays of food and refreshments graced tables next to a half dozen French doors, which opened onto a stone patio that was at least a couple of thousand square feet in size. The view beyond that, into the formal gardens, was stunning.

An elderly male waiter in a tuxedo arrived with a tray of champagne glasses and first approached Lenny, who stood with his mouth open in awe.

"Champagne, sir?"

Lenny exhaled a long breath. "Damn straight."

Once everyone had a glass, Harry raised his and cleared his throat.

"Thank you all for coming so far out of your way to visit. I really cannot thank you enough for all you did for me in Italy, but as promised, I have arranged payment for each of you that will be wired to your accounts."

Ray smiled, and Lenny mouthed "wired to our accounts?" with his brow furrowed and eyes narrowed.

Harry took a sip of his champagne and the rest of us followed suit.

"Now, please avail yourselves of Chef Maurice's delicacies on the terrace, or feel free to stroll through the gardens below."

With everyone tongue-tied. I raised my glass. "Thank you, Harry, we will do that—"

"Not you, Buck," he said. "I'd like you to join me in my study."

Heather's eyes were wide. She was a hawk for everything from fashion to art and all the other finer things in life, which likely had her senses redlined here at Hampshire.

"Don't have to tell me twice," Lenny said. He made a beeline to grab a plate and began to fill it with everything from canapes to foie gras.

I followed Harry through a wide corridor to a room that was cozier, filled with wood bookshelves sagging under more tomes than they could hold, and a fire roared in the central stone fireplace. Another tray of food was set there, between two stately leather chairs framed in wood that matched the coffered ceiling and walls.

Harry pointed me to the far chair, and he sat in the other.

Once we were seated with our glasses of champagne, I sat quietly, waiting to learn why Harry had beckoned me here. He took a sip of the champagne and looked uncharacteristically uncomfortable, shifting around in the chair I'm sure he sat in frequently.

"I have an admission to make, dear boy," he said.

Rather than inquiring further, I held the flute against my lips and savored the fine vintage.

"I asked you to come to Monza on false pretense," he said.

"How so?"

He placed his flute on the side table. "I didn't really care about having you come to fly in that spectacle during the pre-race ceremony. I wanted you there—needed you there—to have my back, which you did beyond my wildest expectations."

"Yeah, I kind of figured that when everything unraveled so quickly after my arrival."

"I do apologize for the indiscretion, and more so for putting you and your friends in harm's way, but even with Tactical International providing security—"

"Which they botched," I said.

"Indeed. There was nobody else I felt I could trust completely."

I mulled over Harry's words but found them somewhat hard to swallow. "Come on, Harry, with all your companies and high society here, there's nobody you could count on?"

"My solicitors and staff, of course, but only so far. I feared things might get aggressive with Himmelman but had no idea just how badly that would play out."

I shrugged. "Truth be told, Harry, that was all way over my head too."

"All of our heads, dear boy, but you never gave up, never

abandoned me—quite the daring rescue effort at the Promontory, by the way, and you prevailed on all counts in the end."

Despite a tray of delicious-looking food within reaching distance, I wasn't the least bit hungry. However, I was thirsty for more information.

"What about naming me in the contract? It was a hundred-million-Euro investment. I mean, I appreciate it, but what gives? I'm assuming there's no real value to my shares—"

"Not so. Upon my demise, you will have full control over those shares, including all proceeds."

When I turned in the chair to face him, the leather squeaked and the chair's feet shrieked against the wood.

"That must be why the Mortician and Himmelman kept referring to me as your partner. I mean, who just cuts a former business partner in on a nine-figure deal?"

His brow creased. "Mortician?"

"Never mind."

He cleared his throat and took a healthy slug of champagne. "Truth is, you're much more than a former business partner to me, Buck."

"And you are to me, too—"

"In fact, worlds more."

Worlds more?"

He inhaled a deep breath. "Your parents have been gone for more than a decade now—adoptive parents, that is—so I think it's time for a long overdue admission."

Harry's mention of my parents caused an immediate pang in my gut that sent erratic signals to my brain. I didn't know where he was headed with this, so I pressed my lips together.

He flashed his eyes in my direction, but quickly looked away. I'd never seen Harry so nervous—

"Truth be told, I'm your birth father, Buck."

His words hung in the air, and I froze.

My mind spun back to my childhood when my parents had first introduced me to Harry. He'd always been a bachelor, but his relationship with them had been close—oddly close. And later he'd been my lead investor in e-Antiquity, which my former partner Jack Dodson ruined when he absconded with all our liquid assets and launched us into

Chapter Seven.

My mind continued to spin as his words sunk in.

"You've nothing to say?" he asked.

"I, ah, don't quite know—then who was my natural mother?"

Harry sank back in his chair with a slow nod. "The one love of my life. Catherine."

"Wait, you were married?"

"Only a few months when you were conceived, and she had a very difficult pregnancy. Confined to her bed the last three months, she grew weak, and, well, you were breached. Our physician was at our home in London, and he tried to readjust the baby, er, you … the simplest way I can explain what happened was that he botched it. She had irreparable internal bleeding and could not be saved."

I sagged in the chair, on one hand gutted by the news, but on the other, astonished.

"I had been friendly with your parents, whom I'd met at Whitehall at a diplomatic affair. So much so that we'd had many dinners together where they'd explained that they didn't believe they could have children, as they'd been trying for years with no success."

"And Catherine?" I asked.

Another deep breath. "She was a beautiful Scottish lass from Edinburgh. Tall, blonde, blue-eyed, absolutely gorgeous. Why she fell for me, I never could explain, but I was much more dapper in those days myself. Athletic—tennis player, believe it or not—and we met at university in Oxford."

I leaned forward, my elbows on the arms of the chair, my hands holding my head up.

Overwhelmed. I was totally overwhelmed.

It was my turn to sit back in my chair—and to take a deep gulp of bubbly that nearly caused me to gag. I'd only learned I was adopted a year after my parents' death in Switzerland by hit and run, but I'd more recently learned that Jack Dodson had planned the hit with Ben, my brother, and it was carried out by Gunner Rostenkowski.

I suddenly sat forward.

I remembered that the day I'd found my adoption papers in the numbered account at Swiss Bank, there had been a document from the United Kingdom relinquishing my natural citizenship.

The penny finally dropped, nearly a decade after I'd been confused by that.

I glanced over at Harry, who now had a mischievous grin pulling at his cheeks.

"I've wanted to tell you forever, but out of respect for your parents, I remained silent. When that awful realization came out last year about your adopted brother being a conspirator in their deaths, I knew I must tell you, but I've been waiting for the appropriate time."

A warmth passed through me as one of the greatest mysteries of my life had just been solved, and the truth was beyond mind-blowing.

"I'm getting old, Buck, and I have nobody to share my life with." He waved his hand around the room. "And all of this." He paused. "While I intend to leave the majority of my wealth to the charities I am most passionate about, you will be the sole recipient of the balance."

I held up my hands, the shock now too overwhelming.

"I don't want your money, Harry."

The pain I saw register in his eyes caused a stab of anguish to my heart.

"What I mean is that now that I know the truth, I'd just like to spend more time with you and get to know you in ways I never have." I bit my lip to stem the quiver that had begun to slur my speech. "And about Catherine, too."

The smile returned to Harry's face, and I realized it was the same smile he'd bestowed upon me after Lenny and I defused the bomb and he arrived with Sterling and Ray on the cart. It was a smile born of pride. Fatherly pride.

The door suddenly swung open, and Heather came in like a whirlwind, all smiles and billowing chiffon designer clothing.

"What are you two conspiring about?" she asked.

"You're never going to believe it," I said.

The End

ABOUT THE AUTHOR

John H. Cunningham is the USA Today bestselling author of the eleven-book, Buck Reilly adventure series, which includes Red Right Return, Green to Go, Crystal Blue, Second Chance Gold, Maroon Rising, Free Fall to Black, Silver Goodbye, White Knight, Indigo Abyss, Purple Deceiver and Buried in Orange, along with the alternative ending fiction novel, The Last Raft, and co-author of Graceless and Timeless.

John has either lived in or visited the many locations that populate his novels, and he mixes fact with fiction and often includes real people in the cast of characters. Adhering to the old maxim, "write what you know," John's books have an authenticity and immediacy that have earned loyal followers and strong reviews. John writes stories that concern themselves with the same tensions and issues that affect all of our lives, and his choices for the places and plots that populate his stories include many settings that he loves. John splits his time between New York, Virginia and Key West.

ACKNOWLEDGEMENTS

Buried in Orange was tremendous fun to research in Italy to review each setting firsthand. Plus, to get the best understanding of the inner workings of a Formula 1 race, I spent time in the paddock, pit lane and attended the podium ceremony in the same location where Buck and Lenny saved the day. All of the locations in Italy were made possible through collaboration with Merrion Charles, a travel consultant who lives there and knows the country inside and out.

My friends at the Hotel de la Ville in Monza were wonderful. Gigi Nardi and his brother are fourth generations owners and operators, and even though the hotel was full of Formula 1 team owners, team principals, and most of the drivers, the staff went out of their way to make us feel just as welcome and important. Special thanks to Riccardo Napoleone, the Front Office Manager and his staff for helping us at every step. Just like Buck Reilly, Holly and I rode the Hotel da la Ville bikes to and from the Autodromo everyday with great ease and joy passing through Monza Park, which was truly beautiful. We will be back!

Lake Garda and the Dolomites were also spectacular. We were there for the Falzarego bike race, took the cable car up to Rifugio Lagazuoi and hiked to Rifugio Scotoni and as you can see, it filled my imagination with ideas. Lake Como was incredible. We stayed at Il Sereno where I sought to provide as much detail as possible without slowing the pace of the action. Needless to say, I'd recommend following in Buck's footsteps to there. And flying out of the oldest seaplane base in the world, Aero Club Como to explore the lake was also helpful and a great experience. Thanks to my friend Carl Grooms for making the introduction there.

Speaking of Carl Grooms, I have him to thank for helping me establish Buck and Ray's flight plan from Key West to Italy. When I first met Carl, he was the original rum maker for Pilar at the Key West Distillery, but his passion for flying, which started as an A6 pilot for the US Navy, pulled him away to becoming a seaplane pilot for Tropic Ocean Airways, where aside from having fun constantly flying the Bahamian and Caribbean islands, he was racking up hours to achieve his next goal, which of course he has now accomplished. Carl now flies 747s for Atlas Air, and when I last saw him a couple weeks ago at his home in Maine, he had just flown around the world in six days to spots that would make Buck Reilly cringe.

Another pilot and beta reader who has been very helpful on the last several books is Dana Vihlen. Thanks for your keen eye and expertise, Dana. Other beta readers included Bill and Linda Klipp, Mary Jones and Fritz Kloepfel, all of whom I greatly appreciate. Thanks also to my friend and fellow author, Nick Harvey, or Brit Nick, as my other Tropical Author friends and I call him. Before becoming an author, Nick had been involved with all types of car racing teams, including NASCAR and Formula 1. His input, advice and suggestions really helped to hone some of the finer points of the story.

Given that this story was a departure for Buck and friends, far away from Key West and the Caribbean, the cover was more important than ever. David Berens once again knocked it out of the park. So good, in fact, you'd think design was all David does, but no, he's another fantastic Tropical Author and I encourage you to check out his work.

Thank you to my friends at The Editorial Department, including Ross Browne, Sean Fletcher, **David Argabright** and Julie Miller for keeping the story sharp, and free of mistakes, which is more than I can say for Buck Reilly.

If you have been enjoying the audio versions of the Buck Reilly series, then you will be pleased to know that Kyle Tait has once again provided an amazing performance. Thank you, Kyle, for putting voices to the many repeat characters, as well as several new ones in each story.

Thank you to Ann-Marie Nieves at GetRed PR, who is both a great friend and one of the best publicists in the business. It is truly an honor to work with you, and I always appreciate your advice and efforts to promote Buck and the gang.

To my friends and colleagues at Tropical Authors, whom I greatly admire, learn from, aspire to replicate and enjoy swapping ideas and stories with, thanks for all you do for the genre, and for me personally.

Finally, and most importantly, thank you to my family, including my brother Jim and his wife Mary, my brother Jay and his wife Beth, Ron and Linda Weiner, and most of all to my wife, Holly and my daughters Bailey and Cortney, along with Will Prendergast for their patience, encouragement, support and love. Bailey and Will's wedding was the highlight of not only the summer, year, and decade, but a real joyous time for our family. As noted in this book's dedication, Bailey and Will got our family hooked on Formula 1 and we enjoy every weekend together during the season and speculate on what's next in the off-season.

If you enjoyed Buried in Orange, please take a minute to leave a review wherever you bought it and let me know what you think about Buck's area of focus increasing beyond Key West and the Caribbean.

Thank you all.

Printed in the USA
CPSIA information can be obtained
at www.ICGtesting.com
LVHW090050071023
760262LV00005B/775

9 798986 920023